I0831777

A NICK FISCHER NOVEL

RODEO REQUIEM

G.D. OBERMILLER

ISBN: 979-8-9938588-3-8 (hardcover)
ISBN: 979-8-9938588-2-1 (paperback)
ISBN: 979-8-9938588-1-4 (ebook)

Cover design by Christian Storm
Interior design by Lisa Gilliam

Published by Frio Press LLC

2026

For all the veterans and rodeo cowboys.
Whoopee ti yi yo.

PROLOGUE

Beau Fahl worked hard at developing his muscles and keeping his body in shape. Staying healthy and keeping himself in peak condition was one way to ensure no one could get the better of him. It worked in Huntsville Prison, a place he vowed never to return, and it worked in the ring or on the street. He'd never been beaten in a fight.

He held his seven-ounce practice gloves up and posed in his fighting stance. At six foot, four inches tall and two hundred and thirty pounds, he cut an imposing figure. He studied the placement of his hands and the distance between his feet reflected in the gym mirror. If there was any weakness, it was his feet. He always felt they were too small for a fighter. A bigger foot would do more damage with fewer kicks, but they had served him well, and he made do with what he had. That had been his motto his whole life.

A bear of a man with shaggy hair and a blond beard shouted from inside the fight cage. "Hey, Fahl. You gonna preen in the mirror all day, or we gonna spar?"

Beau turned his attention to the man in the cage. His name was Joe Garland, and he was not quite Beau's height but was fifty pounds heavier. Beau never understood how people could neglect their bodies. Garland was a street fighter and a barroom brawler who counted on his weight to deter would-be challengers. He'd moved to San Antonio from Mississippi and had a loose southern drawl that emphasized the vowels and added syllables that didn't exist outside the geographic south. Beau had worked hard to drop his own Texas accent while serving in the Marine Corps. In bootcamp, anyone with an accent got pigeonholed and marked with a nickname. His was Tex, of course. Beau was proud of the title at first, then he realized the name implied he was stupid or some kind of country redneck. After that, anyone who called him Tex got a fat lip, or worse, depending on his mood.

Beau strolled into the cage and smiled at the big man. Garland returned the smile, exposing snuff-stained teeth. His beard and shaggy hair reminded Beau that the man was a biker, a patch-wearing member of the Sons of Silence motorcycle gang. Beau had a plan to increase his business and needed a partner who could handle large distribution. He'd planned for two years to make his move. Nothing would stand in his way. Kicking the gang's chapter president's ass would ensure the partnership got off on the right foot.

"They said you was a badass dude," Garland said and spit brown tobacco juice on the floor outside the cage that Beau had set up so that members of his boxing club could tune up for amateur boxing and MMA matches. There were two MMA pros who had free memberships for teaching classes twice a week. Beau sparred with them occasionally just to keep fit. Today's fight was different. This was a business deal.

Beau stood watching the man. He was studying his movements, sizing up his arm reach, and measuring the placement of his feet. Garland stood flat-footed with his arms at his sides. He had a dozen random tattoos on his chest and arms that didn't seem to fit any kind of pattern or unified statement. A skull and crossbones on his left chest and a stick figure Tweety bird on his right obscured by matted hair. Beau recognized them instantly for what they were—prison tatts. Sometimes, inmates got lucky and there was a true artist in the cellblock. But usually, as in Garland's case, the results were crude and telling. Good or bad, ex-cons like him wore the ink as a badge of honor.

Satisfied he'd taken Garland's measure, Beau bounced on the balls of his feet, then threw a few practice punches in the air. It was Garland's turn to watch. He didn't move. He was cocky and sure of himself, accustomed to winning bar fights with his sheer strength and size. Beau had dealt with this kind of fighter his whole life. The kind who thought fat equaled muscle because they could knock out a drunk or a stoned biker with one meaty punch.

Beau turned his back on Garland and stretched his calves and quads. He threw a roundhouse kick with his left leg, then one with his right, reminding Garland that this was an MMA match.

Garland blew a blast of air through his flattened nose. Snot dribbled onto his dirty-blond mustache, and he wiped it on the back of his glove. "You some kind o' fairy? We don't do business with fairies." He grinned at his little joke.

Beau turned and faced him. He smiled even bigger. His teeth were perfect, and he kept his dark hair cut high and tight, like a Marine Corps recruit.

"I'll bet you cozied up to a few fairies in prison," Beau said. He knew how to get under the man's skin. "Were you somebody's bitch?"

Garland turned red. He was impatient. Not the hallmark of a trained fighter. His first move would tell Beau everything he needed to know about his style and how to kill him if it came to that.

"I don't think our arrangement's gonna workout," Garland said and charged across the ring, cocking his massive right arm above his head.

Beau bounced on his feet, weaving side to side and keeping his head loose, watching Garland telegraph his punch like an Amber Alert on a highway billboard. Garland swung with everything he had. Beau easily ducked the punch and landed a left-right combination that rocked Garland's head back. Garland recovered and countered with a left. Beau sidestepped and landed a right hook to Garland's ear. Blood ran down the big man's sunburnt neck. He blinked his eyes to clear his head. Beau saw his opponent was dazed but didn't want to end the fight yet. He was enjoying the exercise.

"We had a deal," Beau taunted him. "You know what happens to people who welch on a deal?" He threw a roundhouse kick that crashed into Garland's other ear. A matching river of blood gushed down the other side of Garland's neck.

Garland mumbled under his breath, "Fuck you," then swung again, connecting with Beau's shoulder.

Beau didn't flinch. "What? I didn't catch that," Beau said.

Garland stood like an angry blind bear in the middle of the ring, swinging at an unseen enemy. Two minutes into the sparring round, and he was exhausted. Most bar fights lasted only a few seconds. The first punch was the only one that counted. If that didn't knock the opponent down, he used a pool cue or waited for his biker buddies to back him up. Fighting someone like Beau was something he'd never done before.

"I said, fuck you. You gonna fight or dance?" Garland yelled, his face beet red and dripping sweat mixed with blood. No matter how hard he swung with his left or right, he came up empty. Beau was too quick and agile for the fat man.

Beau darted in front of him and unloaded another left-right combination that drew more blood. This time from Garland's nose and lip. Garland swung hard, but again he was too late. Beau dodged the ham fist and landed a body shot to his solar plexus and another to his kidney. Garland's breath caught in his throat. He clutched at his chest.

Beau backed off and waited for the man's next move. He had him right where he wanted him.

"Okay, we got a deal," Garland huffed.

"I don't think you can handle distribution," Beau said.

"We can handle anything you got." Garland coughed blood.

"Eighty-twenty split?"

"You said sixty-forty."

Beau moved in while the big man's guard was down and hammered his face with a left-right combo. There was no referee to stop the fight. Only a few bystanders were watching. Those who knew Beau and what he was capable of stood outside the cage smiling, anticipating what was coming like NASCAR fans waiting for a crash.

Garland reeled from the attack. "Okay, man. Eighty-twenty." He tried to raise his hands to block the deadly blows, but Beau was relentless. He rained punches to the man's head until both Garland's eyes were bleeding and his nose was flat against his face.

Beau backed off and watched Garland stagger in a circle, unable to see which direction led to the exit. When he took a step, Beau hit him again, this time with a front kick. Garland sank to the mat. He tried to get up, but Beau kicked him again, and again. First the chest and body and then the head.

Garland tried to speak but only managed a groan like a wounded animal.

Beau grabbed a handful of Garland's tangled hair and began punching him in the face. Over and over until his face was an unrecognizable bloody ball.

When he let go, Garland slumped down on the mat, unconscious. His barrel chest rising and falling was the only sign he was alive. Beau calmly stepped out of the cage.

Kenny Lawrence, a young man with a high-and-tight haircut like Beau's, handed him a clean white towel. "Nice fight, Beau," Kenny said. He was ten years younger and at least thirty pounds smaller than Beau, but he was in peak condition.

"When he wakes up, tell him to clean up and meet me in my office. We have work to do."

"Sure thing, Beau."

PART ONE

Rodeo Cowboys

"I don't care about going down in history as a great bull rider or bronc rider. I hope people will remember me as a great cowboy."

—Ty Murray, nine-time world champion rodeo cowboy

CHAPTER ONE

The San Antonio Rodeo takes place in February over a three-week period inside the Frost Bank Center where the Spurs play basketball. Each year, the team takes a "rodeo road trip" while the hardwood court is covered with over two thousand tons of recycled dirt to a level of twelve to fourteen inches, providing the cowboys and livestock a relatively soft place to land. The arena holds nineteen thousand spectators, and all the PRCA performances sell out. On average, the rodeo organization raises over twelve million dollars for scholarships, grants, and endowments to benefit students attending Texas colleges and universities. Six thousand volunteers and ninety full-time employees entertain a million and a half visitors who watch four hundred contests in a tournament-style format vie for the fifteen-grand top prize in each event. Hungry spectators consume funnel cakes, turkey legs, elotes (grilled Mexican street corn), chicken on a stick, sausage wraps, tacos, and of course Texas barbecue, and pay just under three million dollars to the drink concession contractor for the beer and wine to wash it down.

The night I attended, the local news station reported that the Bexar County Sheriff's Office made thirty-six DWI arrests, recovered twenty-three grams of cocaine, confiscated two illegally carried handguns, and gave out seventy-one warnings. Inside the arena, SAPD reported five cases of criminal mischief, three for petty theft, two for minor assaults, and one homicide. I didn't care about the other reports, but the last one was personal.

I'd scored tickets on the plaza level near the bucking chutes from a former client and season ticket holder. The client owned a string of western-wear stores, and he'd hired me to track down the source of a persistent revenue loss from one of his San Antonio locations. Turned out his cousin was skimming the till. I had my partner, Skeeter Davis, set up a surveillance camera behind the counter and caught him red-handed. They settled it within the family, and I was happy to take a cut of the recovered money. He threw in the semifinals rodeo tickets as a bonus.

Besides being a rodeo fan, there were two other reasons I was at the Frost Bank Center. The first one was an attempt to impress Diana Ochoa by entertaining her and her six-year-old son, Aaron. For the past several months, SAPD Detective Ochoa and I had been dating, but we hadn't quite reached the serious stage. The big obstacle to our relationship was that her life revolved around her son. I admired that, but it only left every other weekend for us to be alone together, and even those times were questionable. Aaron's father, Beto, was also an SAPD officer and frequently worked overtime on weekends. Since Diana had made detective and her ex hadn't, she had an easier time manipulating her schedule.

So far, the rodeo was a big hit. Aaron was wearing the Davy Crockett coonskin cap I'd bought for him at the Alamo gift shop the day before the show. We'd ridden the rides at the carnival and strolled through all the stock pens and the art displays at the expo hall. He liked the pigs the most, so we spent at least two hours in the swine barn entertaining the prize-winning Hampshire sow and her twelve little piglets. Aaron ate two elotes, one turkey leg, and enough sugar-coated funnel cake to fuel a pint-sized rocket ship. When the sugar high wore off, I was hoping he would fall asleep and give me some quality time with his mother.

Diana wore boots and jeans and had curled the ends of her dark, shoulder-length hair. I told her she could get a job on a TV cop show if things went south at the police department. She didn't think it was a compliment. Wherever we went on the fairgrounds, she got hopeful looks from young cowboys and plenty of appraising glances from other females.

The few glances in my direction were focused on the scars across my forehead, courtesy of an IED that ended my military career. The curious gawkers wondered how I could ever score such a beautiful woman as Diana. I didn't have an answer for them. I definitely didn't feel like I had "scored" with Diana. You might say I was courting her in an old-fashioned way. It was something new for me. The fact that she had a six-year-old son gave the dating process a serious side that I wasn't sure I was ready for, but I was willing to try new things.

The second reason I was at the rodeo was to see my brother Colton Macrae compete in the bareback bronc riding. We weren't blood brothers, but brothers-in-arms. Colton was a troubled Marine I'd met at the VFW six months ago. His story paralleled my own. We'd both done three tours in Afghanistan, and we'd both ended our careers after close encounters with an IED. He mustered out missing part of his arm, and I took home a face full of shrapnel.

While I was waiting for Colton's ride in the afternoon show, I was entertaining Diana and her son at the adjacent fairgrounds. Normally, I would avoid riding in any vehicle that spun around in circles, but Aaron insisted I take him on the Zipper. Colton called while I was clinging to the safety rail and left a cryptic message. "*We need to talk*" was all he said. I waited for my head to clear while leaning against the fairgrounds fence, then listened to the message again. He didn't sound drunk, and I hoped he wasn't high. Because of his more extensive injuries, the military hospital gave him all the pain meds he wanted. When he finished rehab, he still wanted drugs, and he found ways, and people, to get the pills he craved. Our conversations at the VFW had covered a lot of ground, from high school football to VA benefits. When he was sober, we mostly talked about the future, but when he was taking pills and sucking on a bottle, things turned dark and inward. I hoped he wasn't on one of his downward spirals.

We shared a common bond because we both had wounds and an unhealthy dose of survivor's guilt. I was still dealing with the latter, but I got help from my late grandpa. He encouraged me to sober up and get on with life using his unique recipe that called for a cup of hard work and a heaping spoonful of history. He said the hard work kept your mind occupied while studying history taught you that you're not the only poor son of a bitch who has ever suffered pain and anguish.

Colton didn't have a grandpa to give him that recipe or a kick in the pants. He wasn't speaking to his father and didn't seem to have anybody except a woman named Lora Michaels, who he'd met at a strip club the week after he returned home. He doted on her, but it was obvious to all but him that the feeling wasn't mutual. I had tried to warn him, but Lora's physical attraction was too much for him, and she knew how to use her assets to her advantage. I knew because Lora Michaels and I had a history.

I steered Aaron and his mother back to the rodeo arena and ordered a beer to settle my stomach. While we waited for Colton's turn to ride, we watched the team roping and the calf roping, two of my favorite events. They weren't as glamourous as bull riding but were definitely more closely tied to real ranch work. The announcer was entertaining the crowd by a steady amusing banter with the rodeo clown. He had wandered into our seating section, which prompted the cameraman to flash our picture on the jumbotron suspended over the arena. We all smiled for the camera. For the moment we looked like a happy family. I wondered if it would last. They flashed the kissing cam, and the audience gave a cheer when Diana and I locked lips over Aaron's head.

"Coming out of chute number three, Colton Macrae from Austin, Texas," the announcer said in his singsong Texas drawl.

"Oh, that's your friend, isn't it?" Diana asked, untangling herself from my arms and almost dislodging my new black 4X Resistol cowboy hat.

I adjusted my hat and nodded. Aaron clambered into my lap and whipped my face with the tail of his coonskin cap. We watched the jumbotron bird's-eye view of Colton screwing himself down on the back of a big palomino bucking horse. His wide-brimmed cowboy hat was jammed down to his ears, and his eyes were focused on the base of the bucking brute's neck. He wore flashy chaps decorated with a red, green, and blue tartan design that he'd found online. He claimed the tartan belonged to his Scottish ancestors and added the design as a joke after I tried to get him interested in his family history, and history in general. I was hoping he would do some research on his own, but Colton couldn't care less about history. He didn't get along with his dad and never knew his grandpa. He was a happy-go-lucky cowboy, and his focus was on the here and now, history be damned. Right now, he was coming out of chute number three.

"Colton is sitting in the lead after three rounds of bareback competition."The announcer's smooth drawl filled the crowd in on Colton's rodeo background. He'd qualified for the San Antonio Rodeo with a string of prize-winning rides that put him in the top ten on the Professional Rodeo Riders money list for this year. If he won the San Antonio event, he had a good chance of going on to the PRCA national finals in Las Vegas.

He was small and wiry and knew how to put on a show during his eight-second ride. He was also a natural athlete who could lie around drinking beer for weeks at a time and still look like he'd been training for a prize fight. Something I could never do.

Colton nodded his head to signal he was ready. The gate swung open, and the big palomino exploded out of the chute, its back arched, its head down, and its four legs stiff. Colton thrust his stub of a free arm high in the air while holding his spurs above the horse's shoulders. The tartan-fringed chaps flashed like Scottish flags in a parade. It was a beautiful thing to watch.

The stout horse hit the ground, then kicked up its back legs like two buggy whips. In the blink of an eye, it sprang skyward again. Colton timed his movements in perfect sync with the animal's. His back met the palomino's spine, and the momentum shot his body forward while the horse lunged for another piece of the arena.

I stood and lifted Aaron to my shoulders. He clapped his hands, eyes glued to Colton and the bucking palomino. Even Diana was caught up in the excitement.

"Look at that cowboy ride!" the announcer shouted.

The clock ticked down to three seconds. Every spectator in the Frost Bank Center stood and cheered. They all sensed that the ride was something special. Colton was in the zone. Riders like him pushed the envelope and were the reason fans kept coming back to the rodeo arena to celebrate their western heritage. Horse and rider were two equal athletes matching their skills in an eight-second contest. Even the points awarded at the end were divided equally between animal and rider.

"That's how it's done, folks!" the announcer chanted when the eight-second buzzer erupted. "It don't get any better than that. Give that cowboy a big round of applause."

While the crowd erupted with applause, Colton grabbed the pickup rider and lowered himself off the palomino horse and to the arena dirt in one smooth, practiced motion, then tipped his hat and flashed his cocky happy-go-lucky grin. He'd just made the ride of his life and the world was his.

"That score of ninety-one puts Colton in the lead and sets a new arena record! How about that?" The announcer played "*We Are the Champions*" by Queen while Colton absorbed the accolades from the crowd. I was happy for him and proud at the same time, thinking I played a part in my brother's success for encouraging him to join the PRCA circuit and turn his life around.

Colton stood in the dirt arena and searched the crowd. I waved my cowboy hat, trying to get his attention. When his eyes settled on me, he gave a little bow. He was a rodeo cowboy in his element, and when he was sober, there was nobody you'd rather be around. His energy was infectious, like a poster boy for rodeo and all things good and wholesome about Texas.

Then he turned toward the chutes and a dark shadow passed over his face that I could see even from my vantage point in the stands. I followed his gaze to a man standing behind the arena gate. Colton pulled his hat back down on his head and hurried out of the arena. He met the man who was dressed in black with short dark hair. He had his back to the stands, and I couldn't see his face.

A shiver ran up the back of my spine. There was something familiar about him that I couldn't quite put my finger on. Was he another veteran I'd met at the VFW? Before I could decide, both walk out of sight.

"You all right?" Diana asked, sensing my change in mood.

I lifted Aaron off my shoulders and set him back into the seat beside his mother. "I'm fine. I'm gonna go congratulate Colton."

"Don't be too long. I don't wanna stay for the concert after the show. It's too late for Aaron."

I gave her a kiss and agreed to make it quick, then walked through the tunnel and out of the grandstands. I fought through the line at the beer concession and found the stairs to the ground floor. Colton would want to hang out behind the chutes at least long enough to accept praise from the other cowboys.

I showed my private investigator license to the security guard and made up a quick story about working for the Shaughnessy family. It wasn't a lie. Martin Shaughnessy was the owner of the western-wear chain and a well-known member of the stock show board of directors. If he called to check my story, Martin would vouch for me.

The area behind the chutes buzzed with excitement because the bull-riding event was next. It was always the last and most hyped event of the performance. I walked past the pen where the menacing bovines bellowed and blew snot, looking for anyone stupid enough to get in their way. I searched the hats and faces for Colton but didn't see him. I stopped a few of the riders and asked if they'd seen him. The cowboys were affable, as usual, but nobody knew where Colton was. They all wanted to talk about his outstanding ride.

It took me twenty minutes to make my way outside the building. Low clouds covered the city, and a steady drizzle soaked the grounds. The temperature hovered just below fifty degrees, cold enough that I was glad I'd worn a jacket. I took out my phone to call Colton, but it rang before I could punch in his number.

"Where are you?" It was Diana.

"I'm still looking for Colton," I said. "He wasn't behind the chutes."

"Okay. The bull riding is almost over, and I'm ready to go." She sounded annoyed.

I promised her I would be with her shortly. It should have been reassuring that our relationship had reached the point where we could make demands on each other's time. Still, it felt a little constricting, and it would take some getting used to. Diana Ochoa definitely had a temper with a short fuse.

I punched in Colton's number and listened to it ring. His voice message made me think he'd answered his phone. "Howdy," his voice responded, then paused.

"Where the hell—"

"Gotcha!" his recorded voice continued. "You've reached the one true Colton Macrae. Leave me a message."

"Colton, this is Nick. Where the hell are you, pard?" I cut through the old Freeman Coliseum that used to house the rodeo. Now it was full of vendors, like a giant western shopping mall, but mostly deserted during the show. The few people there besides the sales reps were trying to stay warm and out of the rain. I figured the best place to find him would be the food court because they were selling beer and had a country music band.

The court was covered with a tent that offered little protection from the north wind. The patrons gathered around the half dozen outdoor space heaters looking like ants globing onto a drop of honey. A few wannabe cowboys waited in line to ride a mechanical bull.

Colton wasn't there. My phone rang. I extracted it from my pocket hoping it was him. It was Diana. I figured she was pissed. I checked my watch. Twenty-five minutes had passed.

"I'm still looking for him," I said, not waiting for her to speak.

"I know. That's why I called." I sensed the change in her tone.

"What's wrong?"

"A kid found Colton in the cattle barn," she said.

"What do you mean?" I didn't like the sound of that.

"A security guard called 911. Dispatch called me." She paused to take a breath.

"Why 911?" Alarm bells went off in my head.

"Colton's dead."

CHAPTER TWO

"That can't be right." I couldn't wrap my head around what Diana said. Colton had made the bronc ride of his life less than thirty minutes ago. He was number one on the leader board. Now he was dead? That didn't make sense.

"One of the stock show kids found the body in his livestock pen. He recognized Colton from his bronc ride. I put a uniform on the scene."

"I'm on my way." I was running for the cattle barn before she finished.

"Stay away from him until I get there," she insisted.

That wasn't gonna happen. Homicide was her job. She'd been promoted two years ago, and we'd met in her rookie year while she was assigned to a mentor detective who turned out to be on the payroll of a corrupt local lawyer running for governor. I was investigating the murder of a young woman found floating in the San Antonio River. The death was ruled accidental, but the girl's mother insisted it was murder and hired me to find the killer. The trail led to the son of a Texas billionaire who was being blackmailed to finance the lawyer's political campaign. When I began to unravel the complicated scheme, the politician put a target on my back and sent the mentor detective to shoot my dog as a warning to drop the case. When that didn't slow me down, he killed my grandpa and tried to kill me and my partner. It didn't end well for the mentor or the politician. The latter added to my collection of scars with a .38 bullet to my chest, but I ended his political career with a .45 bullet to his head.

The next time we met, Diana threatened to arrest me for interfering with a case she was building against a degenerate human trafficker called Dragon. One of his victims was the granddaughter of an old family friend. I tried to give her a chance to make an official arrest, but she moved at the glacial pace of law enforcement bureaucracy, jeopardizing the girl's safety. When Dragon took the girl and headed for the border, I bypassed her police procedure and stopped him within feet of a private plane. In the final shootout, Diana had my back. And, although we still argued over gray areas of the law, she admitted that my unorthodox methods had been necessary to get justice. Whether we could work together on another case remained to be seen.

By the time I reached the open barn doors of the cattle barn, the rodeo was over, and all the spectators who weren't staying for the musical concert portion of the performance flooded out of the building and into my path. I fought my way through the crowd and entered the huge, cavernous warehouse. There was an auction arena on one end and miles of panel fencing on the other holding livestock supplied by agriculture students from around the state. The overwhelming odor of wet hay mixed with urine and manure permeated every surface. The auction was still going on, and the rapid-fire cadence of the auctioneer rattled off the price of a prize-winning Charolais bull. The pint-sized owner stood in a large circular pen wearing a black cowboy hat the size of an umbrella and proudly holding the animal's lead rope.

"Did you hear me?" Diana said.

I glanced at my phone and realized we were still connected. "Loud and clear. I'm in the barn."

"I know. I hear the auctioneer. Wait for me. I'm almost there."

I hit disconnect. She was worried about her crime scene, but I needed to get to Colton before SAPD took over. I had to know what happened.

I jumped up on a stack of straw bales and scanned the expanse of panel fencing. A commotion in the far corner near the toilets caught my eye. A crowd was gathering. Word had spread quickly. Soon enough, if there was a body, everybody in the building would want to take a look. Morbid curiosity.

By the time I worked my way to the back corner, a young female uniformed cop had her hands up, anxiously imploring the curious onlookers to back away from the pen. I needed to get past her and see for myself. I still didn't believe it could be Colton.

I waited until the officer addressed the crowd and slipped through the metal bars on one of the panels. A body lay beside a bale of hay. His knees were bent, and his upper body was twisted, as if he'd been bucked off a horse and landed in a heap. I studied the cowboy hat that was still pulled down on his head. A neat hole cut through the silver crown, and a dark bloodstain coated the underside of the brim.

There was no doubt it was Colton. In his right hand was a pistol. I didn't have to get a closer look to know the make and model—Smith & Wesson .40 caliber M&P Shield. I had given it to him two weeks ago when we were on the pistol range together. He was looking for a concealed carry gun, and he asked to borrow my M&P Shield to try it out for a few days.

I stifled the urge to throw up. Though I'd seen dead bodies in combat, killed my share in self-defense, and held my granddad's murdered body in my arms, I never got used to the sight and smell of human blood. And there was a lot of it here, soaked into the straw beneath his body. The bullet had entered his skull on the right side above and behind the ear. I knew what the exit wound looked like without turning him over. The .40 caliber packed enough power to take out a good portion of bone and brain. No question. He was dead. At first glance, it looked like a suicide. But why would he take his own life? He had just made a bronc ride for the record books, one that would have propelled him to the National Finals. I knew he had dark demons, but how could they have taken over so quickly?

"Nick!" Diana shouted over the murmuring crowd noise. She was standing outside the pen, peering through the panel fence. "I thought I asked you to wait until I got here."

"I didn't touch anything," I said, still studying the body. There was something strange about the scene, but I couldn't put my finger on it. I backed toward the panel and climbed out of the pen. Three more uniformed officers arrived and set up a perimeter. The female cop began stringing yellow crime scene tape across the open pen gate.

I took one more look at Colton, then grabbed the top bar of the panel for support, suddenly feeling weak in the knees.

"Are you all right?" Diana asked.

"It's him. It's Colton. He's definitely dead."

"Could you tell how it happened?"

"He's holding a pistol, and he's got a bullet wound to the head."

"Self-inflicted?"

"That's what it looks like. But it looks strange to me."

"Strange how?"

"I don't know. Just strange. I can't put my finger on it."

Her phone rang. She looked at the caller ID. "That's my team. I've gotta go to work." She put a hand on my shoulder. "You should sit down. I'll bring you some water."

I let her guide me to a bale of straw. "It doesn't make any sense. Colton wouldn't kill himself. Not now. He had too much to live for."

"I'm sorry, Nick," she said. Her phone was still ringing.

"Go to work. I'll be fine."

She was all business when she hit accept and raised the cell phone to her ear. "Detective Ochoa," she said, and walked toward the uniformed officers.

I sat for a moment, collecting my thoughts. I wasn't okay. Colton had talked about suicide when I first met him. He was full of anger, hate, and guilt, as I'd been when I transferred stateside and mustered out of the Marine Corps. My unit had died protecting me after an IED took out my Humvee and left me trapped inside. They held off the follow-up attack until backup arrived. I was the only one left. The windshield glass scarred my forehead, and their memory forever scarred my soul. Colton had returned without part of his arm in the same mental shape I'd been in. I knew what he was feeling, and from the moment I met him in the VFW, I made a promise to help him dig his way out of that dark abyss. The ride tonight should have been his crowing moment, a victory at the end of that dark journey of recovery. Yet there he was with a bullet through his brain and my pistol in his hand.

My sense of despair slowly morphed into anger at myself and at Colton. What the hell had happened? I'd failed him, and he'd failed himself. I needed to know why. I stood and looked around. Diana was still on the phone. The officers had the crowd under control. I saw the prize-winning

Santa Gertrudis steer that might have witnessed Colton's death munching hay in the pen across the alley. The kid holding him must have been the one who found the body. He turned to me as if I had an answer for Colton's death. His face was white, and he looked as nauseous as I felt. He wore pressed Wrangler jeans and a white western-cut shirt. His straw cowboy hat tilted at a cocky angle on his head, and his lips wouldn't completely close over his yellow buck teeth.

I approached him. "Did you see what happened?"

He shook his head. "I didn't really see anything. I came in to check on Gert, and I seen a man in the straw. Lots of blood." The kid looked ready to cry. "I recognized him right away. Watched his bronc ride. Man, he was somethin'."

"Is Gert your steer's name?"

"Yes, sir. He won second place."

"Did you see anyone else in the pen?"

The boy wiped away a tear with his shirt sleeve and thought for a moment, making an effort to force his upper lip over his teeth as if that might help him remember. "No, sir. Just the dead man."

"Did you hear a gunshot?"

"Well, sir, that's why I came to check on Gert. I thought I did, but it's hard to tell in here. Lots of noise. I heard a loud smack, like two board slapping together. I thought maybe one of the steers might have kicked a panel over."

He was right. The acoustics were so bad in the drafty barn that I could barely hear him, and he was standing five feet away.

Diana appeared beside me and took my arm. "I want to ask you a few more questions in a moment. Is that okay?" she asked the boy, holding up her SAPD detective shield.

"Yes, ma'am," he said.

Diana led me to the other side of the pen. "I know what you're doing, 'cause I know how you think. But you're too close to this. Let me handle it."

"I can't stay out of it. This is personal. I was helping him out of a jam. He wouldn't do something like this. Not now and not here."

"You told me his history. Suicide doesn't seem implausible."

"Yeah, but he was turning the corner. Hell, you saw him ride. It doesn't make any sense." My hands were shaking. I took a deep breath. Showing emotions wasn't something the men in my family did. If there was trauma to deal with, we usually did it with a joke in public, then waited until we were alone to let it out. This time, I couldn't think of a joke. So I held it in.

"I know that look, Nick. Promise me you won't get crazy on me." She pulled me close and wrapped her arms around me. She felt warm and I breathed her peppery perfume. I hadn't always had someone to lean on and was glad she was there now. "I know he was your friend but promise me you'll let my team do their work."

I wasn't gonna commit to staying on the sidelines. Instead of answering, I changed the subject. "Where's Aaron?"

"I sent him home with my sister." She checked her watch. It was a little after ten. "It's gonna be a late night."

I smiled at her. "Go to work. I'll catch up with you later."

She studied my face closely. Waiting for an answer. When I didn't give it to her, she kissed me and turned to meet the three-man CSI team. She clicked into detective mode again and quickly took charge. I admired the way she handled herself. She was five-foot-nothing and as pretty as any actor playing a detective on TV, but when the shit hit the fan, she kicked ass and took names.

That didn't change the fact that I was a detective too. Law enforcement was in my blood. My dad had been a county sheriff, I'd been a reserve deputy in Travis County. I'd also spent two years in law school. I respected the law but knew the dirty secret that the system sometimes fingered an innocent man, and a court room was all about what could be proved. Justice, often times, was something never addressed. I was neither and outlaw nor a vigilante, but as a private investigator I was free to play my hunches without covering my ass in triplicate forms. I got out my cell phone and replayed the message Colton left me a few hours ago. "*We need to talk*," he said. Was he anxious or stressed? I couldn't really tell. I played it again. Was it a cry for help from a man in the grip of personal demons? He was near the chutes in the arena when he called, because I could hear the announcer in the background. Maybe he was looking for me in the stands. Maybe he saw someone else who got his attention. I remembered the shadow that fell across his face and the tall man he met.

I approached the pen to wave goodbye to Diana. She and the CSI team were busy working the scene, taking pictures, and combing the area for evidence. I glanced at Colton's body again. They hadn't moved him. He still lay on the straw in a crumpled heap. I realized what was wrong and what had bothered me when I first saw him. His cowboy hat. He still wore his cowboy hat. If he shot himself, Colton would have had to reach up over the brim and point the pistol down. It was possible, but unlikely. He was a rodeo cowboy. His outfit was an important part of who he was. His hat was a 40X Arena that cost eight hundred dollars. He'd bought it with his first winnings. Besides, if he wanted a sure shot, he would have put the barrel in his mouth or jammed it under his chin. Why take a chance on a miss? Colton had weapons training and had witnessed his share of bullet wounds. He knew how to make a kill shot. Also, the pistol was still in his hand. The recoil would have kicked the weapon loose.

All the self-pity and sorrow drained from my system. In its place came anger. Colton Macrae didn't kill himself. Someone had murdered him. I put my hands on the top of the panel fence and spoke, hoping Colton could hear from wherever he was. "I'll get the son of a bitch. And when I do, I'll give him what he gave you—a bullet to the head."

CHAPTER THREE

I sat in the Frost Bank Center parking lot waiting for traffic to thin and my blood pressure to return to normal. I needed time to think away from Diana. She had her procedure and I had mine. She would let me know what, if anything, she turned up at the crime scene. It would take her most of the night to process the livestock pen and interview any witnesses. She was thorough and good at her job, and I respected what she did, but she also had to answer to a bureaucracy. I could move fast and work angles outside of normal procedure. This had cause friction with two prior girlfriends, the last being Kelly, who as on the police force in Lubbock. I didn't know if my investigating Colton's death would cause friction between Diana and me. But this case was personal. Colton was my friend and a fellow Marine. I wanted the killer in the worst way. I wanted justice for my brother, before the perp was swept up in a legal system that I knew from experience might give him a pass.

I opened the console of my pickup and pulled out a new spiral notebook from the stack I kept for new cases. I had a system. Skeeter called it "old school," but it worked for me. He was my partner, and I hired him because he had a knack for research and all things electronic, not my strong point. He saved me from legwork that five or ten years ago would have added days or weeks to an investigation. On my last case, he was able to link the gangster I was after for kidnapping a young girl to a used tire shop and three pawn shops he used for money laundering. The online search took one afternoon, and I was able to act on the information before the thug disappeared out of the country with the girl. In other words, his research allowed me to literally cut to the chase. I would no doubt need him before this case was all over. But before I called Skeeter, my process always started with a notebook.

I started with what I knew, then drove around thinking about hunting, or fishing, or how to keep the neighbor's llamas from breaking into the hayfield. When I wasn't focused directly on the case, I usually had a breakthrough. A thought would jump to the front of my brain, or I would make a connection that eventually led to a suspect. How it worked was a mystery, and as long as it kept working, I didn't question the process.

I wrote Colton Macrae at the top of the first page, then stopped to tap my pen on the steering wheel. Who would want him dead? Six months ago, I would have put his own name at the top of likely suspects. He was addicted to pain pills and Jack Daniels, part of his arm was missing, and he was no longer in combat fighting alongside a tight-knit band of brothers. That camaraderie along with the adrenaline rush was as hard to replace as his missing arm. I knew what it was like because I'd made the same stark transition to civilian life. I'd followed the same path he had, using eighty proof to mask the real world. I watched him hit bottom. I stayed with him when he passed out covered in puck and mumbling about the brotherhood. In a rare sober moment, he told me about riding broncs and bulls before he was a Marine. Just talking about it rekindled a spark that we both thought had died forever. I encouraged him to get back into it. He was reluctant at first because he couldn't do it drunk. I put up his entry fee and watched as a red-roan bronc took three seconds to toss him onto the arena dirt. That was the beginning. He had something to live for. The three seconds turned into five, then six, and finally the full eight seconds. By the time he'd won his first purse, rodeo was in his blood. When Garth Brooks sang about rodeo, he was describing Colton Macrae. "It'll drive a cowboy crazy; it'll drive a man insane. And he'll sell off everything he owns just to pay to play her game." He loved rodeo, and he was good at it. His final ride proved that. He didn't kill himself.

He'd left me a message before the bronc-riding event. "We need to talk." I wrote that down under his name. What was it he wanted to tell me? I remembered the stranger behind the chutes after the ride. Colton had been searching for me in the crowd. When our eyes met, he tipped his hat in salute, but then something or someone caught his attention. Was it someone from his drug-fueled past? Maybe a dealer he had stiffed came to see him, sensing a payday? I wrote the words *drug dealer* under his name and added a question mark. I knew something of what went on in that world from a case I'd worked involving Skeeter. He'd been framed for an apartment fire that killed twenty people. The setup involved a dealer who was trying to take out a rival gang leader. They were a vicious breed and certainly capable of murder, especially if they were owed money. Maybe he made other enemies in that wasted phase before I found him at the VFW. I had encouraged him to sever all ties to that part of his life, but there was one person he wouldn't let go of no matter how much I insisted. Her name was Lora Michaels, a stripper at the Paradise Club. I wrote her name down next.

She was the love of his life, or so he told me. I dreaded the prospect of tracking her down, because I'd once been taken in by her twisted charms and regretted it ever since. I tried to warn Colton. The night before the rodeo, we had nearly come to blows when he insisted on meeting her. We were at Lucky's boxing gym working out. He'd been sober for three months. He got a text message. "*Colton, I'm lonely.*" It was from Lora. I told him to ignore her, but it was like telling Sam, my Labrador retriever, not to jump into the water. I didn't know if she was capable of murder, but if Colton's past had come back to haunt him, she could be the spirit medium.

It was midnight by the time I arrived at the Paradise Club, which was about as far from paradise as anyone could get. I'd met Lora there one night about a month after I mustered out of the Corps. My physical wounds were healed. The only sign of my ordeal were the star-shaped scars on my forehead that linger there today. I did my best to hide the deeper wounds with gallons of Jack Daniels. Single veterans who liked to drink usually ended up in all the wrong places, which was what led me to the Paradise Club one night when Lora was on stage.

It was the same for Colton, only instead of a brief indiscretion, as in my case, Lora had managed to sink her hook deep into Colton's heart. "*I love her,*" he'd told me. "*Don't ask me why, I just do.*" Lora knew how to push his buttons and take his disability check. She loved mostly on the first of the month, when the VA check posted to his bank account. She was his while the money lasted and, like a shot of heroin, left him craving more.

I stashed the notebook back into the console and circled the parking lot searching for an empty space. It was Thursday night, and the gates of paradise were open for business. I found a spot in the back and slipped off the .38 I carried on my ankle and locked it in the glovebox. I didn't want to start trouble; the front door had a metal detector. I just needed to find Lora and ask her what she knew. I opened my door, and the dome light came on. I gave myself the once-over in the rearview mirror. I was dressed for the rodeo, from my gray western snap shirt to my Wranglers and Justin boots, but I wouldn't stand out in a crowd anywhere in Texas. My black Resistol cowboy hat covered most of the scars on my forehead. Skeeter claimed I suffered from "damsel in distress" syndrome and I knew Lora could play the victim like the best of them. *Stay focused, partner. She's gonna have a sad tale to tell and all her assets will be on display.* I practiced my most disarming smile. The words echoed in the pickup cab. I wasn't above a little pep talk.

I handed my ten-dollar cover charge to the porky bouncer at the door and waited for my eyes to adjust to the dimly lit surroundings. There were three mirror-top stages surrounded by drooling patrons. The women on mirrors were working their hips to a hip-hop tune with a heavy bass beat and enjoying raucous cheers, wolf whistles, and generous tips from their admirers.

Lora wasn't on stage, but it didn't mean she wasn't there. I found a seat at the bar in the back and attracted the attention of a waitress in a sequined bustier. She said her name was Dallas and she sold me an overpriced bottle of Shiner Bock. I asked her if she'd seen Lora tonight.

"Ya just missed her, cowboy," she said, touching the brim of my hat. "You know her?" She gave me toothy grin.

"Yeah, we go way back. Would you tell her Nick Fischer is looking for her?"

"She's on her break. You wanna dance? I'm just as good." At least she was self-confident.

When I didn't respond right away, she said, "Twenty bucks. You can pick the song." She chewed her thumbnail, and I took it as a sign she was lying about Lora's whereabouts.

"No, thanks." I wasn't in the mood for a lap dance. I left Dallas, took my beer, and walked toward the dressing room.

The bouncer watched me approach with a hard expression that told me he wasn't going to let me in or answer any of my questions. He was bald and a couple of inches taller than me. He had a recent scar on his left cheek and a flat nose like a prize fighter. I dug out my private detective license and held it up to his face.

"I'm looking for Lora Michaels," I shouted above a heavy metal song that had followed the hip-hop masterpiece.

"So what?" he said.

"She's in trouble." I was making it up as I went along. "I'm Nick Fischer."

"You'll have to wait till she comes back to dance."

"How long will that be?"

He checked his wristwatch as if he could tell time.

"I just need to talk to her. Ask her a few questions."

He took a closer look at my creds. "You ain't a cop. Fuck off."

"Thanks for your time." I put my license back in my wallet and headed for the front door. Out of the corner of my eye, I saw the bouncer get off his stool and hustle into the dressing room. I wondered if he would warn Lora that someone was looking for her. I asked the porky bouncer for my cover charge back since I hadn't been in the place more than ten minutes. He laughed like he heard that one a dozen times a night.

"You paid for a look."

Yes, I did, I thought. And I wasn't proud of it. "Name's Nick Fischer," I said. "As in fisherman, get it? I just came in to see Lora Michaels." I wanted to make sure she knew who'd been looking for her. The bouncer nodded like a bobblehead doll. I fished a business card from my wallet and handed it to him. I was proud of the design, two crossed swords over the Marine Corps motto. He stopped bobbing long enough to read it.

"Semper Fi," he said, giving me a little salute. At least he didn't mispronounce it. "Yeah, I heard of you. You the guy who busted those dudes at Club Forty-Four?"

"That's right," I said. All the better if he recognized me. The gangster who trafficked in young women provided dancers to a rival strip club. When I found out, I went looking for him and the girl I was after. When the manager wouldn't cooperate, I took the place apart. That was five months ago, and the place still hadn't reopened.

"This place is clean, man. Don't repeat that shit here."

"That's good to know. I don't have anything on you. I just wanna talk to Lora."

"Sure thing. I'll pass that along."

Back out in the cool, damp parking lot, I hustled around to the VIP entrance in the back of the building. All three employees had reacted a little strange, like they were covering for her. I found her car, only she wasn't getting in. Lora Michaels was getting out of her white BMW. She wore a black hoodie sweatshirt and jeans. She tugged at the hood, trying to cover her face, then hustled toward the VIP entrance. Nothing she wore could cover the figure that made a cowboy want to sell his horse and saddle just to see her smile.

I stepped out of the shadows. "Hey, Lora. Been a long time."

She froze for an instant but recovered quickly. "Nick. Wow, good to see you."

"Did you talk to Colton tonight?"

I caught the edge of the hoodie before she could turn away. There was a fresh cut on her cheek. "What the hell happened to you?"

"Must've bumped into the wall."

"Where you been?"

"What're you talking about? I've been here workin'. I came out to get some fresh air."

I put my hand on the Beemer and felt the heat from the engine.

"I had the engine running with the heater on," she said.

"So, when did you talk to Colton last?"

"A week or so, why?"

"You're lyin'. He texted you yesterday. I saw him do it. I know he went to see you last night."

"Okay. Yeah, he told me you said to forget about me. Why was that, Nick?"

"You know why."

She pulled away and wiped her streaked mascara with the sleeve of her sweatshirt. "I can't talk now." She shot a frightened look toward the VIP door. "I'm due on stage soon."

I grabbed her wrist and forced her to face me. "Colton's dead, Lora. Someone shot him in the head after his bronc ride tonight. When did you talk to him last?"

Her eyes grew bigger, and her face turned pale under the halogen streetlamps. I couldn't tell whether she was acting or genuinely shocked. A second later, tears flooded her face.

"Oh, my god. Not him. Not Colton."

"Where were you during the rodeo tonight? Did you go to see him?"

"No, I told you I've been here working. Everybody inside will vouch for me."

"Come on, Lora. I know you're lyin'."

"Please, Nick. Just let me go."

"Not until you tell me what's going on."

"I can't. There's nothing you can do."

CHAPTER FOUR

Lora Michaels was lying. She hadn't been at the club. The staff was covering for her. The question was, where had she been? Could she be involved with Colton's murder? I knew she was a gold digger, but I didn't think she could pull a trigger and shoot someone in cold blood. Maybe I was soft on women. Maybe Skeeter was right about my "damsel in distress" syndrome. But I'd been taken in by her once already. I wasn't going to let it happen again.

I waited in my pickup and watched the Paradise parking lot through the steady drizzle. It didn't take long for her to hustle back out the VIP door and into her white BMW. I pulled out of the parking lot behind her. She wasn't wasting any time. She got on the 410 Loop heading south. The traffic was still heavy, and I stayed a few cars back in case she was worried about a tail. One thing about her, she wasn't stupid, and she dealt with the kind of scum that lurked just below the Alamo City's happy green façade, the kind of people who might tail you across town just for the hell of it or something worse. When she took the exit north of downtown, I knew where she was going. Lora Michaels lived in a new condo complex near the old Pearl brewery that had been converted to a trendy San Antonio shopping and entertainment district. The rent wasn't cheap, but she could afford it. It was only a block away from the North River Walk, where my ex-girlfriend Sylvia lived when we were dating.

I parked on the street, jogged to the front entrance, and took the stairs up to the fourth floor. The route made me uneasy, and by the time I reached her door, I realized why. The last time I'd walked up her steps, a fifth of Jack chased by a six-pack of Shiner urged me to break down her door because I'd watched her leave the strip club with a Navy squid home on leave. I woke up the next morning on her floor with a broken knuckle and a screaming hangover. I never knew what happened to the squid, and Lora was passed out on the couch. That afternoon I drove back to Grandpa's ranch near Fredericksburg. He locked my pickup in the barn and let me wallow in my own self-pity until I was sober, then he put me to work building a fence in the brutal Central Texas summer heat. He had a two-part recipe for rehabilitation the consisted of equal parts manual labor and the study of history. He said work kept your mind off your personal problems, and history taught you that you weren't the only poor son of a bitch who's ever suffered heart ache. He started me with a book by Spanish explorer Cabeza de Vaca. He survived a doomed expedition to Florida in 1527 and spent the next eight years crossing North America on foot, eventually catching a boat ride back to Spain. Along the way he was held as a slave by the Karankawa and the Coahuiltecan tribes in Texas, promoted as a faith healer, and forced to suffer hunger and physical hardships beyond imagination. His account supersedes the concept of a "noble savage" and instead describes the brutal reality that life in primitive societies was indeed "nasty, brutish, and short." My own suffering in combat was by comparison nasty, brutish, but considerably shorter than eight years. But like Cabeza de Vaca, I did make it home alive. Grandpa reminded me that life goes on. At least, for everyone except Colton. And I was here to find out why.

I shook off the memory and knocked on Lora's door.

"You shouldn't be here," she said when she opened the door. I pushed the door open and walked into the living room. It was just like I remembered it, only dirtier, decorated all in white like a hospital room except it smelled like Lora's sweet perfume mixed with vodka and stale cigarette smoke.

I noticed she poked her head out the door and glanced up and down the hall before she shut and bolted the door behind me.

"You scared of someone?" I asked. The Lora I remembered wasn't scared of anybody.

"What if I was? You gonna protect me, Nick? Is that why you're here?" She kicked off her shoes and tossed her keys on the kitchen bar. I had tried to save her once, or at least I offered her a ride out of the strip club business. It was after I'd sobered up and started college. I went back just to see if she was still around. She was. Places like that don't look the same when you're sober. I offered her a sober lifestyle and a life on the outside, but she didn't want to be saved. She'd found her calling and was more than happy with what she was doing.

"I'm not gonna make the same mistake again. I'm not here for you. I'm here for Colton."

Lora took off her black hoodie sweatshirt and tossed it on the back of the couch. "You wanna drink?" She had on a thin pink cotton T-shirt with a V-neck. There was nothing underneath. She was never shy about her body. "Still drinking Jack?"

"Not so much anymore." I kept my own jacket on, not wanting to get comfortable. "When did you talk to Colton last?"

She went into the kitchen and opened the cabinet below the counter.

"You might as well tell me. The police will check his phone records," I said.

"He texted me tonight," she said and set a half-empty jug of Jack Daniels on the bar.

"And?"

"And that's it. He was a rodeo cowboy living his dream. He said he had a good draw. The horse was a high scorer, whatever that means. I wished him good luck. I was working. I couldn't go to the rodeo." She put ice into two bourbon glasses and poured one full of Jack and one full of Tito's vodka. She slid the Jack across the bar to me. "Cheers," she said and raised her glass. "To Colton."

She held her glass up until I reluctantly joined her. "To Colton," I said. I took a sip. Lora drank half the glass in one gulp. Tears filled her eyes and streaked mascara down her cheeks.

I put my arm around her waist and guided her over to the once white couch.

"You're wrong about me," she said. "I loved him." She could barely get the words out between sobs.

"You have to tell me what's going on," I insisted. "I wanna know what happened to Colton. Who was after him? I saw him meet a tall guy in black with a short military haircut. It was after his ride. Behind the chutes. Do you know who I'm talkin' about?"

Lora caught her breath and held it, trying to hold back her tears. Either she was putting on a good show of being all broken up about Colton's death, or she really did love him. I couldn't decide which. If she did, it would be a first for her.

I took her hands and pulled them away from her face. She looked at me with bloodshot eyes. Her shoulders trembled. "Will—you—protect—me?" she managed to say. Her eyelids dropped to half-mast and pulled my hands against her surgically enhanced breasts. She leaned close, pressing herself into me. Her hands dropped to my lap. Her breath smelled like vodka mixed with peppermint Altoids. I felt the sucking sensation pulling me into her twisted world, like a sailor drawn toward the rocks by a siren's song. I froze, feeling her fingers on my belt buckle. *Damn it!* I thought. She almost had me again. Even after all I'd been through with her. I grabbed her hands.

"Cut the crap, Lora. You forget who you're talkin' to?" I couldn't believe that I'd almost fallen for her act again, even though I knew exactly what she would do.

She batted her bloodshot eyes. I shook my head. She'd done the same thing to so many men, she didn't know how predictable she was. "Tell me about Colton. You weren't at the club. Not till I saw you. I talked to the staff. They were covering for you. Did you go to the rodeo?"

"I don't know anything, Nick. Please believe me." She wasn't gonna give up that easily.

"I get it. You're in some kind of trouble. If anybody can get out of it, you can. So don't give me that weak and innocent bullshit. Whatever you're into, I know you did it on your own. Only this time you dragged an innocent kid down with you." She had a soft vulnerability that was a natural part of her personality. It was what attracted men to her, besides her surgically enhanced assets. She could make herself look so fragile and delicate that men would line up to protect her. I knew because I'd been one of them.

"It's not like that," she whispered.

"Who gave you the mark on your face?"

She chewed her bottom lip.

"I never wanted to hurt you," she said, tears flowing now.

I grabbed her shoulders and hauled her to her feet. "Stop it. I know you. I've seen all your moves. It hasn't been that long ago. I'm sober now. Your BS doesn't work anymore. I tried to warn Colton about you, but he wouldn't listen. Now he's dead. Tell me what you know, or I will drag your ass down to the police station right now."

Lora's expression changed like the surface of a lake on a cloudy day. I caught her slap on my left cheek. She had muscles from daily workouts. I felt my cheek burn red. Her fragile expression morphed into anger. Her green eyes flared like tiki torches at a beachfront Puerto Vallarta bar. She'd been acting her whole life and could have easily made a living in front of the camera if she hadn't been born with a dark side. I caught her hands before she could land another slap. "This isn't about you or me. It's about Colton. He was murdered."

She jerked her hands away from me. "Up yours, Nick. I don't know anything about it. Colton cared more about the rodeo than me." She walked back to the kitchen and poured herself another glass of Tito's.

"That's more like it. Now we're making progress. That's the Lora I know and love."

She downed the vodka in one gulp. "Fuck you, Nick. Get the hell out of here."

CHAPTER FIVE

I drove back to my fixer-upper in the King William neighborhood a few miles south of the Alamo. It was one of the oldest neighborhoods in the city, named after Kaiser Wilhelm I of Prussia and built by prosperous German businessmen in the nineteenth century on the banks of the San Antonio River. Many of the houses were ornate Victorian style, and those that were maintained or renovated gave the area an old-school charm. I'd purchased a fixer-upper on the fringe of the district with the idea of doing the renovation myself and making a profit on the resale. That was five years ago. The last time I pulled into the Home Depot parking lot, I got a call from a client. It's always urgent. "Nick, you have to help me." If there's a paycheck involved, I can't turn them down. Maybe after this case, I'd get started on the renovation.

The rain had stopped, but it was still cold outside, and the streets were wet and empty at four a.m. Winter painted the normally green canopy of trees over the Alamo city a dull gray with occasional patches of olive-green live oaks and cedar.

I parked in the driveway. Diana's car was already there. I hadn't expected her to be off before I got home and wondered if she'd decided to pass Colton's case off to another detective. A light from my neighbor's kitchen window flicked on, and Rose Gustafson waved at me. She was a good neighbor, even if she was a bit of a busybody. I loved her cooking, which she shared almost as frequently as her opinions. She was a retired biology professor and an insomniac who kept a notebook beside every window in her house to write notes about people coming and going in the neighborhood. She never showed me the contents, but I got the feeling my activities featured prominently. Her other neighbors were retired, in bed by nine, and never had armed guards protecting their house.

I fought the urge to breakout my notebook and work over my notes. Seeing Lora hadn't really added anything new. She was lying, that much was a given. But I couldn't yet see a direct connection between her and Colton's murder. It was time to put it out of my mind and trust the process. My best solutions came when I wasn't thinking about the problem.

I got out of my pickup and waved back. "Hello, Rose," I said in a normal voice, knowing she was reading my lips. "Mark the time down." She raised her pen and notebook. I saw her smile. It was comforting knowing somebody was keeping tabs on me. I walked to the front door. Inside, the room was warm and smelled of perfume and hot tea. "Anybody home?" I called. It was an odd sensation that, added to the evening's events, left me briefly disoriented. For most of my adult life, minus the four years I spent in the Marines, I'd lived alone with my canine companions. For the last five years my roommate had been Sam, a chocolate Lab, who brought his own set of standards and demands—we went for a run whatever time I got home, even if it was four in the morning. He finished anything left over from dinner. And we didn't miss an opening day of dove or duck season. That had all changed when Diana entered the equation. She took over the closet in the spare bedroom and kept feminine products in the bathroom and quickly dismissed any demands Sam made on my time if they interfered with her plans. I knew he was jealous, but he mostly kept it to himself. It was hard not to like Diana.

Sam instantly planted himself between my legs and began inspecting my pants and boots for unfamiliar smells. There were a lot of them tonight, and he made an anxious bark, which made me think it didn't take him long to unravel my backtrail. His Sherlock senses were locked in, and if he could speak, I'm sure he'd have questioned me about the Paradise Club and Lora's condo. Even I could still smell her sweet perfume and vodka on my Wranglers.

"Can we talk about this later?" I asked him. "I'm kinda beat."

He licked my hand and wagged his tail, absolving me of all my sins. Now, I felt guilty for not taking him out for our usual nighttime run.

"In here," Diana responded.

Sam and I looked toward the voice, then back at each other. I shrugged. We would both need time to adjust.

I found Diana stirring a cup of hot tea in the kitchen. She stood and studied my face. "You okay? Where were you?" She wrapped her arms around me. "I was worried."

I kissed her neck. She felt warm and I didn't mind the concern in her voice.

"I'm fine. I went to talk to Colton's girlfriend." I felt her stiffen.

"The stripper?"

"Yep."

"And?"

"She's got an alibi."

"She doesn't need one. You saw the body. The preliminary report shows suicide. Nothing I found changes that. So, it's not my case. That's why I got home early."

It was my turn to stiffen. I expected her to say suicide, but in the hours since I'd left the cattle barn, I'd been in investigation mode, focused on who had shot Colton in the head and what I would do when I found out who did it.

Sam sensed the serious tone in our conversation and crouched beside the table, looking at us with Labrador concern.

"Talk to me," she said, resting her head on my chest. "I have to follow the evidence. So far, nothing says he was murdered."

"I understand."

"But you think it was murder."

"It was murder." I let go of her and grabbed a bottled water from the fridge.

"You wanna share your theory?"

"Not at four a.m."

She put her arms back around me and kissed me on the cheek. "You're still upset. I can feel it. I know you. You have a hunch and you're gonna let it play out no matter what I say."

"You okay with that?"

She smiled. "Do I have a choice?"

I relaxed and kissed her on the lips. "Truce."

"Truce."

I worked my way down past her neck and kissed the top of her shoulder blade.

She wrapped her arms around me and pulled me tight against her. "I thought you were tired?"

"If I don't take Sam for his run, I need my exercise."

"Don't let me interrupt your routine."

"Sam will understand."

Sam heard his name and barked.

"You're sure?"

I pulled her close and ignored Sam. The scent of manure and straw lingered on her clothes. "You smell like a cattle barn."

She sniffed at her own clothes. "Oh my god. I'm gonna shower." She tried to push me away.

I held fast. "It's an aphrodisiac to a country boy."

She laughed as I unbuckled her belt and tugged off her jeans. She kicked them to the floor and wrapped her legs around me. I needed to feel someone like Diana. Someone pure and honest to wash the bitter taste of Lora away and replace the numbness I felt after Colton's death.

I shuffled to the kitchen table, set her down, and pulled her T-shirt over her head. She had olive skin over toned muscles that I couldn't keep my hand from caressing.

"You're harassing a police officer," she whispered.

"So, arrest me."

• • •

We woke the next morning in my bed. It hadn't taken us long to realize that the kitchen table only looked romantic in the movies. Sam had his front paws planted on my side of the bed. He gave a little huff, reminding me that I'd slept passed his breakfast.

Diana opened her eyes and smiled at me. "We'll never be sleeping in, will we?"

"Not with Sam and your son around." I kissed her, and she snuggled into my chest. "So, what did you find at the scene?" I asked her.

"Back to business?"

"Sorry, can't help it."

She pushed up on her elbow and faced me. "Everything points to suicide. We're waiting for the autopsy."

"There's no way he pulled the trigger. Look at the angle of the bullet."

"It doesn't prove he was murdered."

"Be serious."

"Hey, I'm trying to give you some wiggle room."

"Why me?"

"He had your pistol in his hand."

"I told you it was mine."

"Goddamnit, Nick. Why would you give a pistol to a wounded veteran with PTSD? The DA wants to charge you with aiding suicide or criminal negligence. Maybe both."

"That was quick. How does she already know about the case?"

"It was on the evening news. She came to the station personally to get my preliminary report."

"Colton didn't kill himself."

"If that's true, we better come up with some hard evidence very soon." She studied my face. "Nick, I'm worried. None of this looks good. The DA would like nothing more than to take your license and toss you in jail."

"You really think I aided him?"

"No, of course not. I know you were trying to help him." She put her head back down on my chest. "It doesn't matter what I think. When you shot Marcus Lopez, you made a lot of enemies. They all wanted him to be governor. One of them is now an assistant DA."

"Sylvia Flores."

"That's right. Your old girlfriend."

"She should have been charged." I pointed to the angry scar on my left breast. "She's responsible for this."

She kissed the red mark on my chest. "I know. She's a bitch."

Sam's whining switched to loud yips.

"I better go feed him before he goes after one of Rose's cats for breakfast."

"He would do that?"

"He wouldn't eat it, but he wouldn't be against chasing it to get my attention." I got up and slipped on a pair of sweatpants.

"We're not done here," she said as I was walking out.

I refilled Sam's food and water dishes and watched him devour a cup of dry chow like he hadn't eaten for a week.

Diana was right about the DA having her sights set on destroying my career. She'd been one of Marcus Lopez's biggest supporters, and he'd been a shoo-in for governor. Smart, charismatic, ruthlessly ambitious, Lopez encapsulated the qualities necessary to turn Texas into a blue state. One minor problem. He blackmailed a wealthy family to finance his campaign. When I caught up to him, he put a bullet in my chest, and I blew his brains out.

In public, the DA had to express outrage when Lopez's corruption was revealed. In private, she directed her outrage at me for exposing him and ruining her own statewide political ambitions that would have resulted from the huge political change in Texas. As it stood, that change wouldn't be happening for the foreseeable future.

When I came back inside, Diana had made a pot of coffee and laid out the crime scene photos CSI had taken in the cattle barn. I warmed my hands on the leftover coals in the fireplace, then poured myself a cup of coffee and examined the pictures. The pistol was definitely my .40 caliber. I recognized the last four digits of the serial number.

Another picture showed a Copenhagen snuff can. My name and phone number were written on the bottom. I recognized the handwriting. I had written it there the night I'd met him. I wondered why he still had the old snuff can in his pocket, until I looked at the next picture. The can was full of hydrocodone tablets. He had wiped the inside clean and used it as a convenient pill container. No one would think to question a rodeo cowboy with a can of snuff in his pocket.

I studied the picture of the entry wound in Colton's cowboy hat. A neat hole cut through the silver crown, and a dark bloodstain coated the underside of the brim.

"This is the key right here. There's no way he held the pistol over his hat brim. He would have taken his hat off if he had done it deliberately." The logic was obvious to me.

"Why would he take his hat off? You never do."

"That's a custom-fit eight hundred hat." I showed her Colton's name embossed on the inside hatband. "He never took it off, but he would fight anyone who laid a hand on it. He would have taken the hat off and placed it crown-down in the hay if he was gonna shoot himself in the head."

"What's with you cowboys and your hats?"

"You wouldn't understand."

"Obviously." She put her hand on my forearm and studied my face. "Only three people went into the pen. Colton, the boy with the steer, and you."

"Did you find the slug?"

"No. It passed through the body and must have hit the concrete under the straw and bounced. Or maybe one of the metal poles on the pen. We couldn't find a trace."

"I'll bet you that my pistol isn't the murder weapon."

"Come on, it was fired. It was in his hand. After the official ME report, I won't even be on the case. Because there is no case. Which means that—"

My cell phone rang, cutting her off. Whatever she wanted to say next, she kept it to herself. I let it go to voice mail. It might have been Lora, and I didn't want to answer while Diana was in the room. I heard a beep when whoever it was left a voice message.

Diana turned to the counter and poured herself another cup of coffee. "Aren't you gonna see who it was?"

I picked up my phone off the counter and looked at the message. "It's from John Macrae."

"That's Colton's father," she said. "I tried to reach him last night. Why's he calling you?"

I dialed the number he left. When John Colton answered, I introduced myself, then listened. He wanted to meet me right away. We set up a place and time, and I disconnected.

"What'd he want?"

"To find Colton's killer."

Diana twisted her lips into a frown, showing her displeasure. "Can we talk about this first?"

"Gotta go. I'm meeting him at City Market in Luling."

"At least bring home some barbecue," she called after me.

CHAPTER SIX

The City Market in Luling served beef brisket Texas style, slow-cooked to perfection. They served other things too, like sausage, pork ribs, and baked pinto beans, but when Texans refer to barbecue, they're talking about beef brisket. City Market served the best in the state. John Macrae suggested we meet there because the town was roughly halfway between my house in San Antonio and his in Austin, but I was always looking for an excuse to drive to Luling and eat barbecue. The occasion could have been happier, but I was hoping the brisket would ease some of the pain.

I'd only gotten snippets of information from Colton about his relationship with his dad. The picture he painted was of a hard-ass with extremely high expectations. He'd been a Navy doctor and served in Iraq during the Gulf War. When Colton came of age, he'd heard his father talk about his exploits enough to recite them word for word. According to Colton, his dad was a prick who pressed Colton never to show weakness. He wanted Colton to excel at sports and encouraged him to play football and go to college, but Colton never liked team sports. The only thing he liked to do was ride broncs. His dream was to compete in the National Finals Rodeo. His father didn't approve, so Colton joined the Marine Corps. He admitted it was partially to prove to his father that he could survive the training, but it was also because he wanted to prove it to himself.

He'd gotten my name from Colton. Once he'd sobered up and started to turn his life around, I'd encouraged him to contact his dad, if nothing else, to give him an update on his progress. Family was everything to me, and I knew Colton disagreed, but I couldn't help but think his self-destructive behavior began well before that IED took part of his arm.

As I made the hour drive to Luling, I thought about what John Macrae said on the phone. He refused to believe that his son could commit suicide. He not only refused to believe it, he challenged me to disagree with him. But there was something more to what he said. I got the impression that he felt the idea of suicide was a negative reflection on him as a father. Whatever his motivation, I agreed with him that Colton was murdered.

Luling was a sleepy town of less than six thousand people on the banks of the San Marcus river. It started out as a rowdy drover town on the old Chisholm cattle trail in the nineteenth century and survived long enough to witness the discovery of oil and gas in the early twentieth century. A handful of active pumpjacks in the city limits were a testament to the petroleum boom. Even with the windows rolled up to shield against the wintery weather, the putrid sulfur smell of natural gas enveloped the town like a dirty undershirt forgotten for months in the clothes hamper. I wondered if knowing your town has the best barbecue restaurant in the state was any consolation for enduring the smell twenty-four seven.

I drove over the railroad tracks and parked on Davis Street a block down from the restaurant. The street was lined with false-front buildings and, except for pickups instead of horses, hadn't changed much in the last hundred years. A line spilled out the front door of the City Market as it always did around noon on a weekday, rain or shine. Bitter cold or blistering heat. Nobody ever complained about the wait. I clamped on my cowboy hat and slipped into my blanket-lined barn coat in case the line was slow.

I spotted a tall man in his late fifties with a military bearing wearing a dark suit and tie under a knee-length raincoat. I studied the man before he turned to face me. He resembled Colton. They both had blond hair, although John's was turning gray, and each had a distinctive cleft chin. He'd spent twenty years in the military, and it showed in his squared shoulders and air of authority.

"Howdy," I said, stepping in line behind him. "I'm Nick Fischer."

He turned and studied my black hat and barn coat. His expression was grim, what you'd expect from a father who'd just learned of his son's death. He held out his hand.

"Thank you for coming, Nick," he said.

He had the grip of a man who kept up his military workout routine and held my gaze like every Navy commander I'd ever met, ready to give an order.

"You come here a lot?" I asked and held the door open for him to enter the restaurant.

"Not as often as I'd like. Colton and I..." He hesitated for a moment before going on. "I used to bring Colton on my motorcycle when he was in grade school. I had a Harley Ultra that we put quite a few miles on."

"I ride a BMW dual sport."

"You must like the dirt roads," he said.

While we waited in line, I told him about a trip I'd made last spring on dirt roads through New Mexico and up into Colorado. We compared notes about the Three Twisted Sisters ride west of Kerrville, so called because the two-lane blacktop had dozens of hairpin turns that wound through picturesque limestone hills. Most Texas motorcycle enthusiasts made the trip at least once a year. Some were out there every weekend.

When it was our turn to order, we walked through a screen-door entrance to the pit room in the back of the restaurant. A middle-aged man in a white T-shirt and Buddy Holly glasses stood behind the counter. The smell of slow-roasted meat permeated every surface in the room, and years of woodsmoke painted the walls black. Behind him, two meat cutters sliced and diced sausage, brisket, chicken, and turkey with the precision acquired over a lifetime of experience.

I ordered two pounds of moist brisket, and John Macrae ordered four. I liked him already. When you came to a place like City Market, you always took home enough to last a few days. The pit master scratched our order onto a receipt pad with a number two pencil, then added the total in his head. They didn't take checks or credit cards and didn't use a calculator. You paid with cash or left empty-handed. The pit master scooped our order onto butcher paper, gave us the choice of dark or white bread, and offered us jalapeños and sliced onions on the side. The choices were endless.

I let John Macrae pay for lunch since it was his meeting, then followed him out to the drink counter. We both ordered tea and a side of beans and coleslaw, which came in pint-sized insulated foam cups.

"I'm sorry for your loss, Mr. Macrae," I said when we slid into an open booth near the front door.

He clenched his teeth, controlling his emotion. I suspected I was one of the first to say that to him. I'd recently been on the receiving end of the phrase and knew the words didn't help. The difference was I'd caught the man who'd murdered my granddad red-handed, standing over the body. He'd drawn me into an ambush expecting to kill me, but I turned the tables on him. I hoped to do the same with Colton's killer.

"Call me John. And thank you," he said after he'd recovered. "I guess you know that Colton and I hadn't spoken much since he got out of the Marine Corps."

I sank my teeth into the mouthwatering brisket and felt the meat melt over my tongue. I didn't comment on their past relationship. I didn't think it mattered to the case. It was something John would have to live with.

"He told me you were the one who encouraged him to call me. I appreciate that more than you know," he said.

"His injury hit him hard. Losing a limb is tough. A lot of guys don't make it back from that," I said. "Colton was making a comeback. The ride he made last night at the semifinals was really something to see. He scored a ninety-one."

"He had you to thank for that. He admired you. You were true-blue to the end. It couldn't have been easy to stay with him."

"We were brothers. I lived through the same shit he did."

"Colton didn't share much with me, but I know what it's like. I patched together a lot of Marines." There was anger in his voice and in his expression. "He survived three tours only to be shot dead at a rodeo. That kind of thing isn't supposed to happen. Civilian life is supposed to be tame and devoid of real danger."

I knew what he meant, but because of my chosen work, I'd discovered that both danger, and its twin brother evil, could raise their ugly heads anywhere. "Bad things happen to good people."

"You saw his body. What was your impression?"

I told him what I'd found at the scene and what Diana had showed me. He listened patiently and absorbed every word. I got the feeling he could have repeated everything I said, exactly as I'd said it. I also told him about the DA and the charges I would face if it was suicide. When I was finished, he chewed his brisket and studied my face. Finally, he wiped his mouth on a brown paper towel.

"Sounds like you have double incentives to find Colton's killer."

I swallowed a spoonful of beans and washed it down with tea. He was right, of course, but I didn't want him to think that my being on the case was about anything other than getting justice for Colton.

"Is Ochoa a competent detective?" he asked.

"One of the best SAPD has to offer."

"Then why is she saying Colton committed suicide?"

"She's looking at the evidence at the scene and going by the book. She'll wait for an autopsy."

"You say the pistol in his hand was yours?"

"That's right. He'd had it for about a week. We both used it on the range."

"Why would you give him a pistol given his state of mind?"

The question caught me off guard and put me a little on the defense. "Colton was a mixed-up kid, but he wasn't suicidal. If I'd thought that, I never would have given him the pistol."

John Macrae drank his tea and studied me again in his probing way.

"I agree with you. I wanted to hear you say it. I don't want Detective Ochoa or SAPD to mark Colton's death as a suicide and close the case. But I'm afraid that's what will happen. They won't be any help once that happens. I want you to find his killer."

"I'll do what I can."

"When can you start?"

"I already did."

He wiped his hands again on a paper towel and offered his hand across the table. We shook. "You can send a formal contract to my office. I'll pay your normal fee, but I do want regular updates."

I laid it on the line from the beginning. There was no reason not to tell him everything I knew. "Colton was into drugs," I said. "They found opioid pills in his snuff can."

"I figured that much. He smoked dope in high school. Most of the Austin kids he hung out with did also. You think drugs had something to do with his murder?"

"It's possible. I don't wanna speculate until I dig a little deeper."

He waited for me to say more. When I didn't, he said, "I respect that."

I grabbed a paper to-go sack from the counter and wrapped up the leftover brisket. John Macrae did the same, and I followed him out to his pickup. He wrote out a check for five grand, and I gave him a receipt.

"Catch the son of a bitch," John said. "Colton deserves justice." Without another word, he climbed in his pickup and drove away.

CHAPTER SEVEN

Since the case was official now, and the firm had a paying customer, I called my business partner and asked him to meet me at Lucky's Gym. I'd skipped my morning workout and couldn't afford to lose my edge. I'd made some powerful enemies in my short career. Pissing people off was an occupational hazard, and a little voice was telling me finding Colton's killer wouldn't make me any new friends.

Skeeter and I had been working together since I got him out of prison. He was facing the death penalty for allegedly sparking an apartment building fire that killed twenty people. I found the gangster who set him up, and gave Skeeter his life back. It was one of my first cases. I'd taken it pro bono in order to build my reputation. So far it was working. Although I'd have gone after Colton's killer on my own, having John Macrae paying the bills allowed me to bring in my partner and focus on it full-time.

I hired Skeeter full-time because he had a special talent for computers and electronics. He stumbled onto his calling after a car accident ended his football career. He'd put together a standout career with the University of Texas, but on the night he was drafted by the Washington Redskins, before the name change, he wrapped his Chevy Chevelle around a tree. The EMTs had to cut off his arm just below the elbow to extract him from the twisted metal. In its place, he wore a metal hook as a prosthesis.

I was halfway through my fourth set on the speedbag when Skeeter arrived. The regulars all knew him, so they didn't give him a second glance.

The newcomers, including the high school kids that Lucky let work out for free, turned to stare at the six-foot-seven black man that tipped the scales at three hundred pounds. He claimed to have lost ten pounds, but I couldn't tell. A guy that size with a metal hook for an arm always made a grand entrance.

"What's up?" he asked in his hoarse whisper that seemed to emanate from below the earth's surface.

I kept going until the three-minute set timer went off, then wiped my face with a towel and sank onto the bench against the wall. "We're on a case."

"'Bout time. I wondered when you gonna stop playing daddy and get back to work."

"I didn't know you were that concerned."

"Two months is a long time to go between jobs."

"Why didn't you say something?"

"I didn't want to crowd you. I know how you are when you have a new girlfriend."

"You're so full of shit."

He laughed his baritone chuckle. The rumble was so deep and powerful that a skinny high school kid working a jump rope backed away to a safe distance.

"You could've used the time off to get some exercise."

"I'm still recovering from my last workout."

"That was ten years ago."

"It was a hell of a workout. What have you got for us?" he asked.

"Colton Macrae was murdered last night at the rodeo. He was found in the cattle barn after his bronc ride."

"Read about it online. Any theories?"

"Yeah, and it has to do with opioid pills and Lora Michaels."

He pursed his lips together and shook his head. "Man, I don't like the sound of that. What's the connection?"

"Colton was in love with her."

"Him and every swinging dick at the Paradise Club. You been to see her?"

"I questioned her last night."

"And?"

"She lied, cried, and threw me out."

"So, she ain't changed."

"Not a bit. She claims she was at the club last night. When I questioned the staff, they covered for her. But I found her in the parking lot getting out of her warm Beemer. She'd been somewhere, and someone had smacked her around."

"And you offered to help her out."

"What did you want me to say?"

"You know that girl is the devil."

"You don't have to remind me. She had her hooks into Colton, and now he's dead."

"I'm warning you, man. She's poison. Women like Lora twist you around their little finger. All they gotta say is 'Help me, Nicky,' and you turn into Roy Rogers."

"I love Roy Rogers."

"I know you do, but look what happened with Sylvia. When you thought she was in trouble, you put on your white hat and pulled your six-shooters. You almost got me killed."

"I don't own a white hat, and you know I carry a Springfield .45."

"You know what I mean."

"Besides, that bullet you took was your own damn fault. You left the shotgun in your pickup."

"Still, I'm supposed to be the brains of the agency, and you're the brawn. You're supposed to take the bullet."

"Since when are you the brains?"

"Since I'm the only one in this company who knows anything about the internet. You still stuck in the twentieth century. You'd rather ride your horse or drive around in your pickup, yellin' yippee ki-yay cowboy."

I laughed. "Yeah, you're right. Just think, all that talent would have been wasted if you'd played pro ball and cashed in that million-dollar contract."

"God had other plans for me."

"Well, yippee ki-yay, pardner, we're on a case now, and Lora's involved. And no, I'm not wrapped around her little finger. I like to think I learn from my mistakes."

"You think she pulled the trigger?"

"Could she? Yes. She's got ice water in her veins. Did she? I don't know, but I'm gonna find out."

"Just be careful. That's all I'm sayin'."

"Thanks for the advice. I'll be sure to put on my white hat and grab my six-shooters."

Skeeter's chest rumbled. I was glad that I amused him.

"See what you can find out about the opioid trade in town. Buying, selling, people involved. Everything you can. Colton had pills on him when he died. Maybe that's the connection."

"What's Diana say about this?"

"I haven't talked to her."

"But she's on the investigation?"

"Yeah, but her initial take is Colton shot himself."

"You don't buy that?"

"No way in hell."

"So, SAPD has no case?"

"Except against me. The DA's considerin' charges."

"You? For what?"

"He had my pistol in his hand."

CHAPTER EIGHT

The oldest VFW post in Texas guarded a bend on the San Antonio river north of downtown in a white Victorian-style mansion with ornate Greek pillars supporting three stories and porches on the ground and second story. Spanish-American War veterans started the club and began holding meetings there in 1917. These were the men Teddy Roosevelt recruited on the steps of the Menger Hotel across the street from the Alamo. A picture of the scene hangs on the wall in the hotel bar along with a bull moose head and the uniform Teddy wore charging up San Juan Hill and into the history books.

The post was where I'd first met Colton Macrae. I went back to retrace our relationship from the beginning in the hope of finding a trail or a pattern that might account for his actions. I had already convinced myself that Colton didn't kill himself. His father supported that theory, but that didn't explain the pills hidden in his snuff can at the scene. When Colton was sober, he was charming and charismatic, a happy-go-lucky rodeo cowboy that made everyone around him smile and feel good about themselves. Although I knew what he was going through because I'd been there, his mood was infectious. I wondered now if I'd missed the clues that said Colton wasn't on the road to recovery because of his good ol' boy charm. Had I been so caught up in the barroom back slapping that I'd missed signs that he was still an addict? I wanted to think I was immune to that kind of deceit because I'd lived through my own recovery. But maybe I was wrong, and maybe my M&P Shield pistol did make me an accessory to his death. The thought left a churning cauldron of guilt in the pit of my stomach. From an early age, my grandpa taught me never to second guess my actions. He said, always do what's right the first time and you'll never have to feel guilty. Had I done the right thing giving a pistol to Colton? One way or another, I had to find out the truth.

The lot was full, so I parked my pickup on the street a couple of blocks away and walked to the building. There was a country band playing on the outdoor stage and a collection of patrons on the downstairs porch listening and drinking beer. As I got closer, I recognized a few of the regulars and waved in their direction. They were the type who wore caps that read Vietnam Veteran and leather vests with unit patches and merit ribbons. Some were full of shit and had spent their time in the military shuffling paperwork or moving supplies, but they told good stories and occasionally sprang for beer. Others had faced the enemy and now were spending a lifetime getting over it. I liked the place because it was a mixture of crusty old-timers and the new vets like Colton.

I went inside and walked down the photo-lined hallway to the bar. I spotted Jerry Muth, aka Sarge, from Lucky's Gym sitting on a stool with his back against the wall. He was the real deal, an ex-Army Ranger and Vietnam vet who taught Brazilian jiu-jitsu to wannabe MMA fighters. He was in his seventies, but I knew from experience he hadn't lost his edge. He was also a man of few words who was quick to pick up on what was happening around him. It was a habit that had a lot to do with his job in the military. He never talked about it because most of the stuff he did was still classified. One look at him was enough to know he had some dark secrets, stories worthy of a Rambo sequel.

"Hey, Sarge," I said, taking the stool beside him.

He shook my hand and waited for me to order a beer before he responded. "Heard you had some trouble." He was never one to beat around the bush.

"Where'd you hear it?"

"Murder has a loud echo," he said, his face grim.

"You remember the kid, Colton Macrae?"

He nodded and took a sip from a longneck Shiner Bock.

"You ever see him hanging out in here with anybody in particular besides me?"

He nodded again, then cocked his left eyebrow to indicate the three men sitting at the other end of the bar. He could convey more information in a nod than most people could in a five-minute speech.

I adjusted my chair to get a better view. They were all about Colton's age. One had a prosthetic right leg. Another had a badly burned face that left angry red scar tissue from his ear to his chin. Both looked to be recently mustered out of the service. Their hair was still cut short in the military fashion. The third man had no outward signs of a disability or traces of scars. He wore a sleeveless vest exposing an assortment of tattoos over clearly defined muscles, and his dark hair was bushy and cut like a surfer dude from the eighties.

I sipped my beer and studied them. The surfer dude caught me staring and said something to his two friends. They all laughed.

"Whatcha lookin' at," he yelled down the bar.

I held up my beer in a salute gesture. Surfer dude smiled with uneven front teeth. He seemed to take my gesture as a white flag.

While I continued to watch the trio, I spoke to Sarge. "What's their story?"

"The two with battle scars are on thirty days terminal leave. The one with the hair's story is a bit sketchy. He claims to have been in the Air Force, but he's a little vague on when and where he served. He could be legit. I heard him tell the guy with the burned face that he was with the 'Air Commandos.'"

"Air Force Special Ops?" I was skeptical, but then, I hadn't known many special ops guys besides Sarge. "What do you think?"

"He's cocky enough."

"What's his name?"

"Daniel Sanz. He answers to Danny." Sarge finished his beer. "Just so you know, he does have some training. He took out a couple of biker vets last weekend. The bastards made fun of his hairdo. Danny boy followed them outside and took 'em apart. Even drunk, he's pretty good with his hands."

"Good to know. Listen, Colton had pills on him when he died. Opioid pills. Could he have gotten them from someone in here?"

"Danny's the man to talk to. He don't push it on the old guys like me, but you can bet he's talkin' it up to the new vets at the end of the bar."

I took another look at them. "You want another beer?"

"Nah, I'm good. The wife's expecting me." He stood up to leave. "Watch yourself. Let me know if you need anything," he cautioned.

I'd known him for at least five years and never knew he was married. He was a good guy to have on your side. He and Lucky had stepped in and covered for me on several occasions. As I watched him exit, I thought of the time in Lucky's Gym when four armed thugs were sent to take me out. Sarge and Lucky stepped up to bat, and when the young punks dismissed them as old-timers, Sarge and Lucky wiped the floor with them. They won't make that mistake again.

I ordered another beer and a round for the three young guys at the end of the bar. I had a plan that would require some finesse, and a few rounds of beer and bourbon would help. I hadn't seen the three guys before, so likely as not, they hadn't seen me with Colton. I decided to roll the dice and ordered a double shot of Jack on the rocks.

When the bartender set them up and pointed to me, I held my Jack Daniels up in salute. All three raised their drink. Danny nodded a thank-you. He excused himself from his friends and walked to my end of the bar.

"Thanks for the round," he said. "I'm Danny."

We shook hands. "Nick," I said. He didn't give a last name, so I left mine off the greeting as well.

"What's your story?" Danny asked. "Where'd you serve?"

"Afghanistan. First Marines."

"Figured. A fuckin' jarhead."

"How 'bout you?"

"Air Force."

"Chair Force. That explains the hair."

He chuckled. "Funny. Special ops," he said.

I waited for more explanation, but none came. Sarge was right. He was vague about his service. Some guys were like that, but those guys didn't usually hang out at the VFW on Friday night where sharing your story was part of the ritual, so I was a little suspicious.

"Cool," I said. "How long you been out?"

"A year," he said. "You?"

"Ten years."

"Old-timer."

"Never gets old for me," I said.

"Yeah, why's that?"

I had his attention. He wasn't trying to act like a tough guy, and he seemed genuinely interested. "Pain," I said. "It never goes away." I decided to push an indirect line of questioning. "This helps." I downed the bourbon in one gulp and ordered another. I could feel the headache coming on already, but I couldn't see another way of getting Danny to trust me. I'd had my share of blackouts and hangovers when I first mustered out and didn't want either one again.

"That works," he said and ordered a double shot of his own.

When the bartender brought our drinks, we clinked glasses and tossed them down. It had been a long time since I'd downed two doubles in less than five minutes, and I was already feeling the effects. I would have to find a way to water my drinks down or I would be a basket case before the bar closed. My tolerance level was greatly diminished.

When Danny excused himself to go to the men's room, I ordered a large iced tea. The bartender approved with a nod and didn't say a word when I substituted the tea for the bourbon in my glass. I asked him to do the same on the next round because I was the designated driver.

The two young guys on terminal leave joined us, and I bought them another round. The more Danny drank, the more he talked. We swapped stories from our time in country. He never said where he'd been or when he'd been there, which added credibility. If a guy's lying about his service, he will invariably drop names from the news or battles that caught press attention, stuff any swinging dick could know from reading CNN.

After forty-five minutes, the two young guys excused themselves. Both said they had girlfriends waiting at home. Danny followed them out the door.

I double-timed it to the second floor and watched them in the parking lot. I could see something changing hands. I couldn't be certain what transaction they made, but I could guess. I wondered if this had anything to do with Colton.

By the fourth double shot and as many longnecks, Danny and I were showing off our battle scars. Mine were mainly on my face and easy to see. I'd added a scar on my chest and one on my upper arm, but they were from PI work from a case tracking down a murder suspect. I showed them off but left out the details. He was too drunk to notice they were only a year old. He had an angry knife cut that he took his shirt off to show me and anyone still in the bar. The mark ran from his left nipple to his beltline. He had taken out his attacker, but not before almost losing his large intestine. He said he held his own guts in place while he turned the knife on the assailant. The Air Force sent him to the military hospital in Germany. I knew the place well. It was where every GI wounded overseas ended up before he was shipped stateside.

He confessed to a great discovery he'd made while confined to the hospital. The drugs they gave you helped not only with the pain but with the extreme boredom of staring at the same four walls twenty-four hours a day. This was the bit of information I was looking for. I told Danny that I had the same experience. I knew that Colton had gone through the same thing.

The VFW shut down at two a.m. on Friday, and by last call, Danny was three sheets to the wind, and luckily, I was sobering up. For the last three hours, I'd been sipping tea and laughing my ass off trying to be a convincing drunk.

Two old-timers were standing on the porch when I guided Danny out the front door. Both had gray hair and beards and wore baseball caps that read Vietnam Vet. They were big men who looked like they spent a lot of nights at the VFW drinking beer when they weren't riding their Harley touring bikes cross-country.

I bumped into the biggest of the two, who probably tipped the scales at two sixty. "Excuse me, sir," I said to him.

He turned to his partner. "I remember when I had my first drink." He said it loud enough for Danny to take notice.

"Fuck you, old man," Danny shot back. Even drunk, he had a cocky edge.

"Go sleep it off," the man said.

Danny pulled away from my grip before I knew what was happening.

"You first, fat ass!" he yelled, and planted a barndoor slamming right fist into the man's jaw. The move was quick and efficient and grounded in his feet and the torque of his waist. It wasn't a drunk barfight move. He'd honed that skill from countless hours of practice.

The vet stumbled backward into the porch railing and collapsed on his butt.

The other vet took two quick steps toward me and threw a ham fist. I saw it coming and ducked the punch, slipped my boot heel behind his legs, and gave him a shove. He tumbled into the rail and landed next to his buddy.

Danny giggled like a schoolgirl. "It's past your bedtime, Grandpa."

The one he'd hit wiped blood away from his cheek and grabbed the railing to pull himself up. "You little shit!" he shouted, his face turning red.

I didn't want anyone to get hurt or thrown in jail. So I put a hand on the man's shoulder and shoved him back down on the wooden porch. "Stay down. He's drunk off his ass, but he was spec ops, and he'll take you apart. I'll take him home. No one needs to get hurt," I said in his ear as forcefully as I could. I knew the old-timers were more embarrassed than mad and they respected special operators more than most because their experience with them would be firsthand instead of through TV or the movies.

When I backed away, the men stayed where they were.

Danny giggled some more. "Ya old fart," he said.

I guided him down the steps and out the front gate. I found a bus bench, and we sat down together. Danny rested his head against an advertisement for a real estate company offering free bedroom furniture for all veteran first-time home buyers.

"What'd you say to them?" he asked.

"That you were gonna kick their asses if they got up."

"You're goddamn right," Danny said and giggled some more. He took a prescription bottle from his pocket and popped a white oval-shaped pill into his mouth. He closed his eyes and let his body relax.

"How 'bout lettin' me in on some of that, brother?" I said.

He handed me the bottle. It was hydrocodone. His eyes were closed, but I made a show of opening the bottle and dumping a handful of pills in the palm of my hand.

"Hey, hey, now," Danny said, opening his eyes. "That's the real deal, man." He scooped all but two pills out of my hand and took the bottle back.

"Where do I get some of that?" I asked.

Danny rested his head back on the bench and smiled. "It was a gift, brother."

He talked with a smile and he closed his eyes on his way to la-la land. The pill was already hard at work on top of the Jack Daniels.

"Come on, Danny. Let me in."

"Take it easy," he said, chuckling at the desperation he heard in my voice. "Doc Frank can hook you up."

"Who's Doc Frank? Where do I find him?"

I shook his shoulder, and his head rolled like a bobblehead doll.

"Come on. Don't leave a brother hanging. I used to get it from Colton, but he's dead."

His eyes focused for a brief instant when he heard Colton's name. "Don't say that name." Just as quickly, his focus was gone.

"Did you know him?"

"He shouldn't have opened his mouth." Danny's voice trailed off. His eyes rolled back in his head. He didn't say anything more. The cab I'd called for him arrived. The driver and I rolled him into the back seat. I paid the driver to take him home.

CHAPTER NINE

The phone rang too early the next morning. Even though I'd stopped drinking two hours before closing time, my eyes wouldn't focus, and my head was pounding. That and the sand in my mouth reminded me that drinking all night was a younger man's game that I was glad I'd outgrown.

I searched the bedside table for my cell phone. Sam heard the commotion and began a steady bark that added to the pain in my head. I found my phone on the floor in the pocket of my discarded jeans, but it was too late. I heard the beep for a new voice message and checked the caller ID. It was Diana.

I pressed play on the message. "Nick, what happened to you? Call me back."

That was just what I needed to hear before breakfast, a pissed-off Latina detective. Before I could call her back, the phone rang.

"Are you avoiding me?" she asked.

"Why would you think that?"

"Because you didn't call me last night. I waited till midnight. What did Colton's father have to say?"

"That Colton wouldn't commit suicide."

I listened to her breathing into the phone, waiting for her to speak.

"So he hired you?"

"What did you expect?" I offered as an explanation.

"Don't you think you're too close to this? Colton was your friend."

"Look, Diana, this is what I do. I'm a private investigator."

"I know what you do. I also know how you operate. Right now, it's still my case."

"We've worked together before."

"That's what worries me."

"I'll share everything I find."

"You'll share everything?"

"Of course."

"I don't believe you."

"Why would you say that?"

"Because we tracked down Lora Michaels. She told us that you and Colton fought over her the night before he died. That you told him not to see her anymore because you wanted her all to yourself."

I laughed. "Bullshit."

"She also said you paid her a visit the night Colton was killed. Were you gonna tell me about that?"

"Of course."

"Yeah, right. Well, she's here now, giving her statement. She also said he was suicidal. She has text messages to back it up."

"Did you see the texts?"

She began quoting from the text in a deadpan cop voice. "Lora, baby, I'll die without you. I have to see you tonight."

"Come on, he didn't mean it literally."

"It doesn't matter what he literally meant. It's her interpretation that counts. She swears he was serious."

"He was texting a stripper. He probably said that every time he had a hard-on."

"And you would know that because you dated her."

She would never let me forget that. I didn't have to be in the room with her to know her jaw muscles bulged and her eyes shot flames.

"That's ancient history. I was like Colton, fresh out of the Marines and wasted every night."

She was silent. I listened to her regular breathing. I knew from experience that she was counting to ten and using her controlled-breathing routine. "Why would she say that about you unless you're still in contact?"

"She's cold, manipulative, and somehow involved. She's lying to cover her ass. Before I met Colton, I hadn't seen Lora in five years." I listened to her measured breathing again, waiting for her to respond.

"Did you ask her where she was last night?" I said.

"She said she was working. The manager and a stripper named Dallas confirmed it."

"They're both lying. When I got to the club, she wasn't there. She arrived after I did."

"I've gotta go back to work. We'll talk about this tonight," she said and disconnected.

I stared at the phone. Sam rested his bulky head on my knee and wrinkled his face into his best "concerned Labrador" expression. I knew it meant he wanted breakfast, but he was a comfort anyway.

"What am I gonna do about her?" I asked him.

He raised his head and barked.

"I know, stop thinking on an empty stomach." Good Labrador advice. I scratched his forehead and stood. He barked once more, then raced downstairs to the kitchen.

Lora Michaels was up to her old tricks. She lived in a world where the end justified the means, and the end always involved money and staying out of prison. If she was cornered, she would defend herself like a skunk trapped in an outhouse. I knew Colton texted her several times a day because he did it while we were together. If he was drunk or high, the frequency increased along with the urgency. If the texts were taken literally, as Diana suggested, Colton was suicidal. The fact that I knew better was irrelevant.

The vehemently anti-gun DA would love to use the texts to prosecute me. At the very least, she could suspend my PI license. If she went all in, she could take my license for good, fine me, and toss me in jail. There were enough sympathetic judges in Bexar County that I wouldn't stand a chance. My conviction would score big political points and pave the way for her own run for higher office. Everyone in her inner circle, including my ex-girlfriend Sylvia, would privately applaud her for taking down the guy who took out Marcus Lopez. Even though he had been a corrupt politician, blackmailing a Texas billionaire to bankroll his run for governor, he was their politician, and the last best hope to turn the state blue. When I ended his career, I became their public enemy. They would rather have a corrupt politician than live with the opposition party in power.

Just the idea increased the throbbing in my head. I needed a double shot of caffeine and a breakfast taco to clear the cobwebs. I took out the leftover barbecue and diced a slice of brisket to go with a couple of scrambled eggs. Sam carefully watched my every move to insure I cut equal portions for him. I cooked the mixture on the stovetop, then dumped it into a tortilla heated in the microwave. I added Sam's brisket slice to his ration of dry food, and we both dug in. Just the fuel we needed to come up with some hard evidence to prove the DA's theory wrong.

After breakfast, my first stop was the police station. I parked in the garage and made my way across the street. The public art display out front consisted of half a dozen twenty-foot white metal poles stacked like the skeleton of a giant off-kilter teepee. I couldn't think of a better representation of the precarious nature of public safety.

Sergeant Vera met me at the front desk. He was a barrel-chested old-timer with a bushy gray mustache, who'd retired once and come back part-time because he said his wife got tired of seeing him around the house all day. He'd known my father when he was the sheriff of Gillespie County and hunted whitetail and axis deer on my family's ranch near Fredericksburg.

"Morning, Junior," Vera said. He didn't bother to shake my hand. He only called me Junior if he thought I'd stepped way out of line.

"Sergeant Vera," I said, feeling twelve years old.

"You mind if I give you some advice?"

"Do I have a choice?"

Hugo Vera had known me since I was in grade school in Fredericksburg and had always looked after me. If he felt like I was getting off on the wrong track, he didn't hesitate to let me know.

"You're messing up a good thing."

"What's that mean exactly?"

"Detective Ochoa's pissed, and I know it has to do with you and this Colton Macrae business." It was partly because of his subtle suggestions that Diana and I'd gotten together in the first place. He loved playing matchmaker.

"Let me guess, she didn't bring you any donuts this morning."

"And I love my morning donuts. What did you say to her?"

"I'm on a case. She happens to think I'm too emotionally involved."

"Are you?"

"No. My brother Marine was murdered. I'm not gonna stand aside and let the killer walk."

"The preliminary report says suicide."

"It's wrong."

"You know something she doesn't?"

I laughed. The cops I knew were all gossips, but Hugo Vera could swear on his mother's grave at breakfast not to tell a secret, and by lunchtime a dozen people somehow knew all the gritty details. "Yeah, I think you did it," I said.

Vera smiled. "You little pissant. You're not gonna tell me anything, are you?" When calling me Junior didn't work, I was a little pissant.

I smiled back. "Are you gonna tell Detective Ochoa I'm here to see her, or do I have to walk in on her unannounced?"

He buzzed me through, and I rode the elevator up to Diana's floor. We'd made it clear from the beginning of our relationship that we would keep a strict separation between our personal and professional lives. It had worked out great, until now. Getting through this investigation would either strengthen our commitment to each other or completely wipe it out.

Diana sat alone at her desk, staring at her computer screen. She didn't look up when I walked into her cubicle.

"I tracked Lora Michaels down after I left the cattle barn because she was the likely person to have talked to Colton before he was murdered."

She stood and walked around to the front of the desk, gave me a brief hug, and kissed me, indications that I wasn't completely in the doghouse. "Do you understand what's going on? The DA wants to come after you for giving Colton the gun. That's a class A misdemeanor. You would lose your license and do jail time."

I sat in the office chair facing her desk. She took the chair beside me. "You believe Lora?" I said.

"You know it doesn't matter what I believe. The DA's breathing down my neck. She saw the snuff can with your name and number on it and the hydrocodone inside."

"I wrote my name on the can, so what? That was six months ago. I didn't give him the pills."

"The DA's not convinced."

"So, I gave him drugs and a gun just in case he wanted to get high and shoot himself in the head after he won the bronc-riding event?"

She sighed and put her hand on my forearm. She was used to my sarcasm, but I saw a flash of anger in her tense face. "You studied law. You know it doesn't have to make sense for her to charge you."

"Did you get the autopsy results?"

"Not yet."

Her hair was pulled into a tight ponytail, and she wore a cream-colored blouse that accentuated her figure in a professional way. It was hard to be mad or stay mad at anyone who looked as good as she did.

"Why couldn't you have taken him fishing or something?" she asked, taking my hand and squeezing it.

She felt warm, and the faint hint of peppery perfume penetrated my hungover head. "You believe that would have made any difference?" I asked, but it sounded lame. She ignored me.

"My hands are tied. The DA wants results. She calls me every couple of hours for an update."

"Give me some time."

"As soon as she gets the autopsy report, she's going to file charges. You know she's been waiting for a chance to rip you to shreds ever since you took out Marcus Lopez."

"He was a crook."

"Yeah, but he was their crook."

"You make him sound like a martyr."

"For them, he was."

CHAPTER TEN

I took Loop 1604 south to my lunch meeting with Skeeter. The outermost road circling San Antonio posted a 70 MPH speed limit, but traffic and perpetual construction limited forward progress to under 50 MPH. The pace gave me time to think. I pulled the spiral notebook from the console and dug a pen out of the side pocket of the driver's side door in case anything important percolated to the forefront of my brain.

Diana sympathized with me, but I could tell she didn't completely agree that giving Colton a pistol was the right thing to do. She thought like a cop. Evidence first. I admired that, but she didn't know Colton. Hadn't spent time with him. I looked at the evidence too, but I also had my hunches. Impartiality only took an investigation so far. I'd seen too many cases like Skeeter's where the evidence led to the wrong conclusion. SAPD and the DA had pushed for his conviction based on what they thought was solid evidence. It turned out that most of it was planted. My hunch that he was innocent saved his life. I had to come up with something soon before the autopsy results ruled Colton's death a suicide.

I flipped to a blank page and wrote the word *suicide*. Colton had a gun in his hand. No one saw anyone come or go from the pen. There was one casing found. There was one hole in his head. True, the angle didn't fit with a self-inflicted wound, but the DA would skip over that unless she had something more specific. The .40 caliber pistol belonged to me. This was the part the DA would use to nail my hide to her trophy wall.

Under that I wrote *Lora Michaels*. Colton sent text messages to her that he would kill himself if she left him. If you didn't know Colton or Lora, the words he wrote did sound desperate. The DA would use that as proof. I knew suicide had to be the furthest thing from his mind when he climbed on that rank bronc in the rodeo arena and scored ninety-one points. A rodeo cowboy doesn't finish a ride like that and shoot himself in the head. It takes a certain amount of brute strength to stay on a bucking animal, but the main weapon for a champion like Colton is concentration. If a cowboy isn't focused, he won't make the eight-second ride. That left the possibility that he received information after his ride that caused him to shoot himself.

Under that I wrote down *Man in black*. Colton met a tall man with a buzzcut and a black coat behind the chutes. The two talked and left the arena together. I made a note to ask Diana for the surveillance videos. Frost Bank Center had to have cameras everywhere. He seemed familiar, but I searched my memory and couldn't come up with a name or even a place I might have come in contact with the man. What could he have told Colton that would have sent him over the edge?

Finally, I wrote down *hydrocodone* and underlined it. Colton's empty snuff can contained pills. The same can I had written my name and phone number on. We were drinking beer at the VFW, and he asked if he could call me. I used the snuff can because I figured he wouldn't lose it. Never mind that I didn't give him the pills. The name and number were in my handwriting. He told me he used pills, but that he was getting his addiction under control. I had believed him, which was why I took him to the shooting range and let him borrow my spare pistol. That didn't explain the pills. Someone who is kicking the habit doesn't walk around with drugs in his pocket.

By the time I pulled into Isabella's Mexican restaurant across the street from Mission San Juan Capistrano, my head still ached, and I needed a handful of Tylenol and a plate of Isabella's barbacoa to chase away the hangover. Bright orange paint accented with Christmas lights decorated the restaurant year-round. At noon on a Saturday the southside eatery was full of blue-collar workers, two SAPD cops, and a fire crew taking a noon break. I made my way to a table on the patio and sat down to wait for Skeeter.

A young woman in a Spurs basketball T-shirt brought me a basket of tortilla chips and a bowl of salsa, along with a much-needed glass of water.

"Where's your sister?" I asked her. I was a regular and had watched the girl and her twin sister grow up waiting tables when they weren't in school.

"She has weekend classes. You wanna beer, Mr. Nick?"

She called me that because that's what her mom called me. It was a family-run business that included the twins and an older brother who helped his mother in the kitchen. I could never tell which sister she was, Theresa or Margarita.

"Not today. Iced tea. How're your classes goin'?"

She rolled her eyes. "I dropped out. Business has been slow. Mom said she could only afford for one of us to go to school at a time, so I volunteered to work this semester while Theresa goes to school."

"Good for you," I said. I ordered the hangover-curing barbacoa tacos with beans and rice on the side and leaned back in my chair. The ice water tasted good, and I pressed the cold glass against my forehead. I wore a jacket against the cold late-winter breeze, but the ice felt good on my pounding headache. She went back to fill my order.

Skeeter made his usual grand entrance. A man of his size and unusual appearance always turns heads. He liked to tell me that people only looked at him because they wondered who was crazy enough to sit next to me, but a three-hundred-pound man with a prosthetic hook was something people didn't see every day.

"You look like shit," Skeeter said and tossed a small black backpack with his assortment of electronic gizmos into the opposite chair and sat down. He wiped his sweat-soaked face with a paper napkin. He'd walked the mile from his mother's house and was sweating like he'd just finished a workout on the gridiron. It could be ten degrees below zero and Skeeter could work up a sweat walking across the street. The man put out heat like a human furnace.

"Thanks for being honest," I told him, and finished my glass of water.

"That's why you like me. I always tell it like it is."

Rita brought my tacos and iced tea. Skeeter ordered a hamburger. He didn't like Mexican food or anything spicy.

I pulled my spiral notebook from under my coat and opened it on the table. "There're two completing theories of Colton's death. One of them is suicide, and one of them is murder. The DA and, so far, SAPD favors suicide. If that theory wins out, we're out of a job and Fischer and Davis Investigations is history."

"I thought it was Davis and Fischer, you know, alphabetical."

"Until you finish your PI application, it stays Fischer and Davis. But regardless of the order, the business is kaput, and you and I will have to seek alternate employment. The DA wants to charge me for providing the weapon Colton used to shoot himself."

"I don't like the sound of that."

"And I might have to move back to the ranch or move in with you."

"Let's not go there. What about theory two?"

"Theory two starts with Lora Michaels. The police verified her alibi, but I saw her getting out of a warm car in street clothes." I read over my notes. "Colton met a man behind the chutes after his ride. I only saw his back. Big guy, maybe my height, buzz cut, wearing all black. They walked out of the arena together."

"What about surveillance video? Frost Bank Center should have multiple cameras."

"Put that on your list. Find out where the cameras are and who has the backup tapes."

"We are on a paying gig, right? Tell me we ain't just doin' this to save your ass."

"As if that wouldn't be enough."

"We do have to pay bills."

"You're right. And yes, we're on Colton's dad's payroll. He believes theory two that Colton was murdered. Since Colton only called him once since he mustered out of the Marine Corps, I didn't add him to the suspect list. He's an ex-Navy doc, still practicing. Lives in Austin."

"Good to know. I don't like it when there's family involved. Ruins my faith in human nature."

"Yeah, well, that still might take a hit. If Colton was murdered, the killer most likely came from his drug connections. The fact that he had pills on him when he died tells me that either someone planted them, or Colton was backsliding."

"If he was backsliding, where'd he get the dope?"

"That part may be our first lead."

I told him about my misadventure last night at the VFW and how Danny Sanz had suggested Dr. Frank could hook me up with as many pills as I wanted, but he passed out before he could fill me in on the details.

"So, you got wasted with a drug dealer. That explains why you look like shit."

"I switched to iced tea halfway through the night. Danny kept pounding 'em, or I'd have more information. What we need is Danny's supplier."

"The DEA just made a bust in Houston I read about," Skeeter said. He pulled his laptop from the backpack and tapped a few keys with his prosthetic hook. He showed me the latest drug bust in Houston that involved a half dozen doctors running a pain clinic, along with several pharmacists and nurses. "It's all about money. The docs in Houston were making it hand over fist and dumping millions of pills on anyone who could afford it."

"You think this Dr. Frank is running a pill mill?"

"One way to find out."

Rita refilled my tea and brought Skeeter his hamburger. While we stuffed our faces, Skeeter booted up his laptop and did a search for Dr. Frank. It always amazed me how fast he could type with one hand and a metal hook.

Before Skeeter came to work for me, this was the point in the investigation where I would grind out some old-fashioned legwork with phone calls and miles on the pickup. It worked, but it took time. More time than I had. He compressed a week's worth of legwork into the time it took for the barbacoa and jalapeno peppers to work on my hangover. I never told him how good he was because I didn't want him to get a big head or ask for a raise.

I needed some hard evidence that someone else was behind Colton's death besides his demons and my Smith & Wesson.

CHAPTER ELEVEN

Skeeter traced the name of a Dr. Frank to an urgent care clinic on the southwest side of town not far from the sprawling Lackland Air Force base. His name was linked to three clinics in town that he owned or managed and another two in Austin. I wasn't sure it was the same one Danny referred to, but it was a place to start.

It was after eight p.m. The sign on the door said they were open until midnight. A dozen men and women waited ahead of me. None of them looked up when I walked in. Skeeter sat in the parking lot with the live feed from a pinhole camera in my jacket streaming to his laptop. An earpiece designed to look like a hearing aid put us in communication. We'd successfully used the setup on an insurance fraud case to catch a woman collecting four grand a month disability while she trained for a half marathon and worked out at LA Fitness.

"Testing, testing, one, two, three," I said in a normal voice. A man in his fifties with an Astros baseball cap glanced up from his cell phone. Unfortunately, people talking to Bluetooth earbuds was not an unusual sight these days.

I smiled and opened my mouth to speak, but he quickly diverted his glance back to his cell phone. He was curious, but whatever he was looking at on his phone was more interesting.

"I hear ya," Skeeter said into my ear. "The camera's working too. Looks like Doc Frank's doin' a boomin' business."

I studied the patients, trying to figure out if anyone in the room was here for pain pills because they were chasing an addiction. An older woman in the corner stared blankly at the pictures in a dog-eared *Texas Parks and Wildlife* magazine. A teenage boy with a swollen ankle sat next to his mother, and a man my age wearing a City of San Antonio work shirt and a homemade sling on his arm stood by the water fountain. Both boy and man seemed to be in legitimate pain. I didn't know what I was looking for, but I didn't see anyone in a trench coat with a sunburnt face and missing teeth.

I glanced at my reflection in the mirror above the back row of chairs. I wore a baseball cap featuring an American flag pulled low over my forehead scars to avoid unwanted stares and the surveillance camera in the ceiling near the front counter. I had on the same sweaty long-sleeved T-shirt I'd put on that morning under a canvas barn jacket, and since I hadn't seen Diana in two days, I hadn't bothered to shave. Out of all the people waiting, I decided I was the one most likely to be an opioid addict. There was no way to tell about the others. From what I'd read about the opioid epidemic, there was no real pattern for who was addicted. The old woman looking at wildlife pictures was just as vulnerable as the kid with the swollen ankle or the city worker with the makeshift sling.

I'd spent the afternoon at Lucky's Gym sweating out the rest of last night's Jack Daniels. I hadn't heard from Danny Sanz. I suspected his hangover was much more severe than mine. After that, I'd put in a run along the River Walk with Sam. He was always up for exercise.

"Mr. Wallace?" the receptionist called.

I smiled and looked around the room. I'd been waiting for an hour and a half despite the fact that the patients moved through the back rooms at an unusually fast rate. Skeeter had gone to sleep. I could hear him gently snoring in my ear.

"Mr. Wallace?" she said again louder, looking directly at me.

I realized she was talking to me. William Wallace was my go-to fake name. It was the name of my second-favorite Texas Ranger, William "Big Foot" Wallace. The first was John Salmon Ford, aka "Rip" Ford, but most Texans recognized the name Rip. I learned that if I used the name, people would ask questions and engage me in conversation about the famous ranger. I quit using it because it defeated the purpose of going incognito.

"That's me," I said loud enough to hopefully wake Skeeter.

"Dr. Frank will see you now," she said. "That will be seventy-five dollars."

I gave her cash because Big Foot Wallace didn't have insurance and asked for a receipt so I could bill it to John Macrae.

A young nurse with a tight-fitting light blue one-piece uniform greeted me at the door and led me to a numbered room in the back. She took my vitals with a pleasant smile and had me fill out a patient care form. I indicated the reason for my visit was pain, lots of it. Level ten. I decided to use shoulder pain because it seemed easy to fake and wasn't that far off for me. I'd overworked the heavy weights at the gym, then taken a couple of hard hits from my sparring partner that afternoon that had left a mark. I also told her I'd had an operation, which was true. It was an old high school football injury from my junior year as a Battlin' Billy at Fredericksburg high school. She seemed genuinely concerned. I thought my act was working. She took an X-ray, then left me to wait in the room.

Twenty minutes later I heard a soft knock on the door. Before I could respond, the Pillsbury Doughboy squeezed through the door. "Hi, it's a busy night. Sorry to keep you waiting. I'm Donald Frank," he said. He was a couple inches shorter than my six foot one but pushed the scales at over three hundred pounds, all wrapped up in a white lab coat the size of a king-size bedsheet.

"Hi, Doc," I said, noticing he didn't introduce himself as "Dr. Frank." His name tag read "D. Frank PA." He was a physician's assistant.

"Oh, don't get up. I see you're in a lot of pain." He plopped down on a metal stool on wheels and rested the chart the young nurse had created for me on his protruding belly, which formed a natural shelf below his chest.

"Yeah, it's my shoulder. Gives me hell. I'm a truck driver. Cross-country. I ran out of my pain meds. I've been using hydrocodone for a while. They really help. I don't take 'em while I'm driving, of course. But when I bed down for the night, I can't sleep without 'em." I was making it up as I went along. I heard Skeeter chuckling in my earpiece.

Frank tugged at the ends of his bushy gray mustache, then he made some notes on my chart and made a show of studying the scar on my naked shoulder and the X-ray.

"So, you've had an injury?"

"That's right."

"We'll be sure to document that. Shoulder injuries can be very painful." He traced the outline of the small Chinese character tattooed on my deltoid muscle. I'd had it done as an act of rebellion when I was eighteen. My father had died in the line of duty and left me at the mercy of my grandparents. Both insisted I not get a tattoo, but Grandpa said when I turned eighteen, I was on my own. Naturally, I drove to San Antonio on my birthday and found a tattoo parlor. Grandpa knew I would do it, and to his credit, never said a word about it.

"Don't see many like that," Frank said, referring to the tattoo. "What's it mean?"

"It stands for family," I told him. I didn't tell him about the irony of defying my family with a tattoo that stood for family. I didn't really get it until after I came home from my first tour of duty. The defiant streak never died out which is what led me to PI work instead of following my dad's footsteps in law enforcement or sticking with law school.

"What about the prescription, Doc? How many hydrocodone pills can you give me?" I tried to sound a little desperate. He'd been in the room all of five minutes.

"I'm sorry, son. I know you're in pain, but I'm going to recommend you start with an over-the-counter medication for the inflammation and physical therapy." He held up a bottle of regular strength Motrin. "You're young. The combination should help considerably."

"Motrin? Are you kidding me? It hurts, Doc." I couldn't believe this was the guy Danny said could hook me up. "I'm a veteran," I added, thinking that might be the key word.

"We can consider stronger medication on a short-term basis once we've had a chance to evaluate the effects of the physical therapy." He pushed himself to his feet and crossed his arms over his stomach. "Is there anything else I can do for you?"

"Nope. I guess not," I said.

"Our goal is to help, not harm. People like yourself who are in pain need relief. We're here for you. We're here to treat you and get to the root cause."

"Thanks, Doc," I said, thinking it sounded like a rehearsed speech.

He patted my good shoulder. "Thank you for your service," he said with a pasty smile. "See the nurse on your way out, and she can give you some exercises to do that will help. Meanwhile, get started on the Motrin right away and set up a follow-up appointment. I wanna see you in two weeks." He hustled out the door and to his next patient.

"What the hell was that?" Skeeter said in my ear.

"I just spent seventy-five dollars for a Motrin prescription. That should be illegal."

Skeeter laughed in my ear.

CHAPTER TWELVE

I spent a restless night thinking about the case and wondering whether Diana would side with me or the DA. She'd worked late, then picked up Aaron from her sister's house in Castroville and gone back to her own house. I suspected there were other reasons for not coming over, but when she called to explain, I kept my mouth shut. The unspoken part was that she needed time alone. That was fine by me. I needed time alone. Time to focus on finding Colton's killer.

When I did doze off, I found myself back on active duty riding shotgun in a Humvee. It was the reoccurring scene from my last deployment that always ended with me stuck upside-down in the vehicle while one by one my teammates died protecting me. Sometimes the night demons amused themselves by replacing my team with images of my dad and grandpa. Skeeter made an appearance after he'd taken a bullet in an ambush at the ranch the day my grandpa was murdered. I woke disoriented and needing a run to clear my head.

Sam was all too happy to help out. The trailhead access to the River Walk was a couple of blocks west of my house in the King William neighborhood south of the Alamo on the banks of the San Antonio River. It was still dark at five thirty, but the lights were on over the practice field at the high school, and the spring track-and-field athletes were beginning a cold morning workout.

Sam was never interested in straight exercise. His focus was always on the river and the wild ducks he might find there. It made no difference that we were surrounded by urban sprawl. A duck on the water meant only one thing. The hunt was on. He couldn't care less that I had a twenty-foot lead rope around his neck. When he stopped to explore, he expected me to wait for him to finish gathering evidence of duck activity. I obliged him for the most part by running in place and dropping for burpees. When he couldn't find a duck, the next best thing to chase was a cat. Hunting was a sacred pursuit. The mere presence of cats seemed to annoy him beyond tolerance.

After a quick four miles that took us north past the deserted shopping district loop and into the canyons of new buildings and parking garages, we made our way home. Since there were no ducks, Sam made one final charge toward a contemptuous tabby cat lounging on my neighbor Rose's back porch. I let him go, knowing he didn't stand a chance of catching her. The feline deftly leaped onto the kitchen windowsill inches out of his reach and watched him bark with that contemptuous stare unique to cats.

"He's still chasing my cats?" Rose said, stepping out of her back door.

"Sorry about that, Rose." I picked up Sam's leash and reeled him back to our side of the yard.

"Oh, fiddlesticks. You know I'm teasing you. Glad to see you and Sam finally getting some exercise. You're up early this morning."

"You know how it is, make hay while the sun shines," I said.

"How're you and that pretty detective getting along?" she asked. Rose had been retired from her university job for almost twenty years and filled her time with gardening, caring for her cats, and collecting gossip. My daily life was her favorite subject.

"Time will tell, Rose." I smiled. I didn't want to get into the details or receive any of her thoughtful advice.

"When are you gonna bring that son of hers around again?"

"You know how cops are. She keeps odd hours."

"She's good for you, you know. That little boy of hers dotes on you. How did he like the rodeo? Heard there was an altercation." I knew she'd read the newspaper account of Colton's death and was fishing for details.

"He'll make a good cowboy. And yes, there was a murder."

She raised her sparse gray eyebrows. "Paper said suicide."

I gave her a few details about the case to distract her from my personal life.

"Here's what I think," she said when I'd finished. She was never shy about giving her opinions. "You're a blunt instrument. Don't get me wrong. There are certain kinds of investigations where you excel. If someone was after me or my granddaughter was missing, there's no one I'd rather have on the case. You're tenacious. You remind me of my granddad. He was a lawman in Webb County. Used to patrol the Mexican border on horseback. My point is, times have changed. Sometimes you need a lighter touch."

I nodded in agreement. I knew where she was going with this. I'd heard about her grandpa before. I doubted that things along the border had gotten any easier with the flood of drug and human trafficking, but I understood her point. Everyone I knew told me I was living in the wrong century.

"Diana knows what she's doing. My advice is to stay out of her way," she said.

"Thanks, Rose. Take care now. This guy needs some water." I excused myself and led Sam back to my house. She hadn't told me anything I didn't know. She was right, of course. Diana was good at her job, but I couldn't stay out of her way. Not on this case. I had let Colton down while he was alive. I wasn't going to let him down after he was dead. And waiting for the DA to take me to court didn't sit well with me.

My cell phone was ringing when I opened the back door and walked into the kitchen. I never carried a phone when I ran, only the keys to the house and my hammerless Smith & Wesson .38 revolver. I didn't want the distraction or the extra weight.

The caller ID said it was John Macrae. I checked the time. It was six thirty.

"Good morning, John," I said.

"Nick, did I wake you up?"

"I was out for a run. What's up?"

"Sorry to bother you, but I was on my way to the hospital, and I thought I'd check in and see if you'd made any progress."

I gave him an update including a rundown on my encounter with Danny at the VFW and my visit with Doc Frank that hadn't gone as planned. I'd hoped to track down Colton's pill source, but the doctor didn't seem to give out prescriptions without the usual follow-up appointment.

John agreed that the source of the pills had to be the key to finding out who shot Colton. He knew Frank and had met him at social functions in Austin. He told me he lived in the Dominion, an exclusive neighborhood in northwest San Antonio, and he'd seen him on the golf course at the country club.

"He must be doing pretty good to have a house there," I said.

"You wanna meet Frank socially?" he asked.

I hadn't expected that. "I'm not much of a golfer."

"Not golf. Frank always shows up at our annual sausage-making party. It's a big deal and invitation-only. We meet on a ranch near Willow City. You're from Fredericksburg. You know where that is?"

"Sure. Who's the owner?"

"Max Devine."

I searched my memory but didn't come up with a match. My own family had settled in the area before the Civil War. Some of the old families were still around, but Fredericksburg began a makeover from ranch community to tourist attraction when LBJ was president and opened the Texas White House at his nearby family ranch. Instead of dying out like so many other small western towns, Fredericksburg remade itself into a tourist destination. Seventies music icons Willy and Waylon helped by singing the praises of Luckenbach, Texas, which was also close to Fredericksburg. People wanting to "get back to the basics" naturally needed high-end shopping, wine tasting, and luxury hotel space. Their presence pumped much needed revenue into the town coffers. My grandpa had hated the inevitable surge of traffic, but others embraced the transformation. I sided with Grandpa's point of view, but I understood the other argument.

Max Devine had to be new money, but the sausage-making sounded authentic. Most of the ranchers and hunters in Central Texas still met after the fall hunting seasons were over and pooled together the year's harvest to make sausage. It was a German pioneer tradition handed down for generations as a way to preserve meat without refrigeration. It also helped make the notoriously tough whitetail deer meat much easier to chew.

"You can come as my guest," John Macrae said.

"Frank will be there?"

"I'm sure he will be. He never misses a sausage-making party."

Macrae gave me the details, then signed off. I went upstairs to take a shower. This PA Frank seemed to be flaunting his money with a house in an exclusive neighborhood and a rich circle of friends. I wondered if his interest in the clinics was his only source of income.

CHAPTER THIRTEEN

The Paradise Club parking lot was full at noon on a Tuesday. They served discount burgers and fried chicken along with overpriced drinks and lap dances. The patrons were usually businessmen taking their clients to lunch on an expense account. The dancers who worked the lunch shift could make an easy grand and fought over who was on the schedule. Lora always made the list because she had seniority, and the management was wrapped around her little finger.

I parked facing the VIP entrance and watched a group of men in suits and ties walk into the back entrance, laughing and slapping each other on the back like high school football players in the locker room. By the cut of their tailored suits, I guessed they were either lawyers taking a lunch recess from court or maybe used car salesmen.

I'd struck out with Frank and was still waiting for access to the surveillance tapes from the Frost Bank Center. The only break I caught came when the medical examiner notified Diana of an unexpected backlog and that Colton's autopsy wouldn't happen for another day. Normally, I wouldn't celebrate a surge in violence. But this time it worked in my favor. Those extra cases bought me a little breathing room.

I decided to play a hunch and follow Lora Michaels. Her alibi for the night Colton was murdered didn't add up. I hadn't seen her at the rodeo, but it didn't mean she wasn't there. She'd denied any involvement or knowledge of Colton's death to me, but she'd told Diana that he was suicidal and provided the text messages. She'd also told her that I wanted her all to myself. One thing Lora was good at besides dancing was lying.

I waited an hour and watched similar groups of men go in and out of the VIP entrance. The patrons who used the back door were regulars and spent enough time and money to buy special privileges with the management.

Finally, at two thirty, Lora walked out the back door. She wore sequined jeans and a stylish oversized T-shirt tied above her slim waist. Over her shoulder, she carried a gold designer handbag that matched her six-inch platform shoes. Nothing about her was out of place. I didn't see a trace of the mark from the other night. Makeup worked wonders to mold her face into a porcelain mask. She walked to her white BMW. For the brief time we were together, she would never set foot in my old pickup. That in and of itself should have been a wakeup call for me, but I was young, naïve, and drinking like a fish to ease the transition back to civilian life. All I wanted at the time was the pleasure of her company to mitigate the pain.

I followed her to the 410 Loop heading west. She was going somewhere in a hurry, which was good because it meant she wasn't worried about watching her back. The long winter had left the Alamo city's trees bare, and a somber gray cover of dead branches blanketed the skyline. I was beginning to think spring would never arrive. It was as if the gods had conspired to extend the wet cold misery as punishment for some perceived slight. I thought about my German ancestors in the Black Forest gathering in the woods to offer a sacrifice to Woden. I wasn't superstitious, but maybe the gods had something to do with the increase in the Bexar County death count.

Lora hit eighty-five miles per hour before she slowed for the I-10 interchange. I caught up to her when she took the Wurzbach exit and followed her down the feeder road to a newly opened strip mall hidden behind well-maintained live oak and limestone brick landscaping.

She passed the women's stores and parked in the back behind a boxing gym called Fight Night. I knew about it because Lucky had mentioned it as a place not to work out. He was a little vague on the reasons. From the outside, it looked legitimate. It was definitely in a higher-rent part of town than Lucky's place on the west side. Lora was always keen on keeping in shape, which was an occupational necessity, but I never knew her to be into boxing.

She parked beside a shiny black four-door King Ranch model F-250 that reminded me it was time to upgrade my ride. Maybe after this case I'd have enough money left over to invest in a new used pickup. If I still had a license and a job.

Lora hustled to the back door without a single glance around the parking lot before disappearing inside. She wouldn't be able to get in unless she was a member or knew the owner or manager. I settled in to wait.

Waiting was the worst part of the job. It was like combat deployment. Twenty-three hours of mindless boredom, followed by forty-five minutes of heightened alert, then fifteen minutes of heart-stopping terror, repeated every day until your deployment ended and the flight home.

With time to kill, I called Skeeter and gave him an update on the morning's activity.

"Here's the scoop on Doc Frank," he said. "He was investigated by the state board five years ago, but no charges were filed. Last year, there was a criminal complaint by a patient that ended in a non-disclosed settlement. Again, no charges were filed."

"He must have connections or a good lawyer. Keep digging. There's got to be something. While you're at it, run a background check on the Fight Night boxing gym."

"What's up?"

"Lora paid it a visit, and I don't think she's really taking up boxing."

When I hung up, I called Diana. I had a theory bouncing around in my head. The failure to get pills from Frank was a setback, but I still believed I was on the right track and wanted her to know I was working on something. She let it ring several times before she answered.

"Tell me you have something," she said.

"Am I still a free man?"

"For now."

"I think Colton was going to tell me who his pill connection was. The connection found out and killed him before I could get to him."

"You just think of that?"

"Danny knew Colton. He said he had a big mouth."

"He also said Frank could hook me up with pills, but it didn't happen."

"That's not enough to change Colton's cause of death."

"I don't have all the pieces. I said I'd share whatever I had."

Lora stepped out of the back door of the gym. "Gotta go," I said.

"Nick, where are you?"

A tall man about my age in gym shorts and a red muscle shirt followed her. He towered over her and outweighed me by a good twenty pounds. Not fat, the guy's muscles were chiseled.

"Finding some actual evidence," I said. "I think I just found the guy Colton talked to after his ride."

The man turned his broad, angular back to me. A chill went up my spine. This was definitely the man I'd seen Colton meet behind the bucking chutes at the rodeo on the night he was murdered. This was the mystery man in black. Lora had led me right to him.

"You're sure?" she asked.

"I followed Lora after her lunch shift. This can't be a coincidence."

"Be careful. Let me know how it goes."

"I promised I would."

She disconnected without comment.

I poked the 70-200mm zoom lens of my Canon digital camera out the window and started shooting. Lora's face was flushed, and her eyes were lowered. She put her hand on his forearm. The guy made no effort to reciprocate. I couldn't hear the conversation, but his voice was raised. He was giving her a good chewing out. I'd never seen Lora stand and take a tongue-lashing from anybody, not even from the VIPs in the Paradise Club. The guy could be worth a couple million and pass out hundreds like paper towels, but if he stepped out of line in the club, Lora would put him in his place.

Suddenly, the guy backhanded her across the mouth. Lora flew against the wall. She was small, but no weakling. She worked out and danced six or eight hours a day five days a week. This guy slapped her back against the wall with a small movement of his hand. I didn't like seeing anybody get pushed around when they didn't have a chance of fighting back, but I let it play out. He was toying with her like a kid playing with a rag doll.

She opened her mouth to speak, but the brute put a finger to her lips.

She stayed quiet. Another first for Lora. In the telephoto lens, her eyes pleaded with him. I'd seen that look before. She used it when she really wanted something. The difference was that usually she was in control. The man grabbed a handful of her hair and pulled her behind the dumpster. Whoever this guy was, he was in total control of Lora.

Fifteen minutes later, she emerged from behind the dumpster, pushed her hair back in place, and crossed back to her BMW. The brute emerged behind her with a self-satisfied look on his face. He retied the string on his shorts and scanned the lot. I was backed into a parking spot behind the upscale women's shoe store fifty yards away. I had my seat back, sunglasses on, and my face was in the shadow of the building. I'd done scores of stakeouts. It was at least fifty percent of the private detective's job to follow people around and find out what they were really up to.

The brute looked into the shadows where my pickup was parked and smiled as if he could see into the dark. I held the camera button down and recorded ten good pictures.

Lora got in her BMW and slammed the door.

The brute disappeared back inside the gym.

I reviewed the pictures on the viewfinder. In the last frame, he was looking directly into the camera lens, his cocky expression daring me to do something. I didn't know who he was or how he fit into the whole mess, but I intended to find out.

CHAPTER FOURTEEN

On the drive home, the local radio station offered a recap of the San Antonio Rodeo finals. It was Sunday after the show had ended and Colton's score of ninety-one was unchallenged and probably would remain so for several years to come. He'd been awarded the top prize posthumously. Had he lived, he would have had a chance to complete in the National Finals. You never know in rodeo. It's a brutal and unforgiving sport. The cowboys who rode didn't talk about *if* they were going to get hurt. They talked about *when* and which doctors were willing to work on their more serious injuries and write a clean bill of health to the PRCA so they could compete in the next go-round. Colton had a gift for staying in the saddle. A combination of athleticism and balance that all great riders had. Now, he was dead, and no one would ever know his full potential. It wasn't a tragic accident. His life wasn't ended by a bull in the arena, like Lane Frost. He was shot down in cold blood and deserved justice.

Diana was meeting me at my fixer-upper in King William. It amused her that after four years I still called it a "fixer-upper," but I knew if I stopped calling it that, I would forget my plan was to completely renovate the house. I had stabilized the front porch, repainted the interior, and replaced the cast iron and clay pipes. Refurbishing the hardwood floors was next on the list. Maybe next year.

When I finally got home, Diana's car was parked in my driveway. I was supposed to cook dinner for her because she had a rare night off. I had a gas grill and liked to think my steaks were at least equal to the best in the state. The real secret was the cut of meat. It was hard to mess it up unless you left it on the grill too long. None of that mattered now because I'd forgotten to buy steaks while I was following Lora. I glanced at my reflection in the rearview mirror. My hat brim cast a shadow over my embarrassment. *Maybe you should have called her*, I thought. I got out and put my hand on the car hood. Cold. Diana had been here at least an hour. The fact that she was still here either meant that she was okay with my being late or that she was waiting to chew me out. I walked to the front door, ready to face the music.

Rose waved to me from her kitchen window, and I waved back. I wondered what Rose would write in her diary today: *Neighbor Fischer finally arrives home at 8:52 p.m. He kept his SAPD detective girlfriend waiting for over an hour.* I'm sure she was just as curious to hear the detective's reaction as I was. This was the final night of her son's weekend with daddy, and she had spent most of it working overtime.

"Hey, Lucy, I'm home!" I called when I came through the front door. It was our little joke based on watching ancient reruns of *I Love Lucy* together.

"In here, Ricky," she called from the kitchen.

She was playing along—that was a good sign. I walked into the kitchen and found Sam at Diana's feet salivating over the aroma of leftover barbecue and beans.

"I assumed you planned to eat leftover City Market brisket for dinner?" she asked, sampling a crispy end piece of meat fresh out of the microwave. The smoky aroma filled the kitchen, and Sam took a spin through my legs and around the table anticipating his share of the meat.

"I bought extra just for this occasion," I said and kissed her, tasting the spicy sauce that lingered on her lips.

"That's BS, but if I hadn't found this in your fridge, I would have picked up Aaron and gone home. She wrapped her arms around me and rested her head on my chest. "I hope the surveillance shows us something."

"You got the tapes from the Frost Bank Center?"

"I said I would. Now, you owe me."

"And I always pay back in full." I pulled her chin up and kissed her. "Let's eat first. I'm starving." We shared another sauce-laced kiss. Sam couldn't stand being ignored and grabbed my pantleg. "I take it you've already shared some with him?"

Diana smiled and nodded. I tossed him another piece. "Last one," I said. "Now, go lay down." He did as he was told, but not without a final Labrador look that closely resembled a prisoner given a life sentence.

Diana opened two Shiner Bocks, and I set the food on the table. While we ate, I told her about the afternoon activities and the tall dark-haired muscle man Lora Michaels went to see after her shift at the Paradise Club. The surveillance tapes would hopefully confirm my suspicion that he was the same man who met Colton at the rodeo. There was also something else familiar about him. I couldn't quite put my finger on it, like remembering part of a melody from an old song, but the title remained a mystery. I kept that to myself. It was another hunch, and Diana was tired of hearing about my hunches.

When we finished, I tossed the paper plates and put what was left of the barbecue in the refrigerator. Diana took a flash drive from her purse and plugged it into the TV. I grabbed the remote, and we plopped down on the couch to watch the black-and-white footage together.

"This is so romantic," she said, snuggling under my arm.

"Pretend we're watching *Cops*. Weren't you on an episode?"

"One time, and I was only in the background."

"They're gonna make you a star."

"It aired last year, and they haven't called me back. But thanks, sweetie." She rewarded me with a kiss. "Who's this guy we're looking for again?"

I showed her the pictures I'd taken that afternoon. The brute's smiling face stared up at us from the digital images.

"He should be easy to spot. Guy gives me the creeps."

There wasn't a camera focused on the place I had seen Colton's initial encounter with the man, so we had to watch the video of each of the other cameras pointed at the five exit doors. Switching between cameras stretched a process that should have taken five minutes into an hour.

"There he is," I said.

Diana froze the frame.

The time clock under the picture showed 8:36. That was five minutes after Colton had finished his record-breaking ride. Colton's wide hat brim covered his face, but the brute's face was visible. The image was blurred, as all surveillance tapes are, but it was clearly the same man. He was a step behind Colton and towered above him like a Spurs power forward. His formfitting black jacket showed off his wide shoulders and narrow hips.

"We can't see Colton's face," she said.

"Yeah, that's too bad. We don't know whether he knew what was coming."

"How does this help your case for murder? Colton met a dozen guys behind the chutes. One of them happens to know his girlfriend who's a dancer at a popular strip club."

"The guy's out of place. Look at him. He's not a cowboy. And why didn't Lora mention him?"

"Maybe he came to warn Colton to stay away from Lora. Maybe he's the new man in her life. That could have sent Colton over the edge."

"Look, connect the dots—Colton calls me and wants to talk. He's cleaning up his act and wants to unload on his pill connection. He tells Lora. Lora tells this guy. Boom. Colton's dead."

"Except there's no proof of the boom."

"Maybe it's still out there in the cattle barn."

"What're you saying?"

"CSI could have missed the evidence because they focused on the inside of the pen. Look at the angle of that bullet. The shot came from above and outside the pen."

"You can't prove that. Besides, there's nothing above the pens. What did he use, a drone? This isn't an Afghanistan battlefield. We're in San Antonio."

"We still need to find out who this guy is and talk to him."

"For what? Talking to Colton? A dozen guys talked to him after his ride. You got proximity. That's not enough for me to bring him in for questioning."

I grinned at her.

"I know, you can talk to him." She accepted it, but her tone said she didn't approve.

I stood up and walked into the kitchen. It was useless to argue with her. Our approach to investigation worked on two completely different paths.

"Skeeter's already working on a name. He should have a social security and phone number by now. I'm surprised he didn't call." I took out my phone to check the messages. Nothing.

Diana pulled the flash drive from the TV and tossed it in her duffel bag. "I have to pick Aaron up from his dad's house in Castroville at six in the morning, which means I have to be up at five to beat the traffic."

I checked my watch. "It's almost midnight. Does that mean we have five hours to make passionate love before you have to leave, or you're ready for some rack time?

"How come the military makes sleep sound like medieval torture?"

"A lot of things in the military qualify as torture. Ironically, rack time isn't one of them."

She wrapped her arms around my waist. "In that case, I'll settle for an hour of passion followed by four hours of rack time."

I reached behind her legs and lifted her off her feet. "I'll try to make both as pleasurable as possible."

She rested her head on my chest, and I carried her up the stairs to my bedroom.

CHAPTER FIFTEEN

The alarm rang at fifteen till five, and Diana and I both filled our travel coffee mugs and headed out. She to pick up her son and go to work, and I to Willow City for a day of making sausage. John Macrae had promised to introduce me to Doc Frank. I suspected he was the source for Danny's pills and maybe something he said or did during the day would tip him off. It was a long shot, but if nothing else, I would end the day with several pounds of deer sausage, so my time wouldn't be wasted. There was a slight chance Frank would remember me from the clinic, but I suspected he wouldn't. I'd waited two hours but only talked to him for five minutes. Who knows how many others he had seen that day.

Diana was still skeptical of my theory that Colton was murdered, and if the ME ruled suicide after the autopsy, she would have to close the case. She had to follow her boss's lead. The law didn't deal with gray areas of doubt. Once the verdict was in, that was it. I'd run across the same situation on a case involving a young woman fished out of the San Antonio River. The official ruling was accidental drowning. The girl's mother insisted it was murder and hired me to find the killer. The case was complicated, but the accidental-death ruling was influence by a corrupt detective who, at the time, was Diana's mentor partner. She of all people shouldn't have to be reminded how a case could go off the rails if the ME made the wrong determination. She wrote off the woman's case as an anomaly, something that rarely happened. To admit otherwise would be an indictment on her whole profession. I wasn't ready to condemn all law enforcement, but it was an inherent flaw in any bureaucracy system. I was playing a hunch that told me PA Frank was dirty, and he was up to his eyeballs in dealing opioids.

The sun was out but not up to the task of warming Central Texas above forty degrees. A thin layer of bright green rescue grass covered the limestone hills between patches of gray winter brush. Sam felt the change in the road surface from pavement to gravel and stuck his wet nose on the passenger side window. He'd spent a month in San Antonio, but he hadn't forgotten the spring-fed pond and wide-open spaces where he could run without bumping into the neighbor's fence.

My first stop was the Fischer family ranch located about ten miles southeast of Fredericksburg. I stopped at the front gate. Helen had been out that morning to scatter hay in the field. The cattle lined up face-to-face for a hundred yards where she'd tossed flakes of hay from the flatbed trailer pulled behind the John Deere tractor. Mixed in with the cows were Grandpa's goats. In the summer, the goats grazed in the steep rocky hills on the south side of the property. There was water from a spring, and they could take advantage of the grass that the cattle couldn't access.

Sam was anxious to get out and run. He jumped down when I open the pickup door and took off for the pond between the gate and the house.

I drove across the flat hayfield and up a slight incline to the 150-year-old house built out of limestone rocks that my great-great-great-grandpa had hauled from the backside of the ranch on a wagon pulled by mules. It had two stories with a full covered porch on the ground floor. The matching barn had a wide sliding wooden door and a hayloft that was a pain in the ass to fill with hay because the bails had to be lifted to the second-story window. This year I'd foregone that chore and stacked the winter hay beside the barn and covered it with a plastic tarp. Grandpa would call me lazy, but I did have another job to do.

When I cut the engine and stepped out, Helen walked out of the barn, wiping her hands with a towel. She wore a western jacket and matching designer jeans that she tucked into hand-stitched boots, and her silver cowboy hat highlighted her freshly colored blond hair. At just under sixty, she kept herself looking young with dye and regular injections and never stepped out of her bedroom without full makeup. I knew she'd had surgery too but wouldn't admit it. She wrote a gossip column about new residents for the local paper and volunteered for any group that might include rich eligible bachelors.

"Nicky, what a pleasant surprise. What brings you out so early?" she said.

She was my mother and the only person who had ever called me Nicky. "Sam needs a country vacation." I could tell I'd interrupted her plans. Her country-living look definitely wasn't for me. "Expecting company?"

"A few members of the county fair committee are coming for lunch."

I figured that meant she had a new boyfriend, but I didn't want to know the details. Helen had abandoned the family when my father was elected sheriff of Gillespie County. She claimed that she didn't want to be home waiting for the call when he died on the job, which turned out to be prescient because he was killed on duty two years later when I was sixteen. She didn't return home until Grandpa's murder two years ago. Although she never admitted it, I suspected she returned hoping somehow to cash in on any inheritance from the sale of the family ranch. There was no money because I decided to keep the place as long as I could pay the taxes. Against my better judgment, I agreed to let her stay on as caretaker. She still annoyed the hell out of me by trying to overcompensate for walking out when I was fourteen, but I did have to admit that she took good care of the homestead while I was working in San Antonio, and I didn't have to pay her for it.

"How's the hay holding out? Will we need to buy any more this winter?"

"No, I don't think so. There's plenty of rescue grass, and the weatherman says we'll only get one more hard freeze."

Sam finished his swim and ran dripping wet to join us on the porch.

"Easy, boy," I said while he soaked us both with cold spring water. "How about watching him for a week or two?"

"You're on a new case?"

"Yep."

"Anything to do with that cowboy who died at the rodeo?"

"That's it."

"You gonna share any details?"

"That depends."

"On what?"

"Whether you can keep your mouth shut."

"Nicky, I'm your mother. Of course I wouldn't say anything."

She shook her head. "I'll watch Sam. He's good company. At least he isn't shy about sharing." She put a hand on his muzzle to stop Sam from planting his muddy paws on her shirt.

Helen had a proclivity for gossip. She couldn't help herself. If Doc Frank had friends in Fredericksburg, maybe I could use her network to gather a little more information.

"All right. I'm meeting a client in Willow City. A rancher out there's havin' a sausage-makin' party."

She stopped on the porch. "You're getting paid for that?"

"Somebody has to do it."

"Whose ranch is it? I probably know them."

"Max Devine. I'm going to meet one of the guests. Don Frank."

"Everybody in town knows Don," she said.

Bingo. For once her loose lips might be an asset to my investigation. "What do you know about Don Frank?"

CHAPTER SIXTEEN

Helen lived to flirt and spread juicy gossip with the high rollers in Fredericksburg. She wasn't a native, but because she had been married to my father, she knew all the old-timers in Gillespie County, and because of her position on the local paper, she made it a point to know new residents, at least those with money. Since Doc Frank fit the latter category, I shouldn't have been surprised that she was up on all the local chatter. San Antonio was the nearest big city, and since the LBJ era when the late president made his nearby ranch the "Texas White House," the quaint German community had become a go-to weekend destination. Every year the county added more retirees and weekenders who craved German-themed restaurants and wineries to visit. It was hard to spot a native on Main Street because most stayed away to avoid the crowds unless they owned a business or worked in one.

Helen was all too eager to share what she knew. Donald Frank, or "Doc" as he liked to be called, recently bought and restored a house near downtown Fredericksburg. The restoration made him the darling of the chamber of commerce, who were always looking for ways to exploit the town's pioneer roots. When she and her husband opened the house for tours three days a week, they were given the keys to the city. Frank was also negotiating a deal for a strip of land on Highway 290 a mile outside the city limits. The business he was going to build was a twenty-four-hour clinic with an in-house pharmacy, just like the ones he ran in San Antonio and Austin. There was nothing wrong with an entrepreneur, maybe Doc Frank's operation was all legit. But that's what I was going to find out.

Willow City wasn't a "city" at all, but an unincorporated community north of Fredericksburg with a population of around seventy-five people. There was a beer joint that served pretty good barbecue and catered to weekend motorcycle enthusiasts and a turn-of-the-century schoolhouse that was listed on the national historic registry. If you didn't check your GPS or look on a map, you could drive right through the area, notice the small cluster of houses at the T in the road, and not know you'd been to Willow City. Bikers making day trips to the Hill Country from San Antonio or Austin put it on the map. In the spring, caravans of flora aficionados flocked to the area to take pictures of the overabundance of bluebonnets, the state flower, and other wildflowers blanketing the fields along the roadways.

John Macrae waited for me in the Willow City beer joint's gravel parking lot.

I stopped, ranch style, window to window beside his dark blue four-door Dodge Ram pickup. "Nice day to make some sausage," I said.

"That it is," he said, sipping coffee from a metal travel mug. "I trust you've been to a few of these sausage-making shindigs before?"

"Many times, but ours got canceled this year." I usually went to Helmut Geisler's place to make sausage because he provided the ground pork from the hogs he raised on his ranch. Besides that, he was still paying me off in meat for finding his runaway granddaughter last year. He canceled the event because his wife was back in the hospital.

"Sorry to hear that," he said.

I nodded. Elena Geisler had been in and out of the hospital several times in the last two years, and according to Helmut, both had made peace with her failing health. They were past eighty, and for most of that time, they had been married to each other. I wondered if I would have someone to make peace with when and if I made it past eighty.

When I didn't speak, John said: "I've got twenty-five pounds of elk meat plus fifty pounds of ground pork. I like to cut it fifty-fifty."

"I brought twenty-five pounds of venison to contribute," I said. "That ought to work out just right." I'd thawed out the shoulders and neck meat from the deer I'd shot last season.

"Sounds good to me. No such thing as 'fat-free' sausage. Might as well eat cardboard."

I smiled. There must have been something about him that rubbed his son the wrong way, but in the brief time we'd spent together, he hadn't revealed it to me. He had a friendly and personable way of interacting that he'd probably developed from years of dealing with patients. Maybe his son didn't get to see that side of him.

I followed John out of Willow City on a road that quickly turned to gravel. I faded back a few hundred yards to avoid the dust from his pickup. Except for the dark green layer of late-winter rescue grass, everything but the olive-green oak and cedar trees showed gray exposed branches not yet ready to come out of hibernation.

After several miles, John slowed in front of a limestone rock fence. It was similar to my grandpa's original fence, but on closer inspection, this one was new and reinforced with concrete and six feet taller than the four-foot height of most stone fences built by the German pioneers. There was also an annoying flashing neon sign facing the road advertising exotic animal hunts and featuring an animated cowboy resembling Yosemite Sam chasing deer and buffalo across a pasture. Nothing says "old west" like a flashing red-and-blue neon sign. At first glance, the ranch looked more like Knott's Berry Farm than anything a German pioneer would have built in the nineteenth century.

I stopped behind John's pickup while a guard in a wide-brimmed cowboy hat approached his window. The young man wore a blond, peach fuzz mustache, a friendly smile, and could have been an extra from the *Lonesome Dove* television series. He searched the clipboard in his hand, then pointed toward me. Whatever John told him seemed to satisfy his scrutiny. I wondered if the kid had any training with the revolver he carried on his hip in a western-style leather holster or if, like the hat and high-heeled boots, the handgun was all for show. He punched in the code on the keypad, and the huge cedar-and-steel gate wings slowly swung open, reminiscent of that other famous Hollywood attraction, Jurassic Park.

The road from the gate to the compound was paved. Another sign that the owner wasn't making a living raising cattle and goats like the original German inhabitants. Whoever had it built spent more money on roads and maintenance than the total budget for Gillespie County.

A herd of ten or fifteen shaggy buffalo stood around a giant round bale of hay in the level hundred-acre field to the right of the road. On the left, twice as many full-grown longhorn cattle shared two identical large bales for themselves. Both breeds symbolized different eras of Texas history, as did the replica limestone fence, and added to the theme park feel. The paved road crossed a creek and wound between two limestone cliffs for half a mile before the valley opened up into a well-manicured park-like setting that contained gleaming white limestone block buildings nestled into oak motts and spread out over a ten-acre compound. Each structure resembled Grandpa's house, but the stones were untarnished by age or the weather.

I parked behind John's pickup in a designated area far enough away from the buildings so as not to cast a cloud of dust. Whoever designed the layout had planned for large gatherings and thought of everything, down to clearly marked parking spots so that large crowds wouldn't devolve into chaos.

Off to the side of the designated parking area, a white-and-gray helicopter rested on a paved landing pad complete with a windsock. It had four doors and looked big enough for five or six passengers. I was beginning to get the idea that the ranch owner was in a league of his own. In the grassy field below the compound stood an outdoor rodeo arena complete with metal stands for a hundred people and a covered announcer booth that seemed bigger than the Gillespie Country Fairgrounds in Fredericksburg.

Before we could step out of our vehicles, a young man dressed like the gate guard pulled up driving a horse-drawn cart. He could have been the gate guard's twin or his movie sidekick. The cart was a replica nineteenth-century buggy with four iron wheels and a short box fitted with benches for hauling people and ice chests back and forth from the parking lot to a two-story barn where the sausage-making party was in full swing.

"Welcome to the Devine ranch," the young cowboy driver drawled. He wore a wide-brimmed hat and creased Wrangler jeans tucked into knee-high cowpuncher boots with a neatly tied red bandana around his neck. We nodded hello, and he jumped down to help us swing our ice chests full of meat into the buggy.

"You didn't tell me this was a costume party," I said to the kid, teasing him.

"The boss likes us to dress for the occasion." He had a face full of freckles and an easy smile.

John chuckled. "Max Devine loves to put on a show."

"You from around here?" I asked the young cowboy.

"Yes, sir. I'm from Mason. Name's Glen Zech." He took my hand and squeezed, trying to make an impression. He looked anxious, like he had something he was dying to say.

"Nick Fischer," I said.

"I knew who you was as soon as I saw you. Everybody around here knows you," he said. "You played football in Fredericksburg, then joined the Marine Corps. I read about you in the paper last year. You're a private eye."

I wasn't used to being recognized. I hoped he didn't ask for an autograph. "Glad to meet you," I said. Both my recent cases had involved Fredericksburg and Gillespie County, and both had been in the local paper and made the rounds on Facebook. I guess I shouldn't have been surprised.

"Are you on a case?" he asked.

"We came to make some sausage."

"Oh, yes, sir," he said, with a grin that said he didn't believe me. He jumped into the driver's seat and clicked his tongue at the buggy horse. I hoped he wouldn't blab to the rest of the hired hands before I had a chance to talk to Frank.

"This place looks like it was built yesterday," I said.

"Some of it probably was. Devine's been working on it for the last ten years. Each year he adds another building or another herd of exotic animals. He installed the rodeo arena last year and invited all the National Finals qualifiers to join in a private competition. He put up the prize money and paid for their travel. Tonight, after the sausage-making, there'll be a chuckwagon dinner, then a band from Austin will play. Once a week he opens the arena to the public for anyone who wants to practice their rodeo skills."

"I take it Mr. Devine didn't make his money in ranching?"

"Lot of speculation about that. Most people say oil and gas. He didn't show up on the radar out here until about ten years ago, about the time he bought this ranch."

The horse and buggy stopped in front of the double garage door entrance to the limestone barn. We climbed down and helped Glen haul our ice chests into the building. I was glad that most of the twenty-five or thirty guests weren't dressed like western movie extras. The state-of-the-art sound system played "*Tumbling Tumbleweeds*," a hit tune from 1944 by The Sons of the Pioneers. It wasn't music you'd hear on any modern country-western music station; it was music that played in the background while Gene Autry or Roy Rogers rode off into the sunset after a hard day of chasing bad guys and rescuing women in distress.

"Howdy, partner!" Max Devine greeted us at the entrance to the cavernous space. He stood well under six feet tall minus the high-crowned hat and wore a red bandana identical to Glen's. The hand stitching on the upper part of his black, high-heeled cowboy boots featured a cowboy on horseback twirling a lariat that spelled out the word *rodeo*. He could easily have posed for a group photo with Gene and Roy.

John and Max shook hands. Max smiled behind a gray bushy mustache that curved around his mouth and drooped to the point of his chin.

"Who's this young cowpoke?" Max asked, pointing at me.

By agreement, John introduced me as Colton's Marine buddy. I was hoping to talk to Don Frank without him knowing I was investigating Colton's murder. Perhaps catch him in an unguarded moment.

"Nice to meet you, son. Thank you for your service."

Max Devine pumped my hand with the vigor of a much younger man. On closer inspection, the skin on his hands and face wasn't that of someone who spent his time outdoors. I imagined him in the boardroom talking to a group of rich investors and suspected he traded in his cowboy costume for a suit and tie on the weekdays.

"I was very sorry to hear about Colton. I remember him coming out here a few times," Devine said.

"That's right," John said. "You gave him a horse to ride while we made sausage."

"He was always a hell of a rider." Devine patted John on the back and shifted his tone to a concerned level. "How're you doing, John? I know it's a tough thing, losing a child."

"Thanks for asking. I'm doing as well as can be expected. Ready to make some sausage."

"There you go. Keep busy and stay focused. That's the only way to get over the grief. You need anything, anything at all, you just let me know." He pointed at me with his thumb and index finger shaped like a pistol. "That goes for you too, young man. I wanna pick your brain later on. I'll bet you have some great war stories to tell."

Devine turned on his heels and hustled off toward a thirty-foot-long table covered with plastic. "Put on another layer of plastic. It's better protection," he called to a group of men doing most of the setup. In an hour, the table would be covered with huge wheels of sausage meat stuffed into casings and ready to be tied and hung in the custom-built smokehouse.

John and I dragged our ice chests over to a table covered in plastic with bumpers around the edges like a pool table. A commercial-size meat grinder was set up on one end. We both donned vinyl gloves, then tossed the meat from our ice chests on the table. The idea was to mix wild meat with an equal amount of pork to give the lean game meat enough fat to qualify as sausage. John brought his own bag of ready-mixed spices. There was a pan of water on the gas stove heating cloves of garlic that was used to keep the meat moist in the processing.

John activated the commercial grinder, and we set to work. After about twenty minutes, John flipped off the machine, and we stared at a cold, foot-high pile of bloody ground meat. He reached for a plastic container of pre-mixed spices.

"Better put your mask on for this part. This mixture is pretty potent."

I took his advice while he opened the container and scattered it over the meat. We both dug our hands in the cold meat and began distributing the mixture evenly.

"Here comes Don Frank," John said and pointed with his chin.

I paused for a moment and looked up. I recognized him instantly and fought back the urge to laugh. Frank was hard to miss. He was dressed like Woody from *Toy Story*, including a calfskin vest and a cheap felt cowboy hat, but unlike the rail-thin animated character, Frank carried a couple hundred extra pounds, mostly in a keg-sized stomach that bounced when he walked. He stood at the barn entrance with his hands on his wide hips and surveyed the sausage-making work in progress.

"How y'all doin'?" Frank exclaimed to everyone and no one at once.

A few people turned and nodded an unenthusiastic good morning. They seemed to barely tolerate his presence. Devine was busy setting up the hand-crank link sausage stuffer and didn't bother looking up. Frank immediately singled him out of the crowd and walked over.

"Did he bring any meat?" I asked John.

"He never does. He comes just to rub elbows with Devine and his well-heeled friends and eat. I've never seen him get his hands dirty."

"Why does Devine let him come?"

"Good question. My guess is they're golf buddies. Devine likes to play golf, and Frank's a member of the Dominion golf club. He can make tee times for Devine whenever he flies into town."

"Devine gets around in that helicopter outside?"

"Nice way to avoid traffic."

John topped off the ground meat with a cup full of warm garlic water.

The spice he'd added was red in color and made my eyes water. I stifled a sneeze. This was going to be very spicy sausage.

We stuffed the meat back through the electric commercial grinder and into large foil containers. Once we finished, we were ready to load the mixture into the sausage stuffer.

A half dozen other pairs of men had their mixture ready and waiting for the stuffer. While we waited our turn, I followed Don Frank outside to the barbecue pit that was already laden with samples of freshly stuffed link sausage. I grabbed two longneck Shiner Bocks from the ice chest and made my way over to where Frank stood drooling over the smoking meat.

"Mr. Devine sure knows how to throw a sausage-making party," I said, handing him a beer. I didn't normally start drinking beer at ten o'clock in the morning, but I was hoping to break the ice.

"Max loves showing off the latest developments to his compound," he said, smiling.

I waited to see if he would recognize me from the clinic.

"This your first time here?" he asked without a hint of recognition. He twisted the cap off his beer and took a long drink.

"Yeah, I'm a friend of Dr. Macrae's son, Colton."

"How is Colton? Haven't seen him out here in years." Frank seemed mesmerized by the sizzling meat on the grill and barely glanced at me.

"He's dead," I said. That got his attention.

He took another drink of beer and focused his attention on me. "Sorry to hear that. When did that happen?"

"Last week at the rodeo. He was murdered."

He shook his head. "Well, that's a tragedy. He was in the service, wasn't he?" he asked, as if that somehow explained his death.

"The Marine Corps."

"I always wondered why he would make that choice."

"What do you mean?"

"Joining the military. His father's a physician. He had so many other options."

"Maybe he wanted to serve."

"Yeah, well, his father should have talked him out of it. He lost his arm, didn't he?"

I wanted to keep him talking, hoping to get information about the pills he was dispensing at his clinic, but the more I let him talk, the more I wanted to punch him in the mouth.

"That's right. Ever see him in one of your clinics?"

"No. No, I think I would have remembered."

"Do you treat a lot of veterans?"

"We do work with the VA." His Texas accent faded when I asked him pointed questions. According to Skeeter's research, Frank grew up in New York.

"How about hydrocodone. I'll bet you write a lot of prescriptions for that."

Frank sucked down the last of his beer and began tugging on the end of his mustache with his right hand. "Who are you, again?"

I smiled. "Nick Fischer. Pleasure to meet you, Mr. Frank." I held out my hand.

"Yeah, likewise. You can call me Doc. Everybody does."

He shook my hand without gripping it. His skin was soft and moist. I resisted the urge to wipe my palm on my jeans until after he'd turned away.

"Okay, Doc. Enjoy the sausage-making. Did you bring any meat?"

"No. No. I'm not a hunter per se. Max and I are old friends. I come for the party." He quickly excused himself and grabbed a paper plate from the table.

I retreated inside the barn. I found John Macrae already loading our meat mixture into the sausage stuffer. Each guest took turns helping turn the crank for the sausage stuffer, and those who had experience were attaching the casings and guiding the results into large coils. Another team twisted the coils into links and tied the ends with twine.

I stood beside John and took my turn tying. When our shift was finished, John took a portion of the links to a walk-in smoker built into the side of the barn. He would leave it overnight to cure. We loaded the rest of the links back into our ice chests.

I looked for Frank once more before we left and found him perched in a hammock under an oak tree near the barbecue pit. He had a longneck beer in one hand and a plate of cooked sausage resting on his stomach. I guessed he would be in that position for the rest of the day.

Devine stood beside him. The contrast in size of the two men emphasized the strangeness of their relationship. I couldn't hear Devine's words, but they were stern and to the point. Frank laughed and handed him the empty beer bottle.

I expected Devine to hit him over the head with it. I couldn't imagine a man like Devine taking any crap off anyone. Instead, he simply turned on his high boot heels and stomped away, tossing the empty bottle in the trash barrel as he went.

I ducked out of sight and found John waiting for me beside his pickup.

"Thanks for the invite," I said.

"Anytime. Did you learn anything useful?"

"Maybe. I need to dig a little deeper."

A big man with a beard, wearing a brown cowboy hat, drove past us in a dark green Chevy Silverado pickup with dual back wheels. It looked like a game warden truck without the decals. An AR-15 rested in a gun rack mounted on the dashboard.

"Who's that?"

"One of Devine's hired hands."

"He's well-armed for a cowboy."

We watched the Silverado stop at a gate behind the arena. The man got out and unlocked the gate before driving through.

"Pretty high security. What's he keep in the back pasture?" I asked.

"I asked Devine one time. He said that was his exotic game pasture. He charges ten or twenty grand for a hunt."

I examined the ten-foot game fence around the pasture. Dense brush covered most of the land inside. I didn't buy the explanation. There was something else going on at the Devine ranch. I wondered if Doc Frank was a part of it.

CHAPTER SEVENTEEN

I drove from Willow City to Helmut Geisler's ranch. Despite his wife's hospital stay, his fields were plowed and ready for spring planting. The drainage ditch beside his ranch access road was mowed, and all the farm equipment was neatly tucked away in the barn. As I drove into the yard, nothing looked out of place. It was something his generation did without thinking. Like my grandpa, when he was alive, there was a place for everything, and everything was in its place. I liked to think I was carrying on that tradition, but seeing Helmut's ranch reminded me of the many things I'd neglected to maintain. I blamed it on Helen. At Diana's urging, I reluctantly agreed to let her stay at the ranch after grandpa's funeral. Now, if I wanted to do chores, I had to spend more time around her, and I wasn't ready for that. I was fourteen when she left, and the action left a wound that had never healed. I told myself that I was over it, that it didn't affect me anymore, but every time she called me Nicky, I was reminded of the day she left. Someday I'd get over it. But not today.

Helmut walked out of the barn as I shut off the engine. His three dogs recognized my pickup and stood by the door wagging their tails. Either that or they smelled the fresh sausage I had brought their owner.

"*Guten Tag,*" Helmut called to me in his Texas German accent. He was one of a handful of Texas German speakers left in the area. He and my grandpa grew up speaking German at home, and while Grandpa was alive, they met regularly with a group of old-timers who liked to tell tall tales in German and reminisce about the pioneer days they'd heard about from their granddads. My dad had been fluent, but my generation lost touch with their roots. Speaking German wasn't cool when I was in high school. My focus was on girls and playing football. When those two things weren't available, I'd go hunting. I didn't become interested in the language or the history until after I mustered out of the Marine Corps and Grandpa made a suggestion that turned my life around. He said studying history reminded you that you weren't the only poor son of a bitch that's ever suffered in the world, and work kept your mind off the problems that you did have. It was his recipe that allowed me to transition back into civilian society. Without it, I would still be lost in the abyss. Some, like Colton, never completely found peace after their service. Now, Colton would never get a chance.

Helmut used a red shop rag to wipe his leathery hand, then held it out to me. His grip, as always, was firm. He wore a sweat-stained Stetson Rancher hat, and his face and neck were the color of latigo from years of outdoor exposure. His well-worn blue denim work shirt and Wrangler jeans hung on his rail-thin frame like a suit of clothes on a hanger.

"*Wie geht's?*" I said, shaking his hand.

"*Ich habe gute und schlechte Nachrichten.*"

I concentrated on the words I could translate.

"What's the good news?"

He smiled. I must have guessed the correct meaning or close to it.

His granddaughter, Maya, walked out on the porch. She wore trendy distressed jeans with holes in the knees, which I was sure embarrassed her grandpa, and a red high school sweatshirt with the Battlin' Billies mascot, a stylized ram, stenciled on the front. She'd gained weight over the winter and looked healthier than when I'd taken her back from a ruthless trafficker named Dragon and returned her to Gillespie County. Country life had been good to her so far. She had color in her cheeks that came from helping Helmut with the ranch chores. The last time I saw her, she wore a skin-tight dress and a thick layer of makeup. The ordeal had left her with a healthy distrust of men and anyone outside the family circle. There were still signs of stress in her eyes, or maybe it was maturity. She was nineteen now, going on thirty.

"Hi, Mr. Fischer," she called to me.

"*Maya ist die gute Nachricht,*" Helmut said, his weather-beaten face breaking into a grin.

"*Danke, Opa,*" she said without hesitation.

"*Sie lernt,*" Helmut said proudly.

"Only a few words," she said. "Opa's teaching me, and I'm taking German at the high school."

"I bet I know the teacher."

"It's still Herr Beck. He remembers you."

"Probably not fond memories. Tried to get me to try out for the school musical."

"You?" She laughed. "What was it?"

"*Fiddler on the Roof.* He said he needed extra boys to play Russians."

Maya laughed some more at my expense. She was a smart girl and clearly doted on her granddad. It had been less than five months since I'd brought her back home, and I knew it would take time to fully recover.

"I brought you some fresh sausage," I said, pulling an ice chest out of my pickup bed and carrying it to the porch.

"I'm supposed to be paying you off with meat. Why're you bringing me sausage?" Helmut asked, irritated. When he'd hired me to find Maya, we'd agreed my fee would be paid in beef and pork, something, as a working rancher, he had more of than cash.

I opened the chest and showed him the stacks of sausage links packed in ice.

Helmut examined the meat and studied the irregular-shaped links and the mismatched knots of the twine.

"*Wer hat diese Arbeit gemacht?*" he asked.

"The Devine ranch over by Willow City," I said, guessing he wanted to know where the sausage came from.

"*Amaturen,*" he said, closing the ice chest.

"Well, it's the best I could do."

I knew he disapproved of the workmanship, but I let it go. "It will taste almost as good as yours," I said. "When will Elena be home?"

"That's the bad news. The doctor says he isn't sure," Helmut said, taking his Stetson Rancher cowboy hat off and holding it over his heart, saying a silent prayer for his ailing wife or for the doctor treating her. I wasn't sure which.

"We're going to see her this afternoon," Maya said. "I hope they let her come home soon. I'm tired of Grandpa's cooking. All we eat is meat and potatoes."

"What else is there?" I laughed. It was the same for me when I was growing up in my granddad's house. Every meal consisted of meat and potatoes. In the fall we ate venison. During the winter, Grandpa butchered a hog. In the spring we had mutton and goat, and in summertime we enjoyed beef and the sausage we made from all the meat that was left over.

I could see the strain on Helmut's face, but I didn't press him for any more specific information about his wife. Her condition was grave, and her chances of coming home at all were very slim.

When I got back to San Antonio, I washed the ice chests and left them open to dry in the backyard. With Sam staying at the ranch with Helen, I didn't have to worry about everything being reduced to chunks of plastic. I showered and slipped on clothes that didn't smell like a butcher shop. I didn't mind the smell, but my next move was to track down Lora and find out more about the mystery man she'd met behind the boxing gym who was the same man in black I'd seen with Colton the night he was murdered.

It was early evening, and I took a chance on catching her at her condo before she checked into work. After a day of sausage-making, I didn't want to spend the night waiting in the Paradise Club parking lot for her to finish her shift.

I parked on the street and took the stairs to her floor. I knocked and Lora opened the door.

"Nick? What're you doing here?" she asked, but she didn't seem particularly surprised.

"Nice to see you, Lora."

"I'm getting ready for work. What d'ya want?"

I put my foot in the open door in case she decided not to let me in. "Just to ask you a few questions. It won't take a minute."

She chewed her thumbnail. "I don't think I should."

"Somebody here?" I glanced behind her into the room.

"No. There's nobody here." She opened the door as proof.

I took the opportunity to walk in and closed the door behind me. "You didn't tell me everything about Colton the other night."

"You don't wanna know everything, Nick. Trust me." She had on a long T-shirt. Her hair was curled, and she wore a thick layer of stage makeup in preparation for her turn on the mirrored stage.

"Colton's dead, Lora. Doesn't that mean anything to you?"

I followed her into the kitchen, where a half-empty bottle of vodka stood beside a cocktail glass full of ice.

"You wanna drink?" she asked, pouring vodka over the ice.

I took the glass out of her hand and placed it back down on the counter out of her reach. "What is it, Lora? What are you into?"

She chewed her thumbnail and looked down at the floor. "You were always so good to me," she whispered.

"Until you stabbed me in the back."

"I never meant to hurt you."

"No, just drain my bank account."

"It wasn't like that."

"It doesn't matter, Lora. I'm over it. I'm not here about that. You told the police Colton and I fought over you."

"That's what Colton told me."

"Yeah, but not because I wanted you back. Because I knew you were no good for him."

"What's wrong with me?" she asked defensively.

I took her hand and led her into the living room away from the distracting vodka bottle.

"Please, Nick. You should go. I'll be late for work."

"Not until you tell me what's going on. Who are you afraid of?"

She took my hand and squeezed my fingers until they hurt.

"The guy at the boxing gym?" I asked when she didn't speak.

Her eyes got wide. "You followed me?"

Her pupils were dilated, and both eyes were red and moist. "What're you taking?"

"What?" she asked, looking away.

I left her on the couch and walked into her bathroom. I found a bottle of generic hydrocodone pills prescribed by Frank in her medicine cabinet. Someone had scratched off the patient's name. I checked the contents. There were a dozen pills left. I took the bottle back out to the living room.

"How long have you been taking this stuff?" I asked.

She stared blankly at the bottle, then at me. "I take it for the pain."

"What pain?"

"My back. It's always killing me. It's from dancing in high heels."

"Who gave it to you?"

"What difference does it make?"

"Did Beau Fahl give it to you?"

She looked up quickly. I had her attention now. She dried her eyes and stopped chewing her thumbnail. "How do you know that name?"

"I'm a private detective, remember? What's his connection to Colton?"

"Nick, please? I'm begging you. Don't get involved."

"Was he giving Colton pills?"

She put her finger back in her mouth and chewed her nail like a little girl caught by the teacher.

"Did he kill Colton?"

Her eyes began to water.

I pulled her hand away from her mouth. "If you know something, tell me."

She made a quick desperate move to grab the pill bottle from my hand, but I held it just out of her reach. That move alone told me more than she would ever admit to. She was addicted, and Beau Fahl had a big influence over her continued uninterrupted supply.

I wouldn't get anything truthful from her today. I stood and walked to the front door.

"Where're you going?" Lora followed me. Her eyes focused on the bottle. She wasn't concerned that I was leaving, but that I was taking her bottle of pills with me. "Come on, baby. Stay for a while. Like the old days." She flashed a desperate smile and reached for my belt buckle.

I pushed her hand away and walked out the door.

CHAPTER EIGHTEEN

I didn't take her pills because I was under any illusion that I could make Lora kick the habit. I took her pills because I was counting on her craving to force her to track down her supplier. Call me cold and cynical, but if using her addiction to help me find a murderer and get justice for Colton caused Lora a few hours of agony, I didn't care.

I parked on the street a block away from the entrance to her parking garage and settled in to wait. It didn't take long. Five minutes later, Lora appeared in her white BMW. I was close enough to see the cell phone in her hand. Unless I was completely off, she would be on the phone to her supplier and desperate to get her hands on more pills.

She blew through a stop sign at the end of the street and turned onto the Highway 281 frontage road. She wasn't going to the Paradise Club, and she wasn't going to Frank's clinic. Unless she was taking the long way around, she wasn't going to the gym where she met Beau Fahl last time.

Wherever she was going, she was in a hurry. Drunk, sober, or high, she drove one speed. Fast. She counted on her smile and exposed skin to get her out of speeding tickets, and it usually worked.

She took the airport exit, and I followed her past a park-n-ride to a business park with a redbrick office attached to a small warehouse. It looked like an airfreight company, but there was no name on the building, only a street number. I watched a semi-trailer back in to the loading dock of the warehouse, and a two-man crew began unloading boxes.

Lora parked near the office entrance next to the same black Ford F-250 that was at the gym and immediately jumped out of the BMW. I parked on the street, hoping I was out of range of the building's security cameras so as not to attract too much attention. I took a few photos of the pickup and the front of the building.

I focused the telephoto lens on the open warehouse door, but there was nothing to see but wooden pallets stacked with boxes. The place had all the outward appearances of a legitimate airfreight business. I sent the pictures to Skeeter and then gave him a call.

"A little evening surveillance work?" Skeeter said when he answered the phone.

I explained my interview with Lora and how she had left in a hurry after I walked out with her pill stash. Instead of going to see Doc Frank, she'd driven straight to a warehouse by the airport.

"You do like to play with fire," he said.

"We're getting paid for results. At least I'm on the job," I said, teasing him.

"Oh, I'm workin'," he said. "You wanna know about Beau Fahl? I got everything there is to know, starting with his first-grade teacher."

"Why don't you skip ahead to at least high school? I'm on a tight schedule."

"Let me guess, you got a hot date."

"I'm pretty sure I won't have to worry about that for a while."

"What did you do?"

"It's a trust issue."

"That means you haven't told Diana everything you know."

"I told her I'd share. I didn't say when. And I'll handle my own love life, thank you."

"I'm just sayin', you have a tendency to play your cards close to your chest. It's a wonder Diana put up with you as long as she did."

"Some habits are hard to break."

Skeeter's low-frequency chuckle made the phone vibrate. "You're one hardheaded dude."

I let that comment go. I knew I had plenty of faults. I didn't need to be reminded. My methods weren't orthodox or designed to please anybody.

More than one girlfriend had reminded me of my lack of people skills. Maybe I would never change, but I only knew one way to get results in an investigation, and it didn't involve waiting for bureaucratic committee approval.

"Can we get back to business?" I said.

"Fair enough. This Beau Fahl dude may sound familiar."

"Have we dealt with him before?"

"Just listen," he said. "He grew up in La Grange, Texas, played football in high school, did a little rodeo. His father was a DPS officer. He was killed in the line of duty when Beau was fourteen. His mother left him the year after that. Beau spent the last of his high school years living with his uncle on a farm outside of town. When he graduated, he joined the Marine Corps. He did three tours in Iraq and Afghanistan before his Humvee struck an IED, killing everyone else on board. Beau took a load of shrapnel in the chest. He spent three months at the military hospital in Germany before he was discharged and sent home to Texas. Sound familiar?"

"Okay, I get it. This is a joke, right?"

"No joke, man. The dude's your doppelgänger."

"Are you gonna tell me he worked for the sheriff's department after his discharge and went to law school?"

"No, man. That's where your twin took a walk on the wild side. Three months after his discharge, he killed a man outside a bar in Houston. One punch. He knocked him out, then the guy fell back and hit his head on a concrete block. He did eighteen months for involuntary manslaughter. When he got out, he relocated to San Antonio. That warehouse you're watching right now is legit. Mr. Fahl is in the shipping business."

"Where did he get the money for that? Even if he got partial disability, he couldn't afford to buy a business, unless his family had money."

"That part's a little sketchy. The uncle he lived with sold the family property and took off with the proceeds while Beau was overseas."

"Sounds like a nice guy."

"You want me to go on?"

"Only if you have a connection between him and Doc Frank."

"That part I haven't worked out."

"Well, stay on it. While you're at it, dig a little deeper on Frank. Find out if he has any financial ties to Max Devine, the rancher out in Gillespie County."

"What're you gonna do?"

"Wait and see what Lora does. She's in deep and might be the weak link in the operation."

"What about Danny Sanz?"

"Disappeared off the face of the earth."

"Maybe when he sobered up, he realized he'd said too much."

"Or maybe someone else did and shut him up."

Lora walked out the front office door. She wasn't in as big a hurry as when she went in. The self-assured swagger was back in her walk. I focused the telephoto lens. When she opened her car door, she was wearing a smile. That probably meant she'd gotten what she came for.

"Lora just came out of the warehouse. I'll catch up with you later."

Lora drove out of the parking lot and sped toward Highway 281. From there she followed the 410 Loop west. I followed at a safe distance, but she didn't seem to be worried about a tail or the local police. She did her usual eighty to ninety miles per hour. It was almost eight o'clock, and the after-work rush was over. She flew past the Paradise Club and took the exit to Highway 16 west.

By the time she slowed down, we were in a newer suburb on the far northwest side of the city. The light from the Six Flags amusement park sparkled not more than a mile away.

She stopped at the entrance to the Lion Springs housing development. Oak trees framed a limestone brick archway with tasteful landscape lighting accenting a locked metal gate. Two video surveillance cameras kept tabs on the traffic. The deserted guardhouse either meant the personnel worked nine to five or the HOA decided the keypad lock maintained an acceptable level of security and the members could tell their California friends they lived in a gated community.

I pulled to the curb a half block behind Lora's white Beemer and watched her lean out her window and punch in the security code. The gate slowly slid open, and she darted through. I followed before it could close. I guessed the HOA figured the criminals would wait and attempt a legitimate break-in.

The houses were mostly two-story limestone brick with large yards and established trees. They looked to be in the six- to nine-hundred-thousand-dollar range with a few scaled up to a million, all built within the last five years and identical to dozens of similar housing projects popping up on the northwest side of the city.

This one advertised a golf course and a community tennis complex. Lora buzzed by the lit courts that looked well maintained and turned down a street named Back Nine, which I assumed followed the golf course. She parked at the end of a cul-de-sac near a house set back off the street with a circular driveway that was jammed with vehicles. There was a party in progress.

While she sat in her car adding makeup and fussing with her blond hair, a man wearing a black jacket and khaki pants approached the driver's side door. He tapped on her door and shined a flashlight on Lora's face. She smiled, and he opened her door. I saw a bulge on his beltline and knew he was armed. What kind of party has armed guards?

Lora got out, and the man escorted her down the driveway and around the back of the house like she was the hired help.

I didn't see another guard out front, so I took my binoculars out of the console and followed them. I passed a Range Rover, three Suburbans, and a red Maserati in the driveway alongside a couple of pickups crusted with dirt. Nothing unusual, except for the green Silverado parked on the grass near the yard gate. I'd seen it before, on the Devine ranch. I took a closer look. The AR-15 still rested in the gun rack on the dash. I remembered the driver wore a brown cowboy hat and a black beard. John Macrae said he worked for Devine.

I took a closer look. The doors were locked and the floorboards covered with fast food wrappers. I wondered if the driver was on duty protecting Max Devine or taking the night off to party. John Macrae had said Devine traveled by helicopter. So far, I hadn't seen one.

I kept to the shadows and made my way to the backyard fence. A pool surrounded by brush landscaping took up the center of the roughly half-acre yard. Above that, four men stood on a large second-story deck. I froze. The men were armed guards. I waited five minutes to be sure no one saw me. The man in khakis walked off the deck and back around the side of the house.

I worked my way around to the back side of the fence, which bordered the golf course. Through a stand of trees, I saw Devine's white-and-gray helicopter perched on the manicured fairway. I took a picture of the call letters and sent it to Skeeter. I wondered where he parked during operating hours or if this stop was strictly an after-hours destination.

I found a good vantage point behind a live oak branch that rested on the wooden back fence and surveyed the back of the house with my binoculars.

The man with the black beard and brown cowboy hat leaned against the glass wall near the sliding back door and puffed on a cigar. He seemed to be in charge of security. I zoomed in on his face. His stone-cold expression was identical to the one he wore at the ranch. Through puffs of cigar smoke, I watched his eyes constantly searching the darkness beyond the pool. The eyes paused on my location. I put the binoculars down, fearing a flash of reflected light might give away my position. There was no moon, and a heavy layer of clouds covered the night sky. At a hundred yards, the man wouldn't be able to see me. Still, his steady gaze gave me an uneasy feeling, a feeling that I was watching pure evil. Something I hadn't felt since facing off with Taliban fighters on my last deployment.

The men with rifles stood by the deck railing, focused on the steam rising from a built-in jacuzzi linked to the main swimming pool.

I took a closer look at what attracted their attention. Through the steam, I saw Lora with her bare breasts glistening with beads of moisture and a seductive smile, sitting on Doc Frank's lap. He wore a goofy grin, held a fat cigar in one hand and a scotch glass in the other. Another man in the water had his bare back to me, but he wore a high-crown cowboy hat with a Montana crease with a red bandana around his neck. It had to be Max Devine. Both old men looked like potatoes in a pot of boiling water beside Lora's line-free, California tan.

Lora had moved up in the world. Until recently, her list of clientele included gullible veterans like me and Colton Macrae. The fat cats in the jacuzzi with her now didn't need to wait for a government check at the end of the month to pay for her services.

I scanned the rest of the house. Most of the activity came from the upstairs room overlooking the deck. A round table stood in the middle of the room with chairs for a dozen people. A group of men engaged in a poker game occupied seven of the chairs. Every player had a cigar, and every player had a whiskey glass. The pile of colored chips told me the game would probably go most of the night.

A blond female, dressed for work at the Paradise Club, walked out holding a tray of drinks, which she distributed around the table. She paused to sit on one man's lap. Their movements indicated laughter. When she stood, the man slipped a bill in her G-string.

Another female emerged from a back room leading a gray-haired man by the hand. She wore shorts without a top. Her dark hair curled around her shoulders. He wore a dress shirt unbuttoned to the waist. When he sat down, another man stood and grinned at his poker buddies. I recognized him as a Bexar County judge. Poker night for the movers and shakers.

I spent the next thirty minutes watching the game and the comings and goings of the old men mixing with young female entertainment. Frank and the man with the hat left the jacuzzi and joined the poker players at the table. The man with the hat was definitely Max Devine. Lora dried off and refilled her drink inside, then two other players followed her back to the pool.

The one face I didn't see was Beau Fahl. Lora had gone to see him first, before coming to the party. Why wasn't he there? Did he send her to the party? How was he connected to Max Devine? Then it hit me. Beau was hired help. The men playing poker called the shots and had the bank accounts. The men with guns on the deck and Beau Fahl may have wished they were drawing an inside straight with a stripper on each knee, but they were guns for hire.

I risked one last glimpse of Devine's head of security. He'd finished his cigar and walked to the deck rail, where he stood watching Lora entertaining the county judge in the jacuzzi. In contrast to the lascivious looks of the other men, his stone-cold expression never changed.

I'd seen just enough. I wasn't interested in a private poker party with strippers unless it led me closer to Colton's killer. At this point, I didn't see the connection. I was worn out. If I stayed any longer, I might join the party and press my luck in the poker game.

A puddle of water stood in the kitchen waiting for me when I let myself in the back door of my fixer-upper house in King William. One of the major disadvantages of living in a house built over a century ago was that not a week went by without something breaking down.

I tossed an armload of dirty towels on the floor in the kitchen to soak up the pool of water and opened the cabinet under the sink. My phone flashlight caught the sparkly reflection of moisture clinging to the ancient drainpipe that attached to the PVC trap. When I touched the wet spot, the rusty metal dissolved in my fingers like a graham cracker pie crust. I'd been putting off the inevitable since I bought the place. My original intention was to make all the necessary repairs and sell the house for a nice profit. Four years later, I was still fixing one problem at a time when the issue became impossible to ignore, like the swimming pool on the kitchen floor. I'd replaced most of the original water pipes, but I hadn't gotten around to the sinks.

I decided to put it off for another day. The leak was in the drain. It wouldn't leak if I didn't use the sink. I could do dishes in the backyard and pretend I was camping.

I turned off the back deck light and noticed my neighbor Rose sitting beside the window in her upstairs bedroom. She waved, and I flashed her a thumbs-up. *Hello, Rose*, I mouthed. When I first moved in, her ever-watchful eye was a little too focused on me, and I considered putting up a higher fence between our property. But gradually I got to know her, and seeing her in the window was like having my late grandma watching over me. Normally, I would knock on her door and have a "nightcap" with her—a shot of her favorite peach schnapps or peppermint brandy. Tonight, I needed a good night's sleep. Tomorrow I was going to have a little talk with Beau Fahl.

CHAPTER NINETEEN

I drove to the Fight Night gym in the strip mall off the I-10 freeway hoping to catch Beau Fahl during a morning workout or mopping the floor, whatever his morning routine happened to be. I circled the parking lot a little after nine a.m. and found his four-door black F-250 in a reserved spot. This social call might stitch together the missing pieces surrounding Colton's murder or at least shake things up. My specialty. Even if SAPD wasn't looking for a murder suspect, I was. Anyone who came into contact with Colton was fair game.

I grabbed my gym bag and locked my pickup. I had my gloves and boxing shoes in my gym bag along with my S&W .38, just in case.

The inside of the gym hadn't changed. It used to be a Gold's Gym. Sylvia, my ex-girlfriend, had a membership, and I remembered once picking her up here after her workout. The counter faced the glass-door entrance. They still had displays featuring supplemental protein powder, colorful kinesiology tape, and the latest workout gear. A gym rat in his late twenties leaned on the counter staring at his cell phone. He glanced up when I tossed my bag on the floor. His eyes drifted over my red Marine Corps T-shirt and lingered on my forehead scars.

"Howdy, Kenny," I said, reading his name from his plastic name tag.

The gym members working out all looked ready for a photo shoot. At Lucky's, scars and broken noses were as common as blue jeans at a rodeo.

In this part of town, the busy professionals and college student clientele were more likely to conceal physical defects with surgery or makeup.

"Can I help you?" Kenny smirked, dripping attitude like a wet sponge.

I returned the attitude and sneered at the polished surroundings and the ad displays. "Smells like a hair salon in here," I said in mock contempt.

"Excuse me," he said, finally putting his cell phone down.

"I'm lookin' for a place to work out on this side of town."

"We have regular classes if you sign up for a premium membership."

"Classes?" I laughed. "I don't do Pilates. I'm lookin' for a sparring partner. The name suggested you might provide one. But evidently, 'fight' means something else here. Too bad. Good location for me."

"I teach kickboxing. I passed the fifth-grade blue belt last fall." He said it like he'd earned a Silver Star in combat.

"You must be really good, but I'm talkin' 'bout straight boxing."

His jaw muscles clenched. He didn't deal with many redneck customers. I walked to the entrance behind the counter and stood looking into the main gym area. Kenny didn't know whether to give me a pass or ask me to leave.

"I'm off at three, if you're looking for a workout," he said.

"I was looking for some adult competition," I said, emphasizing *adult*.

Kenny bounced back and forth on the balls of his two-hundred-dollar sneakers. "Are ya interested in a membership or just a day pass?"

"Let's start with a *free* day pass. I'll try out your weights and use the speed bag. If I like what I see, I'll go from there."

He tapped a pen on the glass countertop to get my attention. "Sure, you'll have to sign in here and leave your ID. A day pass is twenty bucks."

I kept my back to him and searched the gym floor. I found what I was looking for on a mat in the corner, Beau Fahl practicing combination punches with a partner in focus mitts.

"How 'bout you sign me in, Fifth Grade. I won't be here all day. Mark me down as 'X.' I don't carry ID when I work out. Throws me off balance." I strolled onto the main floor and walked directly to a stretching area near the corner mat, confident that I'd rattled the young man into taking action.

The walls were covered with both male and female MMA fight scenes.

No sexism here. A regulation-size fight cage sat on a raised platform in the center of the main room. All the equipment was clean, new, and state-of-the-art. Lucky did his best to keep everything shipshape at his gym, but the sheer volume of high school kids that flowed through after school made it hard to keep up the maintenance with a strictly volunteer staff.

I passed a dozen or so would-be fighters in different stages of working out. Three were slamming the speed bags in the corner. Two women wearing boxing gloves were jumping rope, and several men were practicing kicks on the row of heavy bags.

I dug out my tape and gloves and made a show of wrapping my hands while discreetly studying Beau and his training partner. I was interested in his style. From what I could see, he was good. He had a quick response time and a highly developed set of combination punches. The crisp popping sound his gloves made hitting the mitts told me his punches packed all the power his muscled arms could muster. He also planted his feet and used his hips when he swung, getting every bit of his weight behind each punch. He had skills, and the way he moved his head side to side and up and down showed he was a natural or had training.

Lucky usually found young up-and-comers in the heavyweight class for me to spar with. He knew I could take a punch and didn't worry about me getting hurt in the ring. I wasn't a natural boxer. I started while in the Marine Corps and kept it up after I mustered out as a way to stay in shape and keep my edge.

Kenny followed me out on the main floor with a red face and clipboard in his hand. "Sir, I can't let you in unless you give me your name and ID," he insisted. He stood on the edge of the mat, waving his clipboard.

I ignored him until I finished swapping my running shoes for my boxing shoes and taping my knuckles. "I told you I don't carry ID when I'm workin' out. Charge me if you want. I'll settle up when I'm finished here." With that I turned my back on him and walked to the speed bags. Kenny hustled over to the practice ring where Beau was throwing punches.

A bell rang, and Beau dropped his gloves and accepted a bottle of water from his trainer. Kenny waved him to the side. I couldn't hear what was said, but when the conversation was over, both men were staring at me. I kept up my rapid-fire punches on the speed bag and waited.

Beau pulled his gloves off and walked toward me. I'd taken his picture from across the parking lot. From a distance, he was a big man, especially standing next to Lora. Up close, he was even bigger. Not quite Skeeter's size, but his muscles were chiseled, and he carried himself like a big cat on the hunt.

I pretended not to notice when he stopped a few yards away. Kenny stood behind him with his clipboard still in his hand and a you're-gonna-get-it look on his face.

"I don't carry an ID either," Beau said.

I gave the bag one last punch and turned to him. "Explain that to hotshot," I said, chinning toward Kenny and pretending to be annoyed.

"He's a pussy," Beau said, laughing.

Kenny turned a darker shade of red.

Beau extended his taped right fist toward me. "Beau Fahl," he said, introducing himself. "This is my gym."

I made eye contact and held his gaze for an extra moment, then nodded and bumped his fist with my gloved hand. "Nick Fischer."

Kenny let out an exasperated breath of air and stalked back to the front counter.

"I hear you're looking for a sparring partner," Beau said.

"Just tryin' to get in a workout. I don't have a lot of time."

"You do MMA?"

"I prefer boxing. Started in the Marine Corps." I was hoping he'd get overconfident. I'd never met an MMA fighter who didn't think he could kick a boxer's ass in the ring or out.

"I did a little time in the Corps," he said, like it was a prison term.

"I do straight boxing now, but just for fun. I usually go to Lucky's Gym."

"Yeah, I heard of him. Lucky Hernandez. Welterweight. I liked his style. Aggressive. He still around?"

"Yeah, he's still training. Got a stable full of up-and-comers."

"He kick you out?" He smiled, hoping to get under my skin.

"He asked me to leave after I broke his best prospect's nose."

This caused another smile. I was lying, of course, but it was getting the reaction I wanted. "You're welcome to join me in the cage sometime," Beau said.

"How 'bout now?" I said, returning the smile. I hadn't come here to set up an appointment. I needed to shake things up. The best way to do that was to catch your opponent off guard.

He gestured toward the cage. "Why not?"

I followed him to the cage. Everyone in the gym turned in our direction. Kenny came back out on the floor. I felt their excited anticipation, as if it were feeding time at the zoo.

"What d'ya say to three rounds?" Beau asked, bouncing on the balls of his feet and stretching his bulky, muscled arms toward the ceiling.

"If you can last that long," I said.

He laughed. "Pretty cocky. I like that."

"I watched you with the focus mitts. You looked a little rusty," I lied.

His trainer stepped into the ring. "MMA rules?" He was asking Beau how he wanted to proceed. He also held up two sets of head gear.

Beau turned to me. "MMA rules?" he asked.

"Sure. Keep it clean. No headbutts, no fish hooking, no biting." I stood with my hands at my sides. My muscles were loose and ready to go after the brief work on the speed bag. I was conserving my energy.

"That's right. Stay away from the groin, and no blows to the back of the head," the trainer added.

"I'm a boxer. We're more civilized."

The trainer laughed.

The dozen or so gym patrons quickly assembled outside the wire, no doubt eagerly anticipating Beau's quick takedown of the new cocky upstart. I was hoping to disappoint them.

"Headgear?" The trainer offered me the protective padding.

I held up my gloved hands. "This is my protection."

"Suit yourself," he said.

"Best two out of three?" Beau asked.

"What do I get when I whip your ass?"

Beau laughed. "How about a month's free membership?"

"Make it a year."

"What do I get?"

"I'll pay full price."

"Let's get it on," he said and raised his gloved hand to his trainer.

The trainer hit the bell, and Beau barreled toward me with his big head tucked behind two massive fists. He wasn't out for exercise; he wanted to kill me. His eyes and demeanor shifted from affable club owner to street thug.

I let him go on offense. I'd told him I was mainly a boxer, and that was true. But I also trained with Sarge and had learned a few Brazilian jiu-jitsu moves that I kept in reserve. That and keeping my moves unpredictable was my ace in the hole.

I easily dodged his first left-right combination, surprised he led with punches instead of kicks. That didn't last long. His next move caught me off guard. In one smooth motion, he planted a right foot on my left shoulder. He was aiming for my head, but I ducked and rolled with the hit at the last second.

I countered with a snap kick that caught him in the chest and rocked him backward. I hadn't intended to show him any kicks, but Beau's move prompted my response.

He grinned through his mouth guard, knowing I had tipped my hand.

He hit me with a solid body shot that forced the wind out of my lungs. I countered with a left hook that missed the mark and caught him on the shoulder. He wasn't fazed. His movements were quick and precise.

We stood toe-to-toe and traded blows and occasional kicks until the bell sounded the end of round one. I could feel swelling on my left cheek under my eye. He nailed me good and definitely won the first round.

"Nice kicks," he said. "I thought you said you were a boxer." His affable club owner smile returned, hiding the killer I'd just exposed. We had both used the round as a test of each other's skills, and he knew he came out on top.

"I watch a lot of TV," I said.

He wiped sweat off his face with a towel, then drank a bottled water.

Kenny and the others looked on like Romans thirsty for gladiator blood in the Colosseum.

I went over my options for the next round. I wouldn't give the crowd what they wanted without a fight. Beau had the reach and the speed to land punches and kicks when and where he wanted. Those were style points helpful in competition, but I wasn't here to score competition points.

I'd planned to save the Brazilian moves to the end, if and when I needed them. But Beau's right jab was lethal. He'd nailed me solid, twice. The second one caused the swelling under my eye. I didn't feel like walking out of the gym with more than one black eye. The jiu-jitsu moves helped a fighter put an opponent on the ground where his kicks and punches were less effective. It was time to put Beau on the mat.

Beau tossed his empty water bottle over the cage fence and turned to me, waiting for the second-round bell. The affable smile disappeared again. He could smell blood like a wolf smells a wounded deer. The test was over. If he had any flaw in his fighting style it was overconfidence. He wanted to show his fans a big finish.

When the bell rang, Beau came on fast again with his big head tucked into his muscled shoulders and his fists dancing in front of his face.

I waited for him by the cage fencing. I wanted him to think I was hesitant to face him in round two. When he saw me holding back, he'd go for the haymaker punch, intending to put me down for the count.

The crowd drew an expectant breath in the half second it took for Beau to cock his massive arm and fire it toward my head. They'd probably seen him use the move on more than one opponent.

I ducked under his glove at the last moment and made my play. I saw the instant surprise in his eyes as I dove at his legs. The move was a simple front scissors throw that any jiu-jitsu beginner might pick up in his first lesson. It was easy to counter if you recognized the move, but Beau wasn't expecting it.

I put my left leg on his ankles, wrapped my right leg behind his knees, and put the big man face first into the mat. His six-foot-four, two hundred and thirty pounds hit hard. Then I pinned him to the mat and applied a choke hold.

"Had enough," I said in his ear.

He blew a sharp breath through his nose, struggling against the hold. He wasn't going to give up.

I admired that quality. We had that in common. I wouldn't have given up either. Could have been our shared Marine Corps background or just our mutual stubborn streak. I noticed his trainer didn't immediately rush in and tap him out. We were playing by MMA rules, but they were modified to the owner's advantage.

He held out until the bell dinged for the end of the round.

I let go and stood.

Beau scrambled to his feet. He nodded and smiled through his mouth guard. The affable club owner was back, but only on the surface. "Last round. We're even," he said and walked to the fencing where his trainer stood.

I took a drink from a bottled water. The onlookers talked quietly amongst themselves and nodded in my direction. I took their reaction to mean a newfound respect for my skills, but it also reminded me of the audience at a demolition derby waiting for the lead car's inevitable crash and burn.

The bell rang for the third and final round.

Beau shot from the edge of the ring, not wasting any time.

This time I didn't stay on the fence. I met him in the center of the cage and threw the first punch combination. He was ready for it and countered with his own uppercut and right jab. I managed to deflect the blows, but I felt the lethal power behind his punches. He wasn't holding anything back. Had I gone for the takedown move, he would have pounded me into the mat, so I stayed on my feet, trading blows and kicks in rapid-fire succession.

Beau landed a solid right to my left cheek. Blood ran down my lips and into my mouth. His left hook caught my chin and set me back on my heels. He moved forward, pressing his advantage. I returned punch for punch, but his combinations were connecting with regularity. I threw a front kick to stall his advance. He countered with a roundhouse that nearly took me to the mat. He was strong and fast.

He knew he had me on the run. I switched to defense in order to survive the round. I blocked his next kick and grappled him to the floor. I used the jiu-jitsu Sarge had taught me to neutralize the big man's lethal hands and feet. It wasn't MMA, and it wasn't pretty, but this wasn't a friendly sparring match. It was a street brawl to the finish.

Someone yelled, "Take him out, Beau!"

I locked my legs around him.

He swung his head, trying to headbutt me into submission.

His final effort connected with my left cheekbone, nearly knocking me out. Little pinpoints of light swam in my vision.

The bell rang to end the round.

I let my legs relax and released my hold.

Beau didn't stop. He hit me with a final left-right combination while I was on the ground.

I kicked him with both legs and wrapped my arms around his.

Finally, he stopped and stood up.

His expression slowly shifted from killer wolf back to affable club owner. It seemed like a struggle for him to get himself under control. When he finally did, he said, "Good round."

"Yeah, thanks for the workout," I said. I was dazed, but not out. I tried not to show the effects, but he knew he had me and that in another five seconds he could have put me away.

I grabbed a towel from the table outside the cage and wiped my face. I tasted blood and felt the swelling under my eye. I'd taken a beating but learned my lesson for the day about Beau Fahl—never turn your back and never give up an advantage.

"You took two out of three," I said.

Beau stepped out of the cage and accepted a towel from his trainer. "The last round was a draw. Call it even."

"How 'bout a rematch sometime?"

"Anytime, boss," Beau said.

The onlookers drifted back to their own workouts. Kenny went back to the front counter, no doubt disappointed I hadn't left more blood on the canvas. If I met Beau Fahl again, I had the feeling there wouldn't be a referee and no one would be watching. There wouldn't be any rules to follow other than kill or be killed.

When the trainer left Beau and me alone, I decided it was time to make my visit personal. "How did you know Colton Macrae?" I asked. I watched his expression for any kind of recognition at the mention of Colton's name. I wanted to hear if Beau would deny knowing him or make up a story.

"We had a few beers at the VFW." Beau dropped the towel and stood facing me with his arms at his sides.

I stepped closer to him. "Why did you meet him behind the bucking chutes at the rodeo?"

He dropped the affable smile. "He wanted me to watch him ride."

"Did you kill him?" I was all for cutting to the chase.

Beau's smile returned. "Is that what you came here to ask me, Mr. Private Dick? You investigatin' Colton's suicide?"

"You know me?"

"I saw you in the parking lot. You followed Lora. She told me who you were."

"Colton was murdered."

"That's not what I heard. He was head over heels for Lora. She was gonna leave him. It sent him over the edge."

"You didn't answer my question. Did you kill him?"

He smiled bigger. "You got some big balls."

"That's right. And just so we're clear. If you did kill him. I will nail you to the wall."

He studied me for a full half minute, but he didn't smile this time. "Good luck. Still interested in a membership?"

"I changed my mind. I think I'll keep my membership at Lucky's."

"Suit yourself."

I walked over to my gym bag and stripped off my gloves and hand tape. Beau wasn't going to give me a confession. I didn't expect that. I wanted the wolf to know the hound dog had his scent. With the DA breathing down my neck, I didn't have time to set up a month-long surveillance. My plan was to shake the tree and hope something fell out.

"One more thing." I turned on my way to the front door. "Do you know Doc Frank?" I watched him closely for a reaction. Beau's face was blank. Sometimes the absence of a reaction is more telling.

"Never heard of him," he said.

"That's funny. Frank said y'all were good buddies."

Beau's expression didn't change.

Kenny was on his cell phone when I walked past the counter. He didn't bother to look up.

PART TWO

Outlaws

The belief in a supernatural source of evil is not necessary: men alone are quite capable of every wickedness.

—Joseph Conrad

"She tried to turn me on to Jesus
But I turned on to the devil's ways
And I turned out to be
The only hell my mama ever raised."

—Johnny Paycheck

CHAPTER TWENTY

Beau Fahl drove his four-door King Ranch model F-250 past the Dominion Country Club's signature golf course and stopped at the security gate entrance to the upscale neighborhood on the far northwest side of San Antonio. He'd heard the course was one of the more challenging courses in Texas. Designed by Bill Johnston and opened in the eighties, it attracted high rollers from all over. Beau couldn't care less about playing golf. He had no respect for a game where the players were fat old men drinking scotch and smoking cigars. If they wanted to get drunk and smoke, that was fine by him, but don't call it a sport. They rode around in fancy golf carts making business deals that regular people like Beau could never make. That was about to change. He could barely contain his excitement. After all these years of sucking up to the big boys, Beau couldn't wait to be in one of those golf carts, puffing on a Cuban and sucking on single malt. Once he made his move, he'd buy a membership and beat them at their own game.

The Dominion was home to a few well-known celebrities, several of the Spurs professional basketball players, and at least one reputed cartel boss. The community was a fifteen-hundred-acre master-planned development nestled in rolling limestone hills and covered with live oak trees. It was quiet, secluded, and very exclusive.

Beau knew that Frank used the house to entertain state and local politicians along with some high-placed police and DEA agents. Thanks to

Lora, he knew how Frank had managed to stay off the radar. It was time to make sure the protective shield extended to the hired help.

He stopped behind a Rossello Red Range Rover. The vehicle was the new *Sport V8 Supercharged Autobiography* model that retailed for a hundred and ten grand. It came standard with heated leather seats, alloy wheels, a sunroof, and a power liftgate. He'd test driven one last week and was impressed by the power of the eight-cylinder engine and how the four-wheel drive gripped the gravel roads at high speeds. One day very soon, he would pay cash for his own vehicle. Maybe he would take Lora for a ride. He would finally get the respect he deserved.

The twenty-something security guard waved the Range Rover forward. Beau stopped beside him and unrolled his window. "I'm here to see Doc Frank," he said.

The kid wore a black uniform with a badge and sported a Glock 9mm on his belt. Two more guards stood beside the entrance to the guardhouse. The neighborhood was well protected, and the residents were serious about security. Two surveillance cameras covered the outside of the gate and two focused on the inside. Cameras also guarded the perimeter fence at thirty-foot intervals. Breaking into or out of the Dominion would be difficult, but Beau had a plan for that too, if it became necessary.

Beau waited while the young guard took his ID and wrote the information on his clipboard. He handed the ID back to Beau and walked to the guardhouse, where he picked up a landline phone and called ahead to Doc Frank's house for verification. This was an unplanned visit, but Beau was confident that Doc would see him given the new set of circumstances they were dealing with. Nick Fischer had come to the gym. He was a private investigator working for Colton Macrae's father, and he had connected him to Frank. Beau needed to know why Doc mentioned his name and what he was prepared to do if SAPD turned up the heat and showed up at his front door. He was going to persuade Frank to use his connections to make the investigation go away. Beau could handle the private investigator. In fact, it would be a pleasure taking that smartass Nick Fischer down the next time they met.

The guard returned and handed Beau a card that had the time and date of his arrival. "You're good to go, sir. Place this on your dashboard. Return it to the duty guard when you leave. There's a map on the back in case you get lost."

Beau closed his window, put the card on his dash, and drove up a long winding road to Doc Frank's house. He didn't need a map. He'd studied the Google satellite images of the area. He made it his business to know who he worked for.

Doc Frank's address was at the end of an oak-lined cul-de-sac. The terra-cotta roof tiles, limestone arches, and bell tower resembled the local seventeenth-century missions. The landscape mixed barrel cactus and Texas laurel trees with native purple sagebrush in a tasteful southwest style made popular by *Texas Monthly* magazine.

Beau pulled his pickup into the courtyard that circled a bronze Catarina fountain. The main entrance had two twelve-foot wooden doors designed like the entrance to a church. Two separate entrances were connected to the main building by covered breezeways, making the compound feel like a small village rather than a single-family house.

A man dressed in khaki pants and a black jacket approached the pickup. He wore a pistol in a belt holster along with a two-way radio.

"Mr. Frank is waiting for you on the back deck," Khaki Pants said.

Beau climbed out of his pickup and followed the guard down a brush-lined path that led around the side of the compound.

Beau studied the security cameras attached to the corners of the house and the stone fence. He didn't see any other guards but imagined there were more in the house. The path led to a tile-covered patio shaded by a giant oak tree and facing the country club golf course. The patio overlooked the main backyard area, which featured an oval-shaped pool with a spiral kids' slide and a dozen children's toys floating in the water. An elaborately designed wrought-iron staircase connected the raised patio to the pool area. The heated water radiated a cloud of steam in the crisp morning air.

Doc Frank reclined on a chaise lounge wearing a thick terrycloth robe that barely covered his belly. He held a fat cigar in one hand and his cell phone pressed against his ear with the other.

Beau envied Frank's money, but at the same time, the man disgusted him. He never understood how a man with zero self-discipline could attain so much money and power.

Frank waved his cigar, and the security guard disappeared back down the brush-lined path. "Help yourself to a bloody mary," Frank said and pointed to a glass pitcher on the table.

Beau pulled up a chair but ignored the drink. He never touched alcohol or drugs.

"I can get any kinda broad you want, judge," Frank said into his phone. "Blond, brunette, redhead, big tits, small tits, young, old. You name it."

Two young girls about twelve or thirteen years old ran out of the house wearing matching white one-piece suits and dove into the steamy pool. A smaller boy followed, pulling an older woman wearing a terrycloth robe that matched the one Doc Frank wore. The woman sat on the edge of the pool and dangled her legs in the warm water while she outfitted the boy with floating arm bands. Her face showed obvious signs of cosmetic surgery under layers of makeup, and her unnaturally dark hair hung loose to her shoulders.

Frank waved toward them while still listening to his phone. Beau had never met her, but he'd done his homework. The woman was Frank's wife, and the children were his grandkids.

"You liked the one in the hot tub? I know just who you're talking about. I'll take care of it. Gotta go, judge. Yes, eight o'clock. The usual time. We upped the stakes. Don't forget it's a thousand dollar buy-in next week, you cheap bastard." Frank chuckled and disconnected his phone, then tossed it on the table.

"Pawpaw, look at me!" the little boy shouted up at Frank from the edge of the pool, then waited for Frank to look before he dove into the water.

"Good job!" Frank yelled over the wrought-iron railing.

"Turn up the heat, Doc. It's still too cold in here," his wife called to him.

"Okay, pumpkin," Frank said and refilled his glass from the bloody mary pitcher. "I'm glad you're here," he said to Beau, his voice low enough not to be heard by his wife and grandkids by the pool. "The judge wants that same bitch you sent to the poker game last week. The blond with the big tits. What's her name?"

"Lora."

"Yeah, that's her. She made a big impression, if you know what I mean." He gestured with his free hand indicating Lora's large bra size. Be sure she doesn't get too wasted. I don't want her gettin' sloppy."

Beau knew Lora would make an impression.

"Pawpaw, look!" one of the girls shouted from the top of the water slide.

Frank turned his attention to the girl. "I'm watching, honey."

The little girl plunged down the slide and splashed into the water.

Frank turned back to Beau, not skipping a beat. "Can you handle that?"

Beau folded his hands on the table. His jaw muscles clenched. "We have bigger problems."

"You're supposed to take care of any problems that come up. What the fuck do I pay you for?"

"Pawpaw, come in the pool with us!" the little boy shouted.

"In a minute, sweetheart," Frank yelled back.

"A private dick came to the gym asking about Colton Macrae."

"I'm supposed to care about that?" Frank fired his four-barrel torch lighter and applied blue flame to his dormant cigar. A cloud of smoke filtered into the live oak branches.

"Colton might have told the guy something."

"Who is this guy?"

"Nick Fischer."

"He too tough for you?" Frank sneered.

"He said you told him we were friends."

"That's bullshit."

"Why would he say that?"

"To get under your thick skin, shit stick. He doesn't know squat. I talked to him, but your name didn't come up."

"If he made the connection between me and Colton, then the police will make the connection. You gonna take care of that?"

"You're on your own with that deal. I can't get involved."

"Pawpaw, hurry!" the little boy insisted.

"Okay, darling. I'm coming," Frank shouted over his shoulder.

Beau slid his chair beside Frank's chaise lounge and grabbed Frank's wrist on the side away from the pool that couldn't be seen by his family.

"What the fuck are you doin'?" Frank gasp.

Beau squeezed his wrist, then twisted Frank's arm. The pressure instantly paralyzed Frank's upper body. He dropped the cigar on the Spanish tiles. "Listen to me, Pawpaw. Play your little godfather games with someone else. Stab me in the back, and I will burn you. Understand? I won't stop after I slit your throat. I'll tie an anchor around your wife and throw her in the pool, then I'll take the twin girls while the little boy watches."

"Watch your mouth," Frank hissed under his breath.

Beau twisted his arm harder. "One twitch and I break the arm."

Sweat beads formed on Franks beet-red face.

"Pawpaw, hurry!" the girls shouted in unison and giggled.

Frank tried to lift his free hand to wave but couldn't. "I can't make an investigation disappear."

"When this is done, we move forward with my deal. I've got distribution ready. But only if you get that asshole and the SAPD off my back."

"Okay, okay. I'll talk to Devine."

Beau let go and stood up.

"These moves take time," Frank said, rubbing feeling back in his arm. "I can't just snap my fingers and make an investigation go away. People have to get paid."

Beau walked to the railing overlooking the swimming pool and waved at Frank's wife and the two girls waiting for their grandpa. "Great day for a swim," he shouted, flashing his hundred-watt grin.

"Come in with us!" the girls squealed.

"Maybe next time." He turned back to Frank. "Do what you have to do. I don't want any interference." He walked off the patio.

Frank wiped his face with a white towel and retrieved his cigar from the ground.

"Pawpaw, come on!" the little boy shouted again.

"I'm coming," Frank said, and drained his bloody mary.

CHAPTER TWENTY-ONE

I kicked back on the couch and let Hank Williams Jr.'s *Whiskey Bent and Hell Bound* CD and a cold beer nurse my swollen face and wounded ego. It wasn't quite five o'clock, but I felt justified in drinking a beer because Beau Fahl had thoroughly kicked my ass. He was big and fast and had skills in the ring. I had misjudged his overconfidence for arrogance, but he had the skills to back it up. I still didn't have a direct connection between Beau and Frank. Their relationship held the key to Colton's murder. If there was no relationship, I'd gotten my ass kicked for nothing. Danny Sanz was my last hope. If I could find him, he might be the missing link.

"I hope the other guy looks worse than you," Diana said, coming through the front door with a bag of groceries in her hand.

She caught me off guard. Maybe our relationship wasn't as far gone as I thought. The way things were going lately, it wouldn't surprise me to know I'd totally misjudged her reaction to our fight the other night.

"Turns out Beau Fahl's an MMA fighter. We went two out of three in the cage at his gym." I turned down Hank Jr. and followed her into the kitchen.

"And you got skunked?" She unloaded romaine lettuce, tomatoes, carrots, cucumbers, a small bag of new potatoes, and the best part, two ribeye steaks. Sam would love the leftovers.

"I took him down in the second round. I'm pretty good in the ring myself." I was fishing for some sympathy, but she didn't bite. Instead, she ignored me and took out my cutting board and began slicing tomatoes. There was something else going on. The dinner wasn't just for reconciliation.

I found the large plastic salad bowl and placed it on the counter. "How'd you know I needed a steak dinner?" I took the meat out of the package and sprinkled both sides with salt and pepper. My favorite part of grilling meat was that it required very little preparation. The secret was to pick the best cut of meat. Diana had gone to Bolner's Meat Company on South Flores Street, which had the best cuts in the city.

"I figured you could use a nice final meal."

"Am I a condemned man?"

"I got the autopsy report on Colton." She finished dicing the cucumbers and tossed them into the plastic salad bowl.

I ran water over the new potatoes and put them on the stove. She was making me wait.

"And?" I covered the steaks with tin foil and took them out the back door. Diana followed me. I pulled my gas grill a safe distance away from the house before firing it up to preheat. Sam sniffed the air and instantly flipped on that Labrador look that said, "I haven't eaten for a week!"

"Did you find the slug?"

"No. From the angle, it probably ricocheted off the concrete and got washed down the drain when they cleaned the place."

"Let me guess, the DA is satisfied with the results."

"More than satisfied."

"What about the angle of the bullet?"

"His girlfriend was leaving him. He told her he would kill himself if she left. He was unstable. A recovering addict. He couldn't handle the pressure."

"Bullshit."

Diana came closer and examined the swelling on my cheek. "He really did a number on you."

"Are you the arresting officer?"

"We can go to the station after we eat."

"Ah, now I understand. I thought this was an apology dinner."

"Apology for what?"

"The argument we had."

"Is that why you haven't called me? We have one little argument and you clam up and sulk?"

"You seemed pretty pissed off."

She kissed me on the cheek. "You can't get rid of me that easily."

"So this is a final meal before I go to prison?"

"Don't be so dramatic. If you behave yourself, I might throw in some dessert."

"We who are about to die salute you."

She smiled and gently traced the swelling on my face. "Gladiator? That suits you. The Romans would call you 'the German.'"

"There are parts of Germania the Romans never conquered."

"No doubt those parts were populated by your relatives."

"I have the documents to prove it." I opened the barbecue pit and tossed the steaks on the grill. Sam continued to watch and wait. He had that hunting dog patience. "Do you think Colton killed himself with my pistol?"

"I don't think giving Colton a pistol was a good idea."

"That's not what I asked." I filled the pot of new potatoes with water from the sink, careful not to spill it. One of these days, I would have to fix the sink drain.

"What do you want me to say? The evidence says Colton killed himself with your pistol. That's all we have to go on. The DA is doing her job."

"Suddenly this steak dinner doesn't sound all that appetizing."

"You can post bail and be home by eight o'clock. I took Aaron to my cousin's."

"And if I don't go in?"

"Don't do that, Nick. Don't put my job on the line too. We'll get through this."

I went back outside to turn the steaks. We both liked our meat medium rare, and I'd almost let them cook too long. It had been a tough day. I'd gotten my ass kicked, and now I was about to get arrested. I didn't want to burn perfectly good steaks on top of that. Sam still waited. "Don't worry," I said to him. "You'll get yours."

I took the steaks inside and wrapped them in tin foil to keep them warm. The aroma of cooked meat filled the small kitchen and mixed with the smell of boiling potatoes. A good meal could heal a lot of problems.

Diana turned the stove off and drained the water from the new potatoes into the sink. The water dribbled through the rusted pipe and onto the floor.

"Sorry, I thought you fixed that."

I tossed a towel on the puddle. "One of these days I will." I took two plates down from the cabinet. She took my hands and pulled my arms around her waist.

"We could start with dessert," she whispered.

I pressed her against the countertop. She felt warm and smelled faintly of perfume. She didn't wear any at work, so I knew she put it on in her car for my benefit before coming in the house. Maybe I had overstated our troubles.

"Or we can go straight for the steaks," she said and kissed my neck.

"The steaks can wait." I carried her upstairs to the bedroom.

Sam barked and scratch the back door with his paw. We were trying his patience.

"You call yourself a detective," she said when she slipped off her shirt. "Stop feeling sorry for yourself and find the evidence we need to clear your name." She said it like a challenge.

I pulled my own shirt off and sat on the bed. She made a little show of unzipping her skirt and seductively letting it drop to the floor.

I was starting to feel much better. "You're right." I slipped my fingers inside the thin waistband of her shear panties. "I'm going to find Danny—"

She put the tips of her fingers over my mouth. "I don't wanna hear what you're gonna do. When the DA asks me what I know, I don't wanna lie to her."

"You trust me?"

She answered with a kiss and pushed me back on the bed. Sam barked again and pawed the back door. I heard a door slam next door. I knew it was my neighbor Rose letting me know she was home. I hoped she didn't decide that now was a good time for a visit. I put both of them and my pending booking out of my mind.

CHAPTER TWENTY-TWO

The worst part of getting arrested by your girlfriend was putting up with the snickers of the other officers at the station. I had a mixed reputation among law enforcement. My dad had been a sheriff, and I'd worked in the Travis County sheriff's office while going to college in Austin, but I was also former military. Those who didn't have that active-duty background sometimes resented those who did. They figured we got breaks that we shouldn't have. My argument was that combat veterans had more than enough experience to compensate for civilian training. Sergeant Vera was my supporter, but that didn't stop him from getting in on the humiliation. There was nothing I could do but grin and bear it. The only consolation was that Diana was still on my side. She had to deal with the evidence she had, but after I explained my new information about Lora and Beau Fahl and finding the pills in her bathroom, she admitted that the circumstances surrounding Colton's death were suspicious.

By noon, I had posted bail and polished off a Big Boy cheeseburger. I called John Macrae to give him an update. He said he was willing to keep paying my salary, if I'd keep going. That meant two people were behind me.

I stopped at the minimart to top off my gas tank. When I got out to pump the gas, my phone rang.

"Hey, jailbird," Skeeter said when I answered.

"Just what I needed to hear," I said.

"I called to cheer you up."

"It's not working so far."

"I found Danny Sanz."

"That's more like it," I said.

"Does that mean I get a raise?"

"It means your employer might have a chance to stay in business."

"I was kinda hoping I would take over while you were doing time."

"You wanna be the boss?"

"You do it. How hard could it be?"

"Thanks, I'll keep that in mind next Christmas bonus."

"You never give a Christmas bonus."

"Now you know why."

Skeeter took a moment to control his laughter. "When Danny Sanz isn't getting wasted at the VFW, he hangs around the Eagle Shooting Range."

"I know where that is. Past Lackland Air Force base."

"That's it. You might be able to catch him there now."

"I'm on my way."

"Remember this next Christmas." He laughed. "Good hunting."

I disconnected.

The Eagle Shooting Range was cheap, allowed pistol, skeet, or trap shooting, and offered a thousand-yard target for the long-range enthusiasts. Danny was an ex–Air Force commando. He'd seen a lot of gruesome stuff on deployment. Besides the opioid pills, focusing his mind and body on finding the bull's-eye at a thousand yards was probably the only exercise that kept him sane.

The Eagle range was the only one that wasn't private or overpriced within a hundred miles of San Antonio that offered a long-range facility. Most hunters and sport shooters were perfectly happy to sight in their rifle in or pop off a few practice rounds at one hundred yards. In the field, if you had a longer or shorter shot, you adjusted your aim up or down, knowing your bullet placement at one hundred yards. Making a thousand-yard or longer shot required more patience, hours more practice, and either specialized equipment or an encyclopedic knowledge of ballistic coefficients and the effects of air pressure, altitude, humidity, and wind speed on the ultimate path of a bullet. It was a sport for the ex-military snipers and hobby shooter types who for whatever reason missed their chance to join the military.

I didn't have the time or the patience to be a crack long-distance shooter. I grew up hunting and always came home with game. I'd put in my time on the rifle range in the Marines, but a sharp DI steered me away from sniper school. These days, I hunted mostly in South Texas, where dense brush prevented seeing animals over a hundred yards away, or the Hill Country, where the deer were so plentiful that taking a thousand-yard shot meant you'd passed up at least a dozen at fifty yards.

The gravel parking lot held half a dozen dusty vehicles. A south wind coming off the Gulf of Mexico turned the late winter weather humid. I hoped it was a sign that spring was on its way.

Heavy booms from big bore rifles vibrated the door handle on my pickup. I checked my duffel bag to be sure I had packed earmuffs. I had extra ammo for both pistols and my .308 Winchester rifle. My Springfield .45 ACP rested comfortably in a shoulder holster, along with the .38 hammerless on my ankle. If Danny wasn't here, I planned to put in some time on the pistol range. I didn't have the patience for honing my thousand-yard shot, but I always made time for the pistol range. Those were skills I would use and would lose unless I practiced.

Danny's beater Ford Ranger pickup was parked closest to the front door of the double-wide trailer that served as the retail store and range office. He'd probably been there since the doors opened at nine a.m.

A woman in her seventies stood behind the counter cleaning a well-used Colt 1911 pistol. She was thin and wiry and wore her gray hair in tight curls. Her skin was tan from years of exposure, the color of well-oiled saddle leather.

I stood at the counter while she slipped the pieces of the 1911 back into place as deftly as any bootcamp DI.

"Can I help you, son?" she said when she clicked a full magazine into the pistol and laid it on the counter.

"You do that well," I said, smiling.

"I've had a lot of practice." She studied the scars on my forehead through thick trifocal glasses. "Marine?"

I nodded.

"My late husband served in Korea and Vietnam." She pointed to a picture behind the counter of a stern-looking man in his forties wearing a full-dress Marine uniform. His burial flag rested below that neatly pressed into a triangular wooden box. A dozen medals decorated the exterior, including two Silver Stars and a Navy Cross.

"Must have been a hell of a Marine," I commented.

She smiled warmly. "Oh, he was more than that." She took a moment to gaze at her husband's photo.

I noticed a dozen other pictures of the man in civilian clothes, jeans, and a straw cowboy hat, standing with different groups of men and women on the shooting range. In one he held a large silver trophy.

"Do you hold competitions out here?"

"My husband did. Years ago. He taught classes on the weekends. All these yahoos came out here to learn how to shoot long-range. Not one in a hundred of them were ever any good at it. But they paid the bills. No one could ever match my husband in competition. Even when he was eighty-one, he could hit the bull's-eye at a thousand yards."

"I wish I could have known him."

"Well, you're a year too late." She adjusted her trifocals and abruptly changed the subject. "You here to shoot, I take it?" She didn't want to venture any further down memory lane.

I laid my .308 rifle case on the counter. "That's right. I'm meeting a friend of mine out here. His name is Danny Sanz."

She pursed her thin lips. Deep furrows lined her leathery forehead. "He's here. Been here most of the day. You say you're a friend of his?"

"That's right."

"I didn't think Danny had any friends. He always comes here alone, and he never talks to any of the other shooters. Most of the men who visit want to brag about how good a shot they are or lie about how far of a shot they took hunting last season. Danny never says a word. He stays out there all day sometimes. A few folks will watch his shots with spotting scopes. They say he doesn't miss. His groupings are some of the smallest they've ever seen."

"He's a little raw around the edges."

She nodded in agreement.

I paid my range fee and walked out to the row of platforms set up for the thousand-yard targets. Four other shooters took up one end, each in a team of two studying a laptop computer, a ballistics chart, and an anemometer to calculate windspeed.

Danny was on the other end, alone. He was lying prone on the black rubber mat, holding a composite stock, .338 Lapua Magnum rifle resting on a tripod and staring into a Burris Optics scope. He didn't have a laptop or an anemometer.

I stopped a respectful distance away and waited for him to take his shot. There was a spotting scope mounted on a rail behind the shooting lanes. I adjusted the focus and sighted in on Danny's target. Three minutes later, he squeezed the trigger, and the big rifle exploded in his hands. Danny didn't move or flinch. He kept his eye glued to the scope until the concussion passed and the rifle once again rested solidly on the tripod. He calmly reached forward and worked the bolt action, releasing the spent casing. He left the breach open, letting the weapon breathe and cool down between shots.

I looked through the spotting scope. "Dead center. Two inches to the right," I said.

Danny adjusted the focal length and studied the target through his scope. "There was a gust of wind," he said without looking up.

I peered through the spotting scope again. A length of blue ribbon tied to the top of the four-by-ten-foot plywood target fluttered to the right. I'd talked to enough snipers to know the wind was the biggest problem for long distance shots. You had to calculate the direction, the speed, and how much to compensate. This was the kind of information the other two shooters were feeding into their laptop. Danny was making the calculations in his head.

"Not bad for the fucking 'chair' force," I said, with a dose of mock contempt.

Danny slowly turned his head. He recognized me. "Why does every jarhead think he can do everything better?" he asked, matching my tone.

"Better training," I deadpanned.

Danny pushed himself to his feet. The four shooters at the other end of the stalls shot uneasy glances at both of us, waiting for the fight to follow.

I held out my hand.

Danny took it, and we both laughed.

The other shooters breathed a sigh of relief. They weren't military and didn't get that we were giving each other a standard ribbing. It was expected. If we didn't respect each other and wanted to fight, we'd skip the pleasantries and start swinging. Civilians didn't get it. Especially not in the mixed-up world we lived in now. No one seemed to have a sense of humor.

I left my rifle in the gun rack and followed Danny off the shooter platform to a bench behind the office and out of earshot.

Danny shook out a Marlboro cigarette and handed the pack to me.

"No thanks," I said.

Danny lit up and inhaled deeply. "What brings you out here?"

"I'm gonna be straight with you. The other night at the VFW, I was after information."

He exhaled smoke through his nostrils and studied his hands. "I figured."

"I'm a private investigator working on a murder case."

"Colton Macrae," he said, raising his eyes to mine. His jaw was set tight.

"That's right. He was a friend of mine. We met at the VFW. He was mixed up with opioid pills. I thought you might know something about what happened to him."

"Why didn't you just ask me?"

"I didn't know if I could trust you."

"And now?"

"I think we're a lot alike, aside from joining different military branches. I think you got mixed up with pills and you want a way out."

"What makes you think that?"

"I just watched you hit a target at a thousand yards. You can't do that like you do it—without a computer and all the fancy gear—while high on pills. You know that. Pulling the trigger and hitting that target gives you more peace than getting wasted out of your mind at the VFW."

Danny took another long drag on his cigarette and slowly let the smoke trickle out his thin nostrils. "I can't quit."

"I been there. When I got out, my drug of choice was Jack."

"How'd you kick it?"

"I didn't do it on my own. My grandpa put me to work building a fence. He poured out all the booze in the house, took my truck keys, and locked the front gate. We lived ten miles from town. He said the two things I needed were hard work to break the physical chemical link and reading."

"Reading? Reading what?"

"History. He said history teaches you that you aren't the only poor son of a bitch who's ever suffered in the world."

"You think he could help me?"

"He's dead now, but I know the formula pretty well."

"I tried to quit before."

"No one said it was easy. You have to be willing to work at it."

"You'd help me?"

"Yeah, I would."

"But you want something out of it."

"That's right. Help me get justice for Colton."

Danny chewed his bottom lip, then stood up. "Tell you what…"

I stood and waited for him to speak. The wind picked up a little more. A line of dark clouds gathered on the western horizon. There would be rain tonight followed by another cold front. Spring would have to wait.

"If you can hit that thousand-yard target, I'll tell you who killed Colton Macrae."

I stared at him, waiting for his mouth to curl into a smile. He didn't smile. It was a test. He wanted to know if I was blowing smoke up his ass or if I was on the level.

"Should be a piece of cake for a jarhead," he said. This time he smiled.

I followed him back to the shooting platform. My mind was racing, but I kept my anxiety to myself and under control. I'd made a few long-distance shots before. During combat training after boot camp, we spent a day on the sniper range to give the instructor a chance to pick a few candidates for sniper school. I wasn't selected. I knew the basics: ballistics, trajectory, wind speed, angle. There were a hundred reasons why you miss when you try to hit a target at that distance. A laptop computer will tell you every one of them and spit out a mathematical formula to fix your problem.

I was in a hurry and didn't have a computer. If I took the shot and missed, Danny may not ever speak to me again. On the other hand, he seemed legitimately interested in kicking his pill habit. He was definitely interested in Grandpa's formula.

"Use my Lapua if you want. It's dialed in."

I pulled my Winchester .308 from the case. "I'm used to my .308."

Danny smiled and moved his rifle and gear out of the way and stepped back to the spotting scope. "I'll give you three tries."

"Fair enough," I said. It was more than I expected. I tossed down two sandbags and laid my rifle across them. It wasn't equipped with a tripod, and my scope didn't have the best optics. When I adjusted to full power and peered at the target, the crosshairs obscured the tiny bull's-eye. My chances of hitting anywhere near that point were less than zero. Danny had said "the target." I figured if I could manage to put a hole in the ten-by-four-foot plywood, I could make a case for a true hit and pass his test.

I loaded a cartridge and slipped the bolt into position. The four men on the other end had stopped their own preparations and were watching me. I didn't need more of an audience, but now that I had it, I was even more determined to hit the mark.

I held the crosshairs high and to the left, into the increasing wind, let out my breath, and squeezed the trigger. I felt the recoil hit my shoulder and the sound wave wash over my face.

A puff of dust appeared ten feet in front of the target.

"Off target. Low and to the right," Danny said.

Two more chances. I didn't look up or take my focus off the target. My fingers found the cartridge in my bag and slipped it into the chamber. I pushed the bolt home, let out a breath, and squeezed.

Again, I felt the recoil and the sound wave.

"You're on the target," Danny said. "One foot high and one foot left."

I found another bullet in my pack and loaded the final shot, keeping my focus on the target. I didn't want to lose my mark, or I would have to start over from scratch.

I felt a gust of wind. It suddenly shifted to the west and kicked up a cloud of dust that almost obscured the target. The blue indicator ribbon stood at attention from the opposite direction, which meant that the two previous shots were meaningless. What the hell? There wasn't anything scientific about what I was doing, not on the final shot or in my negotiations with Danny. Both were all about feel and instinct.

I held my aim high and into the wind, let out my breath, and squeezed the trigger.

The four guys at the other end all gave a little cheer. They were watching the target through their spotting scopes.

"Hit," Danny said.

I waited for him to tell me where the bullet landed before I moved.

"Bull's-eye," he said. "Not bad for a fucking jarhead."

I smiled to myself. It was blind luck, but no one would ever know but me. I stood up and packed my rifle back into the gun case.

"Let's go get some coffee," I said. "We've got a lot to talk about."

CHAPTER TWENTY-THREE

I parked beside Skeeter's Dodge Ram pickup in the permit parking lot at the Frost Bank Center. He wasn't happy to be up after midnight, but he was on salary, so I didn't feel guilty about it. I also had him contact his connection with the building security. As luck would have it, Skeeter's ex–University of Texas football teammate was working the night shift and agreed to meet us at the back gate.

My lucky bull's-eye paid off in spades. Danny confirmed my suspicion about Colton's involvement in an opioid pill operation that included Lora, Beau Fahl, and Doc Frank. Colton wanted out. His mistake was trying to take Lora with him. She was too far gone.

The night he was killed, Colton was going to tell me about his plan to get clean. He made his record ride with a clear conscience. It must have been the first time in a long time that he felt free. Then Beau Fahl put a bullet in his head. Fahl had casually ended a life in its prime just so he could continue in business. I didn't need any more incentive than that to nail the bastard and take him out.

Danny explained how Beau used him and Colton to recruit down-and-out vets to visit Doc Frank and get prescriptions for pain pills. Frank handed out ninety at a time. A month's supply each time they went in. The vets got a steady supply of drugs and five hundred dollars each time they filled a prescription. Beau Fahl took the rest of the pills and sold them on the street. Depending on the dose and the amount, he could make anywhere from three to five grand.

If Danny was telling the truth, the evidence would be on the perimeter of the building and not where SAPD had searched. Beau had fired from somewhere near the wall and not from inside the pen.

"You don't ever sleep while you're on a case," Skeeter said, suppressing a yawn when he climbed out of his pickup.

"I figure I'm on the clock. That means so are you, partner."

"You mean if I was still just an employee, you'd let me sleep?"

"Fat chance. We make money by solving cases."

He grinned. "Let's go make some money then."

We walked to the gate where Skeeter's buddy Jamal waited for us. He was almost as big as Skeeter, but not big enough or fast enough for the pros. When he didn't get picked up in the NFL draft after college, an alumnus pulled a few strings and got him a job with a local security firm.

"Hey, Jamal," Skeeter said.

Jamal wore a rumpled black uniform and looked over his shoulder several times before he replied.

"Y'all got thirty minutes. That's how much time before the super makes his rounds."

Skeeter faked a stomach punch with his metal hook prosthesis and laughed when Jamal flinched. "That's why you always on the practice squad."

"Shit, man. You gonna kill somebody with that, Captain Hook," he said and countered with a quick jab to Skeeter's shoulder.

"Yeah, we owe you, Jamal. How 'bout dinner?" I asked.

Jamal laughed. "How 'bout fifty bucks? Skeeter said you good for it."

Skeeter gave me a sheepish look while I produced a fifty-dollar bill and handed it to Jamal. He had failed to mention the bribe money.

"What are teammates for, man?" Jamal said and slapped Skeeter on the back. "Thirty minutes. I'll meet y'all back at this gate." He glanced at his wristwatch, then at me for confirmation. I nodded.

We followed Jamal to the side entrance. There was an enormous mountain of straw in the parking lot just outside the barn doors. The place had been cleaned in preparation for the next event. Jamal found the correct key from the dozen or so hanging from his belt and opened the door. Inside, he used his Maglite to find the electrical panel and flip on the lights.

Another mountain of straw inside reached almost to the ceiling. The stench hit all three of us like a wet towel in the face. The animal excrement smell was so strong it could have been bottled and used as a weapon. Skeeter and I immediately covered our noses. Jamal laughed, already immune to the odor.

"Have fun, y'all." He walked out and closed the door.

"I don't think we gonna find anythin' in here," Skeeter said, looking at the mountain of manure and holding his nose. The portable cattle pens were stacked against the metal walls, and the concrete floor had been hosed clean. I doubted that after seventy-five years of stock shows and rodeos the smell would ever leave the building.

Skeeter and I walked to the place where the kid found Colton's body.

"Colton told Danny he was gonna wait for Beau in the cattle barn. Danny told him it was a setup, but Colton wasn't worried. He had a pistol. My pistol."

"Did he see him pull the trigger?"

"No, but he saw Colton shoot and saw him take a bullet. He knew he was dead when he hit the ground."

"How did Beau find out?"

"Lora. Colton wanted her to get out with him."

"She signed his death warrant. You believe Danny's telling the truth?"

"That's what we're here to find out."

We stood looking at the mound of straw and manure in the middle of the barn.

"Looks like we're too late," Skeeter said.

"Did you bring a shovel?"

"You serious? You really want to shovel shit?"

I laughed. "I just wanted to hear what you'd say."

I walked to the spot I remembered Colton's body was lying, then searched the top of the twenty-foot metal walls.

"What do you see up there?" Skeeter asked.

"Vents," I said, pointing at the north wall of the building. "The shot came from above Colton's head."

There were vents near the ceiling placed after every other support beam. If these were accessible from the outside of the building, it might have afforded a place for Beau to hide.

"What about the bullet Colton fired?"

"He was shooting at Beau. Colton drew my pistol and fired one shot."

"How the hell did he get to the vent without everybody in this place seeing him?"

"Good point," I said and hustled to the exit door. Skeeter followed.

The north wind blew, and the temperature was starting to drop. Rain was predicted before morning. We both paused and took a much-needed deep breath of fresh, moist air.

We circled the building, looking at the vents in the roof that were at least sixteen feet off the ground. Getting to them would require a ladder. Danny's story was starting to sound like an elaborate fiction.

Then we turned the corner of the building. An eighteen-wheeler cattle trailer was parked beside the building. The top of the trailer reached to the bottom of the vent.

My heart raced. I climbed on the cab of the truck and from there to the top of the trailer. From where I stood, I could see through the vent and directly into the corner where Colton was standing. I looked closely at the vent for any evidence. If there were powder marks or fingerprints, the steady rain over the last few days had long since washed them away.

We searched the ground below the vent next but came up empty.

Skeeter followed me back inside. If Beau had pulled the trigger and the brass from the bullet fell outside the building, he would have been able to see it and pick it up, leaving behind no evidence. If the brass had somehow made it through the vent and inside the building, he wouldn't have had the chance to pick it up. He would need to get out of there as quickly as possible before the rodeo grounds were locked down. That possibility was our only hope.

We heard Jamal open the exit door. He saw us and waved. "Time's up," he yelled. His voice echoed in the empty building.

Skeeter saw it first. He pointed to the brass stuck in the gap between the metal wall and the concrete directly below the vent.

"Bingo," I said and knelt down for a closer look. It was a .40 caliber round. I judged the distance between the vent and where Colton had stood in the cattle pen to be about fifty yards.

"Danny Sanz was telling the truth."

CHAPTER TWENTY-FOUR

"You're telling me that a security guard found a shell casing that the CSI team missed?" The assistant DA, who happened to be my ex-girlfriend, Sylvia Flores, rolled her eyes and did her best to sound incredulous. She was putting on a blustery show in Diana's cubicle mostly for me but also for Diana and any of the other detectives within earshot. She liked the attention.

"It happens. The barn's the size of a football stadium, and it was full of animals and people when we did our search. Also, there was no reason to extend the search outside the immediate perimeter." Diana's response was deadpan and efficient. Sylvia neither impressed nor intimidated her, and I admired her even more for it.

"What makes you think the casing is connected to the case?" Sylvia shot back.

"It's a .40 caliber. There are a lot of .40 calibers around, but statistically, a 9mm is more popular. Forensics says it was fired recently, within the last several days. And it matches the caliber the medical examiner believes killed Colton Macrae." Diana's measured response again contrasted Sylvia's theatrics. "We also found a slug in the wall matching the pistol found on Colton. That's consistent with our theory that Colton fired his weapon at the killer, not at his own head."

"So, Colton used Nick's pistol to shoot at his assailant?"

"That's what we believe. It means we have a murder investigation," Diana concluded. She sat behind her desk with her hands folded.

I bit the inside of my bottom lip to keep from laughing. Sylvia paced the small enclosure, searching for a counter-narrative. It was obvious she wanted to go after me in the worst way. Our breakup had followed immediately after I shot her new boyfriend, who was poised to take the governor's seat bought and paid for with blackmailed funds. We'd spent two years together and I thought we were happily cruising toward married bliss, until she went to work for Marcus Lopez's law firm and found someone more ambitious and, more importantly, much wealthier.

"You can't dismiss evidence that also comes with a witness," Diana said.

"Where's this witness?" Sylvia asked.

"We're locating him now."

"She'll want a warrant for Beau Fahl," I added. "The real killer."

"After I see the witness's statement," Sylvia shot back. "Don't you think it's a little convenient that this piece of evidence shows up now?"

Diana stood up behind her desk. "What are you implying?"

The two women were both Hispanic but otherwise couldn't be more different. Sylvia was born with a silver spoon. Her father made a fortune selling furniture and raised Sylvia in the upscale Alamo Heights neighborhood north of downtown.

Diana, on the other hand, was raised in Castroville, a small town just outside the San Antonio city limits. She had a large extended family, and she was the only member to go to college and earn a degree.

"I'm implying that someone in this room is behind the sudden appearance of new evidence because he's implicated in Colton's suicide." Sylvia put her hands on her hips and exposed her ultra-white teeth in a sneer.

Diana stood. She was four inches shorter than Sylvia but much more athletic. If they came to blows, my money was on Diana.

She took one quick step in Sylvia's direction as if stepping across the ring after the starting bell. "This is the police department, Ms. Flores. We find evidence and follow leads so that the district attorney can follow the law."

Sylvia changed tactics and turned to me. "I know you're behind this, Nick. I know the way you operate."

"I'm working for Colton's father. He hired me because he didn't believe his son would kill himself. Turns out he was right." I leaned back in the metal office chair and put my hands behind my head. I didn't want to give her the satisfaction of seeing me get angry. "Justice is my motivation, Sylvia. You should know that by now. Colton deserve to have his name cleared, and his killer needs to go down."

"Justice? Spare me the lecture, Nick."

I recognized the slight twitch in her left eyebrow and the flare of her nostrils, both signs that I was getting under her skin.

"The district attorney is very interested in this case. If there is any indication of foul play on the part of the police or Fischer Private Investigations, there will be consequences." She turned on her high heels and walked out of the cubical.

"I can't believe you and that bitch were ever a couple," Diana said when Sylvia was out of earshot.

I put my arms around her waist. "I was young and naïve."

"It was last year."

"Since I've met you, I've had tremendous growth."

She gave me a hug and kissed me. "I hope so."

"You're making an honest man out of me."

"Don't say that unless you mean it, cowboy."

The moment between us was brief, but the connection was real. Maybe we would get through this.

Her phone rang. Abruptly she was all business. She looked at the caller ID and let it go to voicemail. "That's the captain," she said. "We need to nail this down so I can tell him we have something solid. And that it's not connected to you."

"We have Danny Sanz's testimony, backed up by the casing," I said, taking out my notebook. "We can also place Beau Fahl at the crime scene."

"A murder weapon would be nice."

"I'll work on it. What about the opioids and Doc Frank?"

"I called the DEA. I'm gonna talk to one of their agents this afternoon." She opened a window on her computer. "If we can get your stripper girlfriend to talk, it would help our case."

Diana was never going to let me forget that I had once dated a stripper. "If it means keeping herself out of jail, I think she'll cooperate."

CHAPTER TWENTY-FIVE

Finding Danny Sanz proved much harder the second time. I checked the shooting range and the VFW. Skeeter checked his apartment. Nothing. Diana gave his description and his pickup license plate to SAPD patrol, but no one had reported seeing Danny since I'd talked to him at the range. He'd disappeared like gun smoke from a rifle shot.

I drove north on Navarro Street, passed Travis Park, and looped back down St. Mary's Street looking for a parking place near the Original Blanco Café. I'd finished my morning run, and a Tex-Mex breakfast moved to the top of my list of things to do. Their *chilaquiles plate* was one of my favorite ways to start the day. The restaurant was busy as usual, but I found a table by the window looking out on the busy urban street.

I called John Macrae and filled him in on our progress. I told him we shouldn't celebrate yet. The investigation was ongoing, but progress had been made. Colton's death was officially labeled a homicide. We had his murderer. The link to Frank and the pill mill was less clear. We both wanted to chop the head off the snake. Beau had pulled the trigger, but addiction to opioids was the real killer, and Frank ran the pill mill. It would take time. Bringing Beau Fahl in would at least bring partial justice for Colton. John sounded confident in my ability to finish the job and promised to cover my expenses and continue paying me for my time. I was grateful for that. Although, at this stage, I had no intention of quitting. With or without a paycheck.

I ordered coffee and a breakfast plate from an overworked young waitress and took out my phone to catch up on the news of the day. Before I could read through the first headline, my phone rang. It was Diana.

"Where are you?"

"Having breakfast."

"Are you at home?"

"No. Blanco Café on St. Mary's having *chilaquiles*."

"Get it to-go. Meet me under the Travis Street bridge."

"You wanna have a picnic?"

"Trust me, I'm not here to picnic. And finish your *breakfast* before you get here."

"Why's that?"

"The dead body hanging under the bridge might ruin your appetite."

She disconnected. I canceled breakfast and bought an extra coffee to-go for Diana. I didn't want to speculate on whose body she found. I hoped it was Beau Fahl, but I had a bad feeling it was our star witness.

The Travis Street bridge was only a block from the restaurant, so I left my pickup and walked. A traffic jam snarled the two-lane street approaching the river. Two cruisers blocked the road, and four uniforms held pedestrians from crossing on both ends of the bridge. I approached a tall, skinny officer no more than a few months out of the academy, guarding the stone spiral stairs that led down to the river level.

"Move along. No one up or down the steps," Skinny cautioned.

I set the two cups of coffee down on the bridge railing and pulled out my private detective credentials. "I'm here with Detective Ochoa," I said.

Skinny looked skeptical, but spoke into his radio and listened for a response.

"Okay," Skinny said and lifted the yellow caution tape to let me pass.

I took a sip of my to-go coffee and walked down the spiral steps. I recognized the location. It was the same spot Marissa Luna went into the water the night she was murdered. It was the investigation that had led to my Grandpa's murder. It also left me with a bullet scar on my chest, as if I needed a more permanent reminder.

A half dozen uniformed officers stood in front of the tile mural of the Alamo where Marissa's mother had set up a *descansos* with plastic flowers, an Our Lady of Guadalupe candle, and a smiling high school graduation photo of the recently deceased. Park Services had removed all traces of the makeshift memorial last summer. In its place was a very real dead body, hanging from the concrete bridge railing.

The stark reality of a man swinging from the bridge by his neck stopped me in my tracks. The sight and smell of death took me back to Afghanistan, where human life was cheap. I would never get used to facing it in San Antonio, Texas, although historically, there'd been plenty of bloody battles fought not far from this very spot and plenty of bloodshed.

The scene reminded me of a gruesome news photo taken in the Texas border town of Nuevo Laredo showing nine suspected Los Zetas drugs cartel members hanging from a highway overpass. Those bodies were meant to send a message to the rival cartel. I wondered if this body was meant for the same thing.

The paved trail beside the river was a popular running and walking path that, at this point, wound through a canyon of office buildings and parking garages. A dozen or so people gawked at the body from behind yellow caution tape fifty yards back on both sides of the river.

Diana excused herself from the CSI team examining the body and made her way toward me. "One of those for me?" she asked, pointing to the coffee.

I handed her a cup, and we stood staring at the dead body. In the nineteenth century, a hanging was a festive public event. Folks would come from miles around to view the spectacle. The local preacher would give a sermon, the PTA sold cake and cookies, the soon-to-be deceased said a few last words before the hangman slipped a noose around his neck and dropped him through a hole in the platform. This morning's event didn't have a festive feel. I doubted if the dead man had been given a chance to say any last words, and there was no preacher here to pray for his soul, only me and the SAPD.

"You just thought I'd like to see a hanging after breakfast? Is that why you called?"

"I knew you wouldn't wanna miss it. Thanks for the coffee. Follow me."

She led the way toward the body through the police crowd. Two officers on the bridge above lowered the body down while the CSI team grabbed it and lowered it to the concrete path.

The body was stiff, and the markings around the neck were deep blue. The rope was a thin yellow nylon cord that had cut deep into the skin.

I recognized Danny Sanz instantly.

"Our witness got cold feet," she said.

"You think he killed himself?"

"His hands aren't tied. From what you told me about him, I'm gonna guess he's got drugs in his system."

"The only witness against Beau Fahl turns up dead and your first thought is suicide?"

"You know I have to go by the evidence."

"You're gonna go back to square one?"

"No. In the beginning we thought Colton's death was suicide."

"What about Beau Fahl?"

"Without Danny Sanz, we don't have enough to arrest him."

I turned to walk away. "Maybe he'll give me a confession."

She grabbed my arm. "Don't walk away from me."

Several of the uniforms shot glances toward us.

Diana led me away from the group of officers. "Who the hell do you think you're talking to?"

"Look, Diana. This thing stinks. You know that."

"I'm not giving up on the case. He'll slip up. Guys like Beau Fahl always do. When he does, we'll nail him. Until then, you know the drill."

"It's more than Fahl. What about Frank? Who's gonna stop him from ruining more lives?"

"I talked to DEA. They say he's clean."

"You believe that?"

"What did you have other than Danny? You went to the clinic, remember? He gave you Motrin. Maybe Danny was yanking your chain."

"Then why was he murdered?"

"We don't know that he was."

We walked to the base of the stone steps and watched the CSI team work on Danny Sanz's dead body while the SAPD beat cops laughed and joked a few feet away. This was their job. They were used to it. If they took it too personally, they wouldn't make it through their shift.

"We need more evidence," Diana said. "Until we get it, my hands are tied."

"Mine aren't." I took a step toward the street level.

She grabbed my arm again. "Damn you, Nick Fischer. We need to talk about this."

"I'm done talkin'."

"If you beat a confession out of Beau Fahl, he'll walk free. You know that."

"Not if he can't walk."

"Come over tonight. Aaron's with his dad."

I hesitated. Waiting wouldn't bring justice for Colton. Waiting gave Beau Fahl and Doc Frank more time to hand out pills and ruin more lives. Or skip town.

"I don't wanna have to arrest you, but I will if you step over the line."

"We'll finish this tonight," I said, and left her standing by the river. I had no doubt she would arrest me. Ironically, that was one of the reasons I admired her and stayed in the relationship as long as I had. Despite all the red flags, including her ex-husband and her extended Catholic family, I loved her.

That fact didn't change what I had to do.

I stole a glance at her from the top of the bridge. She was standing beside the body, watching the CSI team do their job. She was all business.

CHAPTER TWENTY-SIX

Beau Fahl wasn't hard to find. His black F-150 was parked behind the Fight Night boxing gym. I wanted to know where he was twenty-four seven.

I called Skeeter and had him meet me in the parking lot. He brought along a tracking device so we could keep tabs on Beau's movements.

"I heard about Danny," Skeeter said when he pulled in beside me. He drove a silver Dodge Ram pickup that he kept polished to a high sheen.

"If our target thinks the heat is off, maybe he'll slip up."

"You think he'll resume business as usual?"

"No reason not to. He knows with Danny gone, SAPD has nothin'."

"Let's do this," Skeeter said.

"It's gonna get ugly. You packin' your shotgun?"

"Always. I learned my lesson." He latched onto the pistol grip of the 870 tactical shotgun with his metal hook prosthesis and held it in the window as proof. The first time I'd given it to him and asked him to use it, he'd left it on the seat of his pickup. Consequently, a corrupt police detective put a .308 round through his shoulder and nearly killed him. I hoped he'd learned his lesson.

He handed over the magnetic, quarter-sized tracking device, and I attached it to Beau's bumper while he stood watch.

"What's the plan?" he asked when I got back into my pickup.

"Keep an eye on him for now. I just wanna know where he goes and what he's doing. And be careful. He was willing to kill Colton and Danny Sanz. He wouldn't hesitate to plug your ugly mug."

"What's your move?"

"I'll keep shakin' things up. I want him to know that I'm not letting up."

Skeeter smiled. "'Cause that's what you do best."

• • •

I left him in the parking lot and drove south on the freeway, heading for Frank's clinic to put the screws on Doc. The traffic wasn't bad for a change, but I kept my speed near the limit. I didn't wanna risk getting pulled over and giving Sylvia more ammunition against me.

Frank's clinic was just as busy in the afternoon as it was the evening I came posing as an addicted trucker. The receptionist at the front desk was the same one who met me the first time. She was just as overworked today as she was on my late evening visit. I showed her my own ID this time along with my private eye credentials. She didn't recognize me, or if she did, she kept it to herself.

"I'm here to see Frank," I said. "Is he in today?"

"Yeah. The wait's about forty-five minutes," she said, focusing on the scars on my forehead. A hint of recognition formed in her expression.

"I just wanna ask him some questions. It's not a medical issue."

"I'm afraid Dr. Frank is very busy right now. I could take your number and have him give you a call."

I looked around the packed waiting room. A few patients studied me, listening to my interaction with the receptionist. A middle-aged guy in a beard diverted his attention from his cell phone and glared in my direction. He looked as if he'd been waiting over an hour and wasn't about to let me or anyone else cut in line. "What're the chances of me getting some pain pills? Doc said I could get a refill."

"I'm sure I don't know," the receptionist said, squirming in her chair. "I'll see if Dr. Frank can see you." She disappeared into the back of the clinic.

The guy with the beard turned to glare at me. A woman came in carrying a small teenage girl wearing a soccer uniform. She held her ankle, and her eyes were red and swollen from crying. The woman set the soccer player in a chair and approached the empty reception desk.

"Anybody here?" the woman asked me.

"She'll be back in a moment. What happened?"

"My daughter twisted her ankle at soccer."

"It's broken, Momma," the girl whimpered.

"Let the doctor decide," the mother said.

The daughter winced. I bet on broken.

The receptionist opened the patient entrance to the exam rooms and beckoned me inside. "He only has a few minutes," she said.

"Take the girl," I said, pointing to the young soccer player. "I can wait."

The man with the beard stood and opened his mouth to speak, but thought better of it when I picked up the girl.

The mother smiled at me, and I helped her carry her daughter into one of the exam rooms.

The receptionist tapped her clipboard while we set the girl down, then she escorted me down the hallway to Frank's office. I let myself in.

Frank sat, leaning back in his chair, licking red sauce from the fingers of his left hand while folding the remains of a barbecue sandwich back inside the paper wrapper with his other.

"It gets so busy around here, I rarely have time to stop and eat," he said with a half smile.

I was skeptical. Frank looked like he found plenty of time to eat. He gestured toward a metal folding chair in front of his desk. As far as I could tell, none of the money he was making on opioids was going into office furniture. I declined the offer and stood by the door.

His cell phone rang. He read the caller ID. The half smile disappeared. "Excuse me one second. I have to take this." He picked up the phone and swiveled his chair so that his back was to me. I heard him mumble "okay" a few times but couldn't hear the caller's voice. I wondered if it was Beau Fahl.

While I waited, I studied Frank's diplomas displayed on the wall. His physician's assistant degree came from the University of Nebraska Medical Center. That was curious. John Macrae had said something about Frank being from New York but didn't mention Nebraska. There was a framed picture of a platoon in army-green fatigues. The caption on the bottom said CSH unit. I recognized a younger Frank, less portly but still a big man, kneeling in the front row with a big smile on his face.

"Sorry to keep you waiting. What can I do for you, Mr. Fischer?" Frank swiveled his chair back around to face me and tossed his cell phone on the desk beside his half-eaten sandwich.

"So where were you stationed in the army?" I asked, hoping to establish more of a rapport before getting down to business.

Frank showed his teeth but didn't really smile. He pointed to the picture of his unit on the wall. "That was in Iraq. The first war."

"Is that what brought you to San Antonio?"

"Yeah, PA school at Fort Sam."

I pointed to the Nebraska diploma. "Not Nebraska?"

"Nebraska sponsors the army program."

"Was it a good program?" I asked. My effort to build a rapport was getting nowhere.

Frank snorted impatiently. "Why is it you're here, Fischer?"

"You don't remember me, do you?"

"Of course. You were at Devine's ranch with John Macrae. Hope you enjoyed the sausage-making. It's a unique experience."

"I was here before that. I came in last week. You wrote out a prescription for hydrocodone." I decided to test his memory further. Maybe he saw so many vets he didn't keep track, or maybe Beau kept the list of names. "Danny Sanz sent me over. We met at the VFW. He gave me five hundred bucks for the bottle. The problem is, Danny's dead, and I need more pills."

That got his attention, but Frank didn't skip a beat. His demeanor shifted into comforting physician mode. "I don't have any idea what you're talking about."

"Cut the bullshit, Frank. Danny told me how it works. Maybe that's why you killed him or why you had Beau Fahl kill him."

"Just a goddamn minute," he shouted. His bedside manner jumped out the window along with his fake Texas accent. "You can't come in here and make baseless accusations. I will sue your ass."

"Maybe Beau did all the work, but y'all are working together. That makes you an accessory to two murders."

"I've never heard of this guy you're talking about."

"Really? That's what you're gonna go with? How 'bout Lora Michaels?

Ring a bell?" She's a real looker. Works as a stripper at the Paradise Club. You should remember her from the poker game."

Frank pushed his great bulk to a standing position and pointed to the door. "I think you need to leave. I'm very busy."

"The pill party is gonna crash and burn. Tell me what you know about Beau Fahl and you might be able to get off with less than twenty years."

Frank's face turned beet red. His eyes dropped to his top desk drawer where I guessed he kept a pistol for personal protection.

I stepped around the side of his desk and tapped him on the shoulder. Not anything hard, just enough to force him back into his chair. "I'm not a policeman. I'm not with the DEA. What I wanna know about is Colton Macrae and Danny Sanz. Both were murdered. I know Beau Fahl did it, and I will take him down. If I find out you helped him in any way, I will take you down with him. Do you understand?"

The half smile came back on his face. Frank wasn't intimidated. "You think you can come in here and threaten me?" He pushed himself back to his feet. "Get the hell out of here. Who the fuck do you think you are?"

"I'm just giving you a chance to separate yourself from Beau before I take him down."

"Yeah, here's some advice. I will crush you. Come back here again, and I'll call the police. You will no longer be in the private eye business. When my lawyers are through with you, you'll be the one in jail." He pointed at the door. His head was ready to explode.

I could imagine him having a heart attack in front of me. I wouldn't help him. There was plenty of nursing staff around. "Have a nice day," I said and walked out.

CHAPTER TWENTY-SEVEN

I called Skeeter and checked on Beau's whereabouts. He'd gone to the warehouse near the airport, then paid a visit to Lora Michaels. He was still there now. Skeeter had stopped off for a cheeseburger. So far, Beau didn't seem to be worked up enough to make contact with me. I had a feeling that would change soon once he heard from the good doctor.

Diana was still at work by the time I got to her house. Aaron was supposed to be staying with his father, so I let myself in the back door and was surprised to find my stash of cold beer still chilling on the bottom shelf of her refrigerator. Normally, tonight would be pizza night, so I got on the phone with Casandra's and ordered a large sausage and pepperoni and a couple of Mediterranean salads. I didn't like to argue on an empty stomach. If Diana and I were going to have it out and go our separate ways, pizza seemed like an appropriate last meal.

Her house was on the far west side of the city and a little out of their delivery range, but I was a regular customer and had done some work for the owner last year when his high-school-aged daughter decided to take a mini vacation to the coast without telling him. I tracked her down in Port Aransas with a boy from Austin. He was happy to have her home.

I heard Diana's Crown Vic in the driveway and saw shopping bags stacked in the passenger seat, so I went out to help her with the groceries.

"You're early," she said suspiciously.

"You wanted me to keep my nose clean."

"Don't bullshit me." She handed me a case of Shiner Bock in cans and a supersized box of laundry soap to carry inside. The beer surprised me. On her own, a six-pack lasted her a month.

"I did a little surveillance work. I'm still on John Macrae's payroll," I said, following her into the kitchen.

She spotted the open beer bottle on the counter. "Looks like you started without me."

"I ordered pizza. Should be here any minute."

She put away Aaron's milk and Cocoa Puffs.

"He still hooked on chocolate cereal?" I asked.

"Won't leave the house in the morning unless he has a big bowl. I hope he grows out of it soon. It cost more than a carton of eggs."

I opened a beer for her. She took a long drink, then studied my face.

"You wanna fill me in now or after pizza?" she asked.

"I was hoping to get pizza."

She laughed. "I thought so."

I began to think I'd misjudged her. She wasn't coming after me with a wire brush. I had my argument ready to go. I wasn't going to bend to any demand for change, but she brought home a case of beer and stood in the kitchen laughing at my lame attempt at levity, so I decided to take a wait-and-see approach.

"Is Skeeter involved?" She finished putting away the groceries and hung her business jacket across the back of the kitchen chair. Her 9mm was still clipped to her belt.

"He's my partner." I took a drink of beer, waiting to gauge her reaction.

She slipped off her pistol and laid it on the counter. "What do you hope to accomplish?"

"I promised Colton's dad I would get justice for his son."

Her eyes flashed with anger. She had a knack for checking her emotions that came from years on the police force, but she also had a temper.

"You promised justice? Are you kidding me? Who do you think you are, Zorro? You should start wearing a mask and riding a black stallion."

I reached for her hand, but she pulled away. "That would make you Catherine Zeta Jones. I like where this is going."

"Stop! Just stop," she insisted, turning her head away to hide her smile. "This is serious."

"You don't think I know that?"

"Well, you act like this is a game." She got her expression under control and faced me.

"It's work for both of us. You're a cop, and I'm a private investigator. How many referrals am I gonna get if I give up on every case at the first sign of trouble or suggestions from SAPD?"

"That's BS and you know it. This is personal with you. You got your butt kicked by Beau Fahl, and you want a rematch." She narrowed her eyes and touched my chest with her outstretched finger. "Admit it. Your macho pride is offended because he gave you a black eye and took you down in the ring."

"Fine, I admit it. But Beau Fahl is still a bad guy, and he's still out on the streets."

"Let me handle that. That's what we do at SAPD."

"And Doc Frank? He's dealing drugs and playing poker with a county judge. Isn't that a little suspicious? What's SAPD doing about that?"

"What did you do, Nick?"

Her white teeth flashed from her dark complexion, and her brown eyes took on a lighter shade, like coals in a fire ready to spark into full flame.

"I went to see Frank at his clinic," I said and filled her in on my afternoon activities.

Her eyes caught fire. "How's that gonna help us get Beau Fahl?"

"You don't pull off the hounds when they have the scent."

"You're acting on a hunch."

"Someone's gotta do something or Beau Fahl gets away with murder."

"Let SAPD handle it. It will be legal, and it will hold up in court."

We'd covered this ground before. I didn't want to argue. "You're right. I'll back off."

"Don't do that, Nick Fischer!"

"What?"

"Give in just because you think I'm getting mad."

"I'm trying to agree with you."

"Liar."

"Fine," I said. "I don't completely agree with you. I think my methods get better results." On impulse, I stepped toward her and put my arms around her waist. When she didn't push me away, I continued, "Can we just..." I hesitated, trying to think of a way to tell her how I felt.

I heard a car in the driveway and expected the doorbell to ring with our pizza order.

Instead, the picture window exploded. Bullets sprayed the inside of the living room.

I shoved Diana to the floor behind the kitchen counter and covered her with my body. The rapid fire continued for another thirty seconds. I drew the .38 revolver from my ankle holster. My .45 was locked outside in my glovebox.

Diana squirmed out from under me and grabbed her 9mm from the countertop. The sound of breaking glass and splintering wood echoed through the small front room and kitchen. When the noise died, Diana started to stand.

I yanked her back down just as another round of bullets ripped through the front room. The blast lasted less than ten seconds, then we heard squealing tires on the street. We both sprinted for the front door.

By the time we reached the porch, the vehicle was turning left at the end of the street. Its lights were off, but we saw the reflection of a black SUV as it sped around the corner.

"Let's go," she yelled.

CHAPTER TWENTY-EIGHT

We lost sight of the perp's vehicle in the maze of backroads somewhere south of Loop 1604. I drove us home while Diana called dispatch and gave a description of the vehicle. I pulled into the Whataburger drive-through on Marbach Road and ordered a Coke for Diana to help her get her adrenaline rush under control.

"Thank God Aaron wasn't home," she said. Her hands shook as she fumbled to speed-dial her ex-husband, Beto.

"Beto, let me talk to Aaron," she blurted before he could answer. She put the phone on speaker.

"Ah… Okay. Give me a few minutes," Beto stammered. We heard voices in the background.

"Beto, put Aaron on the phone right now," she demanded.

"Diana, chill out," he said, sounding nervous.

"Where are you?"

"I'm at the store. Aaron's home playing video games. I'll be there in a few minutes."

"You left him alone?"

I picked up the Coke at the drive-through window and accelerated out of the parking lot.

"Go, go, go!" Diana shouted at me.

"What's going on?" Beto's voice sounded more urgent.

"Beto, if anything's happened to him, I swear to God…" She didn't finish. She closed her eyes and took a sip of cold Coca-Cola.

By then I was on Highway 90, crossing into the left lane and accelerating toward Castroville, where Diana's ex-husband lived. I took over the conversation.

"Listen, Beto. This is Nick. Somebody just shot up Diana's house. Drop whatever you're doing and go to Aaron, now."

"Jesus, was anybody hurt?"

"We're fine! Just go. Hurry!" Diana shouted and disconnected the phone. "I'm gonna kill him."

I turned north at the first stoplight and found Beto's street. His house was a modern single-story ranch style in a row of similar homes, each with a half-acre yard and sheltered with established oak and maple trees.

Diana had the passenger door open and hit the ground running before I stopped in the driveway. We'd beat Beto home.

I cut my engine and followed Diana to the porch. The front door was open. Not a good sign. She yelled Aaron's name and sprinted inside. Her voice echoed through the house. There was no response.

The front room was turned upside down. I wasn't sure whether Beto was just a slob or if this was a crime scene. There were pizza boxes scattered on the floor near the dining room table. Toys and stuffed animals scattered around the living room. I recognized the stuffed horse I'd given him for Christmas. Two of the couch cushions had been chewed to the point that the white cotton filler was scattered on the floor near the open fireplace.

Aaron's giggling voice drifted over the sound of Diana's running footsteps in the hall. He was playing hide-and-seek.

"Aaron, come out here right now."

He heard the edge in his mother's voice and instantly appeared in the living room. He had been hiding behind the TV table, holding his squirming pint-sized dog.

Diana burst back into the room and scooped him up in her arms, angry and relieved at the same time.

"I was hiding good, huh, Mommy?" he squealed.

• • •

Diana gathered Aaron's clothes and repacked his dinosaur backpack. It didn't matter that her son was safe despite being left alone by her ex-husband or that Aaron was completely oblivious to any danger he may have been in. She was taking him home with her.

When Beto tried to protest, she dismissed his argument about this being his weekend. He knew better than to push her when she had already made up her mind. The only impediment to leaving immediately was his missing coonskin cap, the rodeo present from me that came with a coloring book, a leather pouch craft kit, and a set of round cardboard disks with animal silhouettes on one side and their matching tracks on the other. When he got it, Aaron vowed to become an expert tracker like Davy Crockett. I suspected Aaron's dog was involved with the disappearance, but I didn't say anything. After a half hour of frantic searching, Beto found the fur cap outside under the swing set along with the disks.

I drove Diana's car back to her house while she tried to calm down and Aaron slept. I parked in the driveway, and we both stared at the shattered front window. Crime scene tape stretched across the front porch. The CSI team had been here and collected what evidence they could, which included two dozen .223 caliber slugs embedded in the window frame and the interior walls. They also found spent casings in the street. It wasn't a random gangbanger; their weapon of choice was a 9mm. This shooter had used an AR-15, which was more lethal and accurate.

"Any ideas?" I asked quietly so as not to wake Aaron.

"Hard to imagine it's not work related. Some pissed off perp or a moron with an ax to grind with the police."

"You can't stay here. Get a change of clothes and stay with me. I'll put a piece of plywood over the window."

She leaned over and kissed me. "Thank you."

While she gathered her overnight bag, I found a piece of plywood in the backyard. The play fort for Aaron I'd planned to use it for would have to wait. I felt kind of guilty that I'd waited this long to build it. I bought the wood over a month ago. My intentions were good.

I found my portable drill and a handful of drywall screws in my pickup toolbox and dragged everything over to the porch. Before I lifted the board in place, I examined the bullet holes in the wall. They weren't concentrated on one particular spot but scattered across the front of the house.

The shooter wasn't targeting anything in particular. Had he been aiming at Diana or me, he might have hit one of us. We were both standing in full view of the street. I realized either one of us could have been the target.

I finished attaching the plywood. She didn't live in a high-crime neighborhood, but we were still in San Antonio. There was enough crime that you didn't want to leave your door unlocked at night or the front window open.

I put my tools back in my pickup and walked out to the street to see if there were any casings or shreds of evidence that CSI hadn't found or picked up. I shined my flashlight up and down the deserted street. They seemed to have done a thorough job.

I shined the light into the yard, wondering how much longer it would take Diana to pack her toothbrush and a pair of underwear. Hers was one of the few neighborhoods that still had street-side mailboxes. Diana's featured bright reflective sunflowers against a silver background. The lid stood partially open, and the light reflected off a small yellow piece of paper.

Diana emerged from the house and inspected the plywood. "Good work." She was carrying two sandwiches wrapped in paper towels and a banana. We'd never gotten to eat our pizza. "Are you gonna replace the glass tomorrow?" she called to me.

I focused my attention on the mailbox. There was something inside.

"What? What is it?"

"Take a look," I said, shining my flashlight on the small note.

She joined me in the street. I used my pocketknife to open the box and slide the yellow note to the edge so we could see the writing.

In dark, block letters, the note read: BACK OFF. FIRST AND ONLY WARNING.

CHAPTER TWENTY-NINE

I transferred a sleeping Aaron to my pickup and drove him and his mom to my King William fixer upper. I expected to see the front window shot out. It made sense that whoever Beau Fahl had hired to send the message would first go to my house. There was no sign of broken glass nor any bullet holes on the front wall.

I glanced toward my neighbor's house. Rose waved from her upstairs bedroom window. Had there been any violence here, she would be on her way to give me the lowdown on what happened. Instead, she was probably smiling and making a note in her upstairs window journal of my bringing Diana and her son home for the night. She would think I was making progress with my relationship. In the morning she would update the downstairs window journal to reflect the changes.

I asked Diana to wait in the pickup while I searched the perimeter just to be sure. I called Skeeter and held the line while he checked the surveillance footage for this afternoon from the inside and outside cameras. The surveillance was a headache and a constant reminder of the last case that got personal. A corrupt cop broke in, searching for the evidence I'd gathered against his boss. He brought a cheeseburger for Sam, then shot him with a .22 and left him for dead.

I heard Sam whimper from behind the backyard fence. It wasn't a warning. He was a chocolate Lab and didn't give warnings. This sound meant "Where have you been? Let's go for a run." If I'd have been a stranger, he would have barked. The bark would translate to "Come on in, and I'll let you pet me as long as you don't shoot." He was only slightly more wary of strangers after almost being killed.

I let myself in the back gate and scratched Sam behind the ears where there was still a scar from the .22 bullet. I thought of the similarities in the two cases. In that case, the warning came from a dirty cop working for a corrupt politician. Both were arrogant to the point of believing they were beyond the reach of the law because they were the law and could act with impunity. The bastards sending a message in this case acted the same way, only they weren't the law. Something or someone else was backing their work. I needed to find out who or what it was.

Diana tucked Aaron safely into the guest bedroom. Sam circled the bed twice, then settled down on the floor rug beside the bed. Skeeter had switched the surveillance cameras inside and outside the house to live feed so he could monitor my house through his laptop. I stood in the living room and waved to the eye on the wall.

I asked Skeeter to set up the same system at Diana's house. I didn't expect them to return, but having the cameras in place would be a comfort to both of us. More than anything, I hated the intrusion into our privacy.

Diana put on her cotton pajamas and slipped into bed beside me. I turned off the lamp, and we both lay wide awake, staring out the window into the dark Alamo City sky.

"It's got to be Beau Fahl," I said.

I heard her blow a skeptical breath through her nose. "I need more than your hunch to officially go after him. You had Skeeter follow him. Was he at the scene?"

"He was with Lora."

"So you gave him an alibi."

"He won't keep his nose clean for long."

"You're not still thinking of going after him?"

"Tomorrow, I'm going to put a couple more men on the payroll."

"The geriatric duo?"

I raised my head and leaned on my elbow, trying to read her expression in the dark. "You know those two old-timers can still kick ass."

She pinched me hard on the rib cage. "I know that. Sometimes you can't tell when I'm teasing you."

"And it bugs the hell out of me."

We stayed quiet for a long minute, listening to the constant big city noise outside the window. I missed the dead silence of Grandpa's ranch in Gillespie County, where the only night music came from the breeze through the oak trees and an occasional hoot owl or coyote.

"Do you remember what we were doing right before the shooting started?" she asked.

"Yeah, waiting for pizza. I'll bet one of the officers on the scene took it."

"Probably, but I was talking about something else. You were about to tell me why you agreed with me."

I remembered exactly what I wanted to say to her, but the case had taken a turn for the worse, and I didn't want to complicate the issue even more by discussing it now. I needed to think clearly.

I kissed her forehead. "It can wait."

I turned my head and checked the nightstand.

My Springfield .45 was within arm's reach.

CHAPTER THIRTY

A half dozen pickups populated the parking lot for Beau Fahl's gym by the time I arrived. I'd spent the morning replacing the front window on Diana's house. Luckily, it was a standard dimension, and Home Depot had one in stock she liked. Replacing the miniblinds and curtains would have to wait until we had more time. Skeeter came over, and we installed surveillance cameras inside and outside her house. If someone stopped by again, we would know who they were in real time.

Aaron was halfway through the first grade and in his first year of all-day classes. He was no stranger to daycare with both parents being cops and was still at the stage where he looked forward to his time in the classroom. I didn't believe he was in any danger at the school, but I tagged along when Diana dropped him off just to get the lay of the land. The school didn't have a police presence on campus, but the entrance was secured, and I didn't see any need to add extra surveillance.

The warning note had said to back off. We both assumed it meant Colton's murder case and that I had touched a nerve when I paid Frank a visit. While CSI hadn't found anything yet, the forensics team was hard at work looking for anything that might point to a suspect. I knew Beau wasn't directly involved—that would have been too easy. He was much too smart for that. Skeeter was looking into his association with the local chapter of a biker gang who were involved in all manner of illegal activity, including intimidation. Shooting up the front of a house was their signature tactic.

I parked as close to the front entrance as I could. This wasn't a clandestine surveillance operation. I already had a GPS tracker on Beau's pickup, which was dialed into Skeeter's laptop. I wanted to show him that I wasn't intimidated. Something I was sure he wasn't accustomed to.

I brought a sandwich made from the same peanut butter and jelly that Aaron took to school. Diana made one for each of us before she went to work. I thought about Aaron sitting in the school cafeteria, munching on his sandwich and listening to the cacophony of elementary voices bouncing off the brick walls. The memory of my own time in first grade gave me a little shiver. I went to a small Lutheran school in Fredericksburg. My father, like Aaron's parents, served in law enforcement. Dad worked for the DPS before the people of Gillespie County elected him sheriff. It never occurred to me, as it wouldn't occur to Aaron, that my dad was in any kind of danger. Aaron showed the same admiration and pride for his mother that I had for my father. People looked up to him and respected the badge. He looked invincible wearing his cowboy hat and an ivory-handled Colt 1911, like Matt Dillon on the streets of a Hollywood Dodge City.

Then one day he walked up to a trailer house parked back in the cedar brush a few miles north of town. He'd gotten a report of a little girl being held against her will. He didn't wait for a warrant or backup. The occupants were cooking meth, high on their own product and armed to the teeth. No one made it out alive, including the little girl. The trailer burned to the ground, fueled by the toxic chemicals used to make the drugs.

All that was left at the scene were the two ivory handles from Dad's Colt pistol. I mounted them in a frame with a picture of Dad in his sheriff uniform and kept it on the mantel as a reminder that only Hollywood heroes are invincible.

The front door of the gym opened, and Beau Fahl stepped out wearing designer jeans and a black muscle shirt despite the forty-seven-degree temperature.

I unrolled my window and waved in his direction. Beau hesitated for a brief moment before continuing on to his black F-250. He didn't smile or wave, but he knew I was there. He started his pickup and sped out of the parking lot. I followed until he took the on-ramp to Loop 410. He was accelerating when I continued on the feeder road. I smiled, watching him cut off a slower-moving semitruck. He was trying to bait me into a high-speed chase as an excuse to run me off the road.

Skeeter texted me his location, and I took a different route to the warehouse near the airport. Beau arrived just ahead of me. He sauntered across the parking lot, headed toward the front door. I pulled up to the gate and honked my horn to make sure he knew I was there. He looked over his shoulder but kept going.

I didn't wait around at the warehouse. Skeeter met me at Lora's condo after lunch, and we installed a battery-powered camera near the entrance. It was the same brand as the one in use by the property manager, only it sent the image to his laptop instead of the building security. If they discovered it and took it down, they wouldn't be able to trace it back to him. I figured that by the time they noticed it, we wouldn't need it anymore.

Skeeter was dressed for the operation in a dark blue cable company shirt and black company baseball cap. Around his neck hung an official-looking ID badge. He'd worked for the company a couple of years ago. It was only briefly, but he had kept the uniform because he liked the way it fit. Not many stores stocked his enormous size. I watched him operate from the parking lot, just to be sure the real cable guy or the building security guard didn't stop by asking questions.

The whole installation took less than five minutes. He mounted the camera on the corner of the building with a power drill. It helped that his giant arm reach cleared close to ten feet. He didn't need a ladder. Back in the pickup, he adjusted the angle with a remote control so that the camera took in the front of the building.

I wanted Beau to feel me over his shoulder. He was smart, and he had showed me in the gym that he was cocky. His record was clean since he'd gotten out of prison. I was going to make it harder for him to keep it that way.

Skeeter finished adjusting the camera and opened the map window showing the location of Beau's pickup.

"You wanna have some fun?" I said.

"I don't like the sound of that," Skeeter replied, his voice a low rumble.

The red dot from the tracker showed Beau's pickup parked at an H.E.B. grocery store about five blocks from Lora's condo.

I pointed to the map. "He's at the H.E.B."

"So."

"I think we need some groceries."

I drove to the grocery store and parked a few spaces over from Beau's F-250. Skeeter stayed in the pickup, and I strolled inside wondering what kind of groceries Mr. Fahl was buying. I hadn't figured a big-time tough guy like him would be making a Waldorf salad for dinner, but that was where I found him. He pushed a shopping cart next to the Gala apple bin and spent the next few minutes selecting half a dozen fresh specimens.

I grabbed a handheld basket and threw in green onions and cilantro, thinking I might surprise Diana and make tacos for dinner. She would be impressed that I thought of dinner, and Aaron loved tacos.

I hovered around the produce section until I was sure Beau had seen me, then headed for the checkout stand. When I walked to the exit, I could see Beau waiting for me by the crosswalk.

I slipped my cell phone out of my pocket and clicked on the recording app in case I could get him to confess. It was doubtful, but this was a grocery store parking lot, and he wouldn't be expecting voice surveillance. Skeeter was also recording the encounter on his zoom lens camera.

"What the fuck do you think you're doing?" He didn't raise his voice. The store wasn't busy. No one took a second glance at the big man with tight designer jeans and a black muscle shirt.

"Buying groceries, Beau. What's it look like?" I held the plastic grocery sack loosely in my left hand and kept my right slightly bent and ready to pull the Springfield .45 from my shoulder holster. I wasn't under any illusion that Beau had stopped me for a friendly conversation. I hoped I was getting under his skin. If he wanted to play rough, I was ready.

"You know what I mean, asshole."

"No, I don't. Why don't you spell it out for me?" I was hoping he would remind me about the warning note and implicate himself in the shooting at Diana's house.

"This is harassment," he said.

"Buying taco mix is harassment? There'll be a lot of folks disappointed to hear that in South Texas."

"Stay away from me," he said in a low growl.

"Or what? Are you warning me—again?"

"You know what I mean."

"You shot up the front of Detective Ochoa's house last night. I know it was you because you left a cute note."

His eyes narrowed, and he clenched his jaw. "I guess you should be more careful."

"I get it. Frank put you up to this. You're just a thug for hire, too stupid to call the shots."

The skin on Beau's neck turned red. Maybe he didn't like being called a hired hand. "Stay away from me or I'll file a restraining order," he spat.

"Do what you gotta do, Beau. Why not take Frank down? Maybe you can plead out of murder and blame it on him."

He showed his teeth at that. It wasn't a smile. It was the same look he showed me on the mat at his gym, like an alpha wolf staring down a challenger.

I waited for him to say more. Instead, he turned on his heels and stomped back to his pickup. I wanted to shake his cage and force a reaction.

Beau slammed his door.

Mission accomplished.

"Did you get all that?" I asked Skeeter when I climbed back in the driver's seat.

"What'd the man have to say?"

"Not much. He threatened to get a restraining order."

"That's rich."

"Crazy thing is, they'd grant him one in a heartbeat. But he won't need it. We're gonna stop followin' him. Keep him off balance. I want him to think his threat was enough to scare me off. We know where to find him if we need to."

CHAPTER THIRTY-ONE

I picked Aaron up from school, and we spent thirty minutes playing catch in the front yard. The kid was getting pretty good. For a six-year-old, he had a strong arm. I promised to take him to a Rangers game when the season started. He brought out the disks from the Davy Crockett kit next and insisted I quiz him on animal tracks. I showed him the track, and he named the animal pictured on the opposite side of the cardboard disk. The only thing better would be real tracks, but that would have to wait for a trip to the ranch when the business with Beau Fahl was over.

He helped me fix tacos using a mixture of ground venison and pork. His mother never let him cook because he was too messy. When we finished, I could understand her position. My kitchen had a new coat of taco mix on the floor and walls, which Sam happily helped clean up.

When Diana got home, we had a family dinner waiting. It was unusual to be all together at my house, and we both felt the tension. On more than one occasion we talked about the next big step. Living together. We were both willing but also comfortable with our own routines. Diana and I were making little changes like sleepovers twice a week. She kept a toothbrush in my bathroom. I kept a six-pack in her fridge, but we were reluctant to cohabitate.

We joined hands at the table while Diana said grace in Spanish, pretending the events of the last forty-eight hours hadn't happened. It reminded me of growing up at the ranch with my grandparents. While Grandma was alive, we never skipped grace. The only difference was that Grandma's prayer was in German. Sam sat a few feet from the table, not begging, but with his Labrador eyes so big you'd think I never fed him. His focus was split between Diana and Aaron, knowing I was immune to his machinations.

"What did you learn in school today, Aaron?" Diana asked.

Aaron responded unintelligibly, his mouth around a soft taco.

"We played catch and practiced naming animal tracks. The kid's a natural," I said.

Aaron washed his food down with a gulp of milk. "I'm Davy Crockett," he beamed.

"What happened in school?" Diana persisted.

"I shared my sandwich with Gerald. He gave me a chocolate bar."

"You're not supposed to exchange food. It's against the school rules," she instructed.

"Seriously?" I said. "Kids have been doing that since the middle ages."

"They didn't have peanut butter and jelly sandwiches in the middle ages."

"You know what I mean."

"Besides, it spreads dangerous diseases."

"Oh, come on. I did it and never got sick."

"And that proves what?" Diana caught Aaron following our argument with rapt attention. "No more sharing lunch with Gerald. Okay?" She arched her eyebrow in my direction.

"Yes, ma'am," he said.

"Of course, you should do what your mom says," I said, smiling at her. I realized my role in Aaron's life was to support whatever his mom said.

When Aaron finally fell asleep, we retired to the couch to focus on the case. I told her about my encounter with Beau Fahl.

"You think the order to hit my house came from Frank?" she asked.

"Yeah, I think I touched a nerve and Frank's just arrogant enough to think he can get away with it."

I moved a little closer and put my arm around her shoulders. "I could get used to this," I whispered in her ear. Always the suave operator.

"I'll bet you say that to all the girls who stay over," she said, turning to face me.

"Only the ones I cook tacos for."

She kissed me. "I feel so special."

I kissed her back and pulled her closer to me. She squirmed on top of me, and we lay on the couch, her dark hair falling on my chest.

"Are you sure you're ready for us, Mr. Fischer?" she said.

I knew she meant her and Aaron came as a package deal. I wasn't sure I was ready, but I was willing to try.

"I'm ready," I said. Her face was too beautiful, her perfume too intoxicating, and her body too warm, pressed into mine, to say anything different. I lifted her in my arms and carried her upstairs to my bedroom.

CHAPTER THIRTY-TWO

The noontime sun filtered through the live oak mott, offering about as much heat as a forty-watt lightbulb. Spring seemed to be waiting somewhere in Mexico, unwilling to cut its winter vacation short and move back north of the border. Beau Fahl zipped his thin leather jacket to his freshly shaved chin and was glad he brought it on this trip to Willow City. The view of Max Devine's roping arena and beyond to the dark green live oak and cedar covered limestone hills brought back memories of his own country childhood and of his uncle's farm a hundred miles east. The thought irritated him. Why anyone wanted to live in the country escaped him.

He waited in the park-like area down the hillside from the main house. The rustic wood furniture looked like it was pulled from a black-and-white nineteenth-century photo. Bright limestone steps led down from the expansive patio, where a man in a brown cowboy hat stood watch. His beard was black and his expression stone cold, like the weather.

Two cowboys on horseback trailed a dozen two-year-old steers into the roping arena a hundred yards away. The riders pinned the animals behind the chutes at one end. In the field along the creek, two horses pulled a buckboard wagon stacked with bales of hay. Docile longhorn cattle lined up waiting for their daily meal.

All the cowboys and workers Beau had observed since driving through the front gate were armed. They all wore nineteenth-century-style boots and cowboy hats, like extras on a movie set. The only things not authentic were the modern automatic pistols tucked into leather belt holsters.

If this were his place, he would have more modern conveniences and replace the arena with a dirt bike track. He'd gotten his fill of animals as a kid and didn't have any interest in rural life. He did admire Devine's setup. It was the perfect place to hide. No one would expect someone with cartel connections to live out in the middle of nowhere pretending to be a cowboy.

Devine walked out of the house carrying a wooden tray with barbecue sandwiches, beans, and potato salad. A pitcher of sweet tea and two glasses already sat on the split-log table beside Beau's chair.

"This is buffalo meat from an old cow we butchered last week. She wasn't producing any more calves, so I put her on grain for a month to fatten her up. Besides elk, it's the best meat on the planet."

Devine set the tray down and served Beau a sandwich on blue-speckled enamel camp plates. He filled the tea glasses from the glass pitcher. "You know, back when the army first moved the Comanche Indians out of Texas, my great-grandfather had a government contract to deliver beef to the reservation north of the Red River. It started as a butcher service. He drove a wagon loaded with whole sides of beef to the headquarters. But the Comanches wouldn't eat it. They preferred to take delivery on the hoof so that they could chase down the animal on horseback and kill it with a lance or bow and arrow. That's the way they used to kill the buffalo. The hunt was woven into the fabric of their culture. Cut meat was an insult to them."

As if on cue, the gate flew open in the arena and a longhorn steer sprinted for freedom. Two cowboys emerged behind it on horseback, swinging their lariats. In a matter of seconds, the header dropped his loop over the animal's horns, and the heeler caught the back legs. The horses stretched the ropes, and the steer toppled to its side.

Devine pointed at the men in the arena. "Those two boys won the team roping this year in San Antonio," he said proudly. "Do you like rodeo, Mr. Fahl?"

"Not particularly."

"Football?"

"I'm not a team sport fan. I do MMA."

Devine looked disappointed. "Kung fu, huh? Well, everybody needs a hobby."

Beau started to explain but thought better of it. He didn't yet know why he'd been summoned to this meeting. He suspected Frank had complained about being muscled, but Frank had it coming. Business was business, and Frank was a weak link in the organization. Devine would understand. Devine wouldn't respect him if he let Frank push him around.

"Thanks for lunch," Beau said and bit into the buffalo barbecue.

Devine watched Beau's face for a reaction. "Well, what do you think?"

"Best buffalo I ever ate," Beau said. He washed the food down with sweet tea.

Both men dug into the food and remained silent for the next several minutes. It was after the noon hour. The cowboys in the arena let one of the steers loose from the small pen and chased it across the arena floor, swinging their ropes.

"Let's get to it," Beau said impatiently.

Devine wiped his chin with a paper napkin.

The man with the brown cowboy hat stood on the patio fifty feet above them. He carefully studied Beau Fahl's movements. His right hand rested on the Colt 1911 pistol strapped to his belt.

"By all means," Devine said.

"Did Frank say something? Is that why I'm here?"

"Frank's an idiot. I don't care if he gets pushed around. He usually deserves it." He pushed back in his chair. "You're here because you have a problem and forced me to step in."

Beau thought for a moment. He knew who Devine must be talking about. "Let me handle Nick Fischer."

"Like you handled Colton Macrae?"

"That was clean."

"Until Nick Fischer showed up."

"I'll take care of him."

"You'll walk away. You've done enough damage. I'll let you know when we're back in operation."

"Okay. I understand," Beau said. He knew better than to question the big boss.

Max Devine smiled. "Hope you enjoyed your lunch."

Beau wiped his mouth on the paper napkin and realized he'd been dismissed.

Beau stood. "You don't have to worry about anything."

Devine didn't stand or offer his hand. "I never do."

Beau walked down the limestone path back to his pickup.

When the black F-250 cleared the horizon, Doc Frank walked out of the house carrying a longneck beer and a plate with a barbecue sandwich.

"Did you straighten his ass out?" Frank asked, plopping down in the chair Beau vacated and immediately digging into the barbecue sandwich.

"I don't know why I put up with you," Devine said, shaking his head.

Frank replied with a mouth full of meat. Brown sauce dripped down his chin. "You know why. 'Cause I make you money."

Devine rubbed his eyes with the tips of his fingers and sighed. "We might need the judge and your DEA friends on this deal."

Frank washed his food down with a swig of beer and smiled. "I'll make some phone calls."

"This Nick Fischer is something different," Devine said thoughtfully. "He's too independent and that makes him dangerous."

"I guess you'd better be extra careful," Frank said around a mouthful of sandwich.

Devine stood and flashed a bloodless smile. "When this is over. I won't owe you any more favors."

Frank stopped chewing and swallowed. "Like hell you won't."

Devine didn't bother to reply. He left Frank and walked up the stone steps to the patio where the man with the brown hat stood watch. "Did you get all that, Z?"

Z nodded, keeping his eyes focused on Frank.

"You're gonna have to get creative. This thing is outta control. Rein it in and put a rope around it. I'm going to the Houston Livestock Show. Take care of business before I get back."

CHAPTER THIRTY-THREE

"Nice to get a few hours off," Diana said from the passenger seat when I pulled into the city parking lot across the street from Nonna Osteria in the old Fairmount Hotel downtown. It was her favorite place, and it was close to my neighborhood.

Despite her ex-husband's dismal record, Diana gave in to his demand for visitation on his scheduled day off, which gave us a rare free weeknight out for dinner.

We had reservations, but we still had to wait twenty minutes for a table. Nonna's was the kind of place people liked to take their time and enjoy the food and the atmosphere. We strolled around the lobby of the old Fairmount Hotel while we waited. A series of pictures showed the building's history from its 1906 beginning to the record-setting move in the eighties from a few blocks south to the present location. They hadn't just moved the business; they took the whole historic building. At the time, it was the largest building ever moved on wheels. However it got there, they had great food in a building that reminded me of simpler times in Texas history.

After dinner we walked down Alamo Street to the River Walk and strolled under the lights with a handful of winter tourists. A mariachi band was playing at the River Theater, and we sat on the stone steps to listen.

"My papa was in a mariachi band when he was younger," she said, enjoying the music.

"Really? Mine was in a singing club. The Germans called it a Sängerbund. They met at Grapetown near the ranch."

"Your relatives sang in a choir?"

"Music's in our blood."

"I've heard you in the shower. I wouldn't call the sound pleasant."

"I'm hurt to hear you say that." I faked a frown. "Truth is, the old-timers got bored with choir practice and combined the Sängerbund with the Schützenbund."

"Let me guess, a singing and shooting club?"

"That's right."

"Why am I not surprised?"

"They still hold a festival every year."

"There's probably beer there."

"Singin', shootin', and beer. It doesn't get any better than that."

She made a half-hearted attempt to smile. The last several days had been hard on both of us. I knew she was thinking of her son.

The north wind picked up. A German family with two small children sat down on the amphitheater step below us. The children were chatting, and the parents looked exasperated. The father was bald and in his thirties, wearing a bright green sweater that matched his wife's long-sleeve dress. There were only four other couples on the steps and dozens of empty seats, but they sat directly in front of us.

I understood a few words the two young children spoke. They wanted ice cream and to go back to their motel room to play video games.

I whispered the translation into Diana's ear. Instead of laughing, she took out her cell phone and hit speed dial. I heard the phone ring and go to voicemail, then Beto's voice say to leave a message.

She stood abruptly. "We have to go."

I hustled to catch up with her. "I'm sure everything's fine," I said, but I was worried too. If Beto left Aaron alone again, I would belt him myself.

She called again when we got to my pickup.

Still no answer.

"Drive," she said.

I took I-35 south to Highway 90 and sped west toward Castroville and her ex-husband's house. Beto finally answered his phone when we cleared Loop 1604.

"Where have you been?" Diana yelled. She put the phone on speaker and set it on the console.

"I—I just stepped out for a minute," he stuttered.

I knew something was wrong.

"Put Aaron on the phone, now!"

"Okay, I'll be home in two minutes."

"You left him alone, again?"

I put my hand on Diana's shoulder. I could feel the tension in her muscles. A volcanic eruption was imminent.

"Beto, it's Nick." I picked up the phone and clicked off the speaker.

I could hear a cashier in the background say, "*Cash or debit to save five percent.*" That was the standard line from a chain discount liquor store.

"Drop what you're doing and go. Call us back when you get home," I said. I didn't share what I heard. Diana didn't need to know Beto was stocking up on booze while he should have been home with his son.

Twenty minutes later we pulled into Beto's driveway. His car wasn't there, and he hadn't called back.

Diana opened the door and hit the ground running before I came to a complete stop. The front door was open, again. I felt an eerie déjà vu.

She yelled Aaron's name, and her voice echoed through the empty house. There was no response. I hurried after her.

Beto hadn't cleaned the house. The front room still looked like it took the brunt of a Texas tornado. I listened for Aaron's dog. This time the house was silent.

Diana yelled again. It wasn't the playful voice a mother uses to play hide-and-seek. It had an edge that a six-year-old wouldn't be able to resist even if he had a really great hiding place.

"He's not here!" Diana yelled, jogging back into the room. She was on the verge of tears. She was a police detective and used to crime and crime scenes, but this was her son.

"Check the yard."

She turned abruptly and ran out the back door.

I heard a car in the driveway and looked out the front window. Beto finally arrived.

"Aaron," he called, as if Diana or I hadn't thought to call the boy's name.

"Is this how you left the place?" I asked.

Beto surveyed the room and stared at me blankly. "What?"

"Where's the dog?"

"Nick!" Diana yelled from the backyard. Her voice trembled.

I ran out the back door fearing what I might find.

The dog was lying dead on the patio. Two pinpoints of blood marked the animal's right side. I knelt and pressed my hand to its side. Still warm.

"We must have just missed them," I said.

I stood and turned to Diana. Her hands were shaking. Tears flowed down her cheeks.

"Aaron! Oh my God." She managed to choke out the words.

"The dog's dead, and Aaron's not here," I said, taking her hands. "That's good."

Anger flared in Diana's eyes. "How's that good?"

"It means Aaron's alive."

She jerked her hands free and leaped for Beto like a mountain lion springing for a deer.

"You left him alone!" she screamed.

I grabbed her around the waist before she could take him down and pulled her kicking and screaming inside the house.

"Kill him later," I said. "Right now, we need him to talk to the local PD."

She took a deep breath and stopped resisting.

I slowly let her go.

Diana took a deep breath and quickly checked her emotions. This was a crime scene, and her cop instincts kicked in. She turned to Beto.

"Get the local PD here, now. Tell them the perps left less than five minutes ago."

"I'll check with the neighbors and see if anyone saw or heard anything. Maybe we can get a description on the vehicle."

"Did you get the security cameras fixed?" she asked Beto.

He shook his head in response, already on his cell phone.

She reached for her cell phone and pressed a number on speed dial.

I studied the trashed room. The only surface not piled with junk was the dining room table. On it was a single piece of paper. I stepped closer. It was a note typed in all caps.

THIS TIME PAY CLOSE ATTENTION. IF YOU WANT TO SEE AARON ALIVE, 1) NO POLICE OR FBI. 2) DROP THE INVESTIGATION.

I heard a voice on Diana's cell phone say, "SAPD Detective Lopez."

I lunged for the phone. "Wait!" I yelled and punched the disconnect button.

"What the hell?" Diana said, looking like I'd just slapped her in the face.

I pointed to the note.

Diana reached for the piece of paper, then quickly remembered her detective training. "Get a plastic baggie out of the drawer," she said.

I held open a gallon freezer bag, and she picked the paper up by the edges and slipped it inside. "Beto!" she yelled through the open back door.

Beto appeared with his cell phone still to his ear.

"Tell them we found Aaron. False alarm."

"What? You found him? Where?" Beto walked inside.

Diana held up the note in the bag long enough for Beto to read it. He wasn't the brightest bulb in the chandelier, but he understood.

"Hey, listen," he said into the phone. "We found him." He listened for a moment, then continued. "That's right. He was playing at the neighbor's house. Really sorry to raise the alarm. These days, you know how it is." He disconnected and turned to Diana. "What the hell does this mean?"

"I think this is directed at me," I said before Diana could respond.

"What're you talkin' about?" he said.

"A friend of mine was killed at the rodeo last week."

"I heard about that," Beto said.

"Yeah, well, I think I know who did it. I turned up the heat and found evidence and a witness."

"That witness ended up dead," Diana added.

"You turned up the heat? Did you harass him?"

"He's guilty of two murders," I said.

"What did you do?" Beto's cheeks were flushed. He was one of those types who wore his shirts a little on the tight side to show off his dedication to the gym. His muscles were cut and chemically enhanced. He also resented ex-military who were cops or had been cops.

"I asked him to confess. Colton Macrae deserves justice. So does Danny Sanz, the witness he killed."

Beto stuck out his chest. It was an involuntary move left over from the high school locker room.

"That's just great. You picked a fight with a murderer. Now, he kidnaps my son!" he shouted.

"Yeah, leave the bad guy alone and he'll just go away."

"Okay, okay," Diana intervened. "None of that matters right now. Aaron is missing. Likely, it's our suspect, Beau Fahl, who took him. The question is, what do we do now?"

Beto pointed a stubby finger at me. "Is he gonna stay out of it?"

"The number one priority right now is getting Aaron back unharmed," I said, deliberately ignoring him.

"So you're gonna drop the case?" he asked, his chest still puffed out like a banty rooster.

"Beto, shut up," Diana said, annoyed. "We need to focus."

Beto blew an exasperated breath through his flared nostrils.

"We'll keep this between us for now. We need to cover this crime scene. Fingerprints, footprints, anything and everything we can find." She turned to Beto. "That's your job. You live here. You should know how much of this crap on the floor belongs here. Find some evidence we can use and find the casing or the bullet that killed Aaron's dog. You're a cop. Do your job."

Beto shifted into work mode reluctantly. I knew our fight wasn't over, but for now he was willing to focus on finding Aaron.

Diana took a step toward the front door and tripped over the stuffing from one of the pillows. "Why don't you ever learn to clean up the house?"

I followed her outside to the front yard. Only five minutes had elapsed between the time we'd arrived and the time we emerged back on the front lawn. My pickup was still running. I cut the motor and took out the keys.

"You take that side of the street," she said. "I'll take this side. Let's see if anyone saw anything."

I took her hand before she turned to go. "We will find him."

She took a deep breath to steady her nerves. "If anything happens to him, I want you to promise me you'll take them apart."

"Of course," I said and kissed her.

CHAPTER THIRTY-FOUR

Canvassing the neighborhood turned up nothing. Two of the immediate neighbors were home but watching television. Gunshots, tractors, barking dogs, cows, and coyotes blended together like white noise in rural Castroville. Whitetail deer and wild hogs roamed the hundred-acre pasture behind the houses, and hogs never went out of season. If a landowner saw one rooting around his property, he'd reach for his rifle. Nothing the neighbors heard was out of the ordinary.

I wished my nosy neighbor, Rose, lived on Beto's street. She would have heard the gunshot, seen the vehicle, got a description of the driver, and written down the license plate number.

We did get invited in for coffee and cookies. No one can say small-town Texas isn't friendly. The older couple promised to look for our missing dog. We used a cover story because it was a small town and word would travel fast. Diana's parents and large extended family lived on the other side of town and would know about Aaron's kidnapping within the hour.

I had no doubt that Beau Fahl meant business. He assumed that attacking Diana and Aaron would force me to back off the investigation. To a point, he was right. I wouldn't jeopardize their safety for any reason. But I would never give up. I would see that Beau Fahl got what he deserved.

Beto turned up zero forensic evidence from the house. I wasn't sure how he could tell the trash from the clues. Diana double-checked his work inside, and I tried to sort out what happened in the backyard.

The dog was small and harmless. True, it barked, but the kidnappers could have locked it in the closet. Why waste a bullet? The entry wound left only a pinpoint of blood. I guessed it was a .22 caliber, which wasn't the weapon of choice for gangbangers or someone who anticipated significant resistance.

With nothing left to do in Castroville, Diana and I drove back toward San Antonio. Being in the same room with her ex-husband surrounded by her son's toys put us both on edge.

During the drive, I tried to think of a way to calm her fear. "Aaron will be safe," I finally said. It was all I could think of.

"How can you be sure?"

"Think about it. Beau's smart, but he's arrogant. So is Frank. They think they're untouchable. But they've gotta know if they kill a police detective's son, no one can protect them."

"What's our next move?" she asked. She was giving me the ball and trusting me not to fumble. It should have felt good, but it gave me an uneasy feeling.

"We're partners on this," I said.

She nodded, then held my gaze.

"Waiting for the posse won't help," I said.

"Then let's go to work."

I picked up my phone and called Skeeter. I hoped the GPS tracker was still on Beau's pickup. When he answered, I briefed him on what transpired.

Diana watched me impatiently for a moment, then took the phone out of my hand. "We're partners, remember?" She put the phone on speaker.

"Hi, Skeeter, this is Diana."

"Hey, kid. How you holdin' up?" Skeeter asked.

"I don't know yet. My heart's still racing."

"I know how you feel."

"Tell us what our man Beau Fahl has been up to," I said.

There was a long pause on the phone, then Skeeter cleared his throat.

"Talk to us, Skeeter," Diana said, her voice betraying rising fear.

"I lost him," Skeeter said.

"You lost the GPS?" I asked.

"It happened late this afternoon. I tracked him to that warehouse near the airport. He must have swept the vehicle. He'd been there about ten minutes, and the signal went dead."

"I was afraid of that."

"I drove over to the warehouse thinking the battery went dead, but his pickup wasn't there. I checked the gym and Lora's condo parking lot. Nothing. I'm checking the surveillance at her condo now."

"All right. We gotta think. Where would he go? What would he do? He can't go out in public."

"Anything at her condo?" Diana asked.

"That's interesting," Skeeter said.

"What?"

"I'm taking a closer look."

"You're killin' me, man."

"Some dude in a brown cowboy hat. Bushy black beard. Looks like bad news."

"Why's that?" Diana asked.

"Just the look on his face. All business."

"Send me a pic. I've got a good idea who he is."

PART THREE

Get Western

"When bad men combine, the good must associate; else they will fall, one by one, an unpitied sacrifice in a contemptible struggle."

—Edmund Burke

"It's about to get western
Around here tonight
Better wear your workin' clothes and pull your hat down tight
It's about to get western
I don't mean it might
It's about to get western
Around here tonight"

—Gary P. Nunn

CHAPTER THIRTY-FIVE

I listened to Diana's argument for not going to see Lora while I loaded two spare .45 magazines and strapped my Springfield into a shoulder holster. I didn't want to be accused of not listening. When she finished, I checked the loads on the hammerless .38 and strapped it back on my ankle.

By that time, she realized I wasn't going to change my mind and shifted her focus to why she should go with me. When she gave me a chance to speak, I explained that Lora would not open the door if she was with me.

"You're a cop. She doesn't trust you."

"And she trusts you?"

I knew in the back of her mind she was thinking of Lora's accusation that I fought with Colton over her and that I wanted Lora all to myself. "No, she doesn't trust me, but I do think she's scared. She thinks I can protect her, or at least I would try."

"What do you mean?"

"I mean, if Devine's bodyguard went to see her, she's in way over her head. She would realize that and look for a way out."

"Meaning he would kill her?"

"That's a possibility."

"If he's there, you'll need backup."

"Not this time."

She started to protest again, but Skeeter pounded on the door.

"Come in," I yelled.

Diana was a police officer and trained to defend herself, but I felt better knowing there was another person in the house.

It was time to distance myself from my personal feelings for Diana so I could think clearly. Had she come with me, I would have at some level always been thinking of her safety. Maybe it was a flaw in my character, a romantic notion that I had to protect the women in my life. Whatever the origin, it didn't matter. I couldn't deny it was there. I knew I had to adjust my strategy to accommodate it. Diana would stay behind. Sam and Skeeter would stay with her.

She followed me out on the front porch. The wind was calm, and the pecan tree, still bare of leaves, allowed the few stars visible in the city to shine through. It was forty degrees. Cold by South Texas standards, but the wind was calm. I wore a gray sweatshirt zipped over my shoulder holster. Diana stood beside me in the same white cotton blouse she'd worn to work. Goosebumps formed on her bare forearms. Her hands were shaking, but not from the cold.

"Get him back," she said, taking my hands. "Do you understand me? Bring him home alive."

Her dark eyes implored me to act. I saw fear, anger, and something else. Doubt maybe. We hadn't known each other that long. I knew trust had to be earned. Her last husband, Aaron's father, had let her down. She was probably wondering if I was any different from the other men in her life.

"I'll bring him home," I said and took her in my arms. I hoped it was true.

• • •

By the time I took the stairs to Lora's condo, it was close to three a.m. It wasn't late by her schedule. On any normal night, she'd just be getting off work.

I knocked. "Anybody home?" I called through the door.

Inside was silent. If she was dead, it would mean one more link to Beau Fahl was cut. Flaky as Lora was, I had a feeling she knew way more than she let on. She was popular not only because of her enhancement surgery. Guys knew she listened and had volumes of information about a lot of high-powered clients.

I heard footsteps inside and the sound of the deadbolt in the lock.

"What're you doin' here?" Lora said, appearing behind the safety chain.

"I was baking cookies and ran out of sugar," I said, smiling. "Spare a cup?"

"Go away, Nick. We got nothin' to talk about." Her eyes were glassy and dilated. She'd been hitting the booze or the pills or both. Maybe her inebriated state would help me get the information I wanted from her.

Lora tried to slam the door, but I had my boot jammed in the opening.

"I was going to bring you cookies when I finished."

"You're not funny." She tried again to shut the door.

I lost my patience. "Step back," I insisted.

She didn't move.

"Suit yourself." I blasted the door with my boot.

Lora caught the door with her face and slumped to the white carpet, holding her nose.

"Nick, you're such a fuckin' asshole," she screamed.

"I warned you." I took her hands away from her face. There was a red mark, but no blood. "Pretty as ever," I said and pulled her into the living room and tossed her on the dirty white couch.

"What do you want?" she whined.

"Who else is in here?"

"Nobody."

"Where's Beau Fahl?"

"How should I know?"

"'Cause he's your boyfriend. Beau is not a nice guy. People who hang around him get killed."

"He's not like that." Tears flowed down her cheeks. I knew she could turn them on or off at will. I handed her a tissue from the box on the lamp table.

"Who came to see you this afternoon?"

She blew her nose in a tissue and tossed it on the coffee table next to half a dozen others. "Nobody."

"You're lying."

She wiped her face with another tissue and smiled like she knew something I didn't. I took hold of her elbow and twisted her arm behind her back.

"You're hurting me," she whined.

"I know he works for Devine. What's his name?" I showed her the picture Skeeter took from the surveillance camera.

She chewed her bottom lip, thinking of a lie to tell me.

"Wait, this is my apartment. How'd you get this?"

"Never mind. Who is it? What's his name?"

"You bastard. You're spying on me!"

I let go of her and scanned the room, searching for signs that someone had been in her apartment recently. The place looked like a bus station. I left her on the sofa and went into the kitchen.

Two empty glasses rested on the counter. One smelled like scotch. I open the lower cabinet and found a half-empty bottle of Macallan 12. I brought the bottle to Lora.

"How come he gets Macallan and you give me Jack Daniels?"

My phone buzzed. It was Skeeter.

"What's up?" I asked.

"That cowboy with the brown hat's here."

"Where?"

"Outside your place. He's sittin' in a green dually pickup about two houses down."

"Have Diana call in a burglary in progress. Lock and load and stay put."

"You think this guy's a badass?"

"I don't wanna take any chances."

I disconnected and pointed to the pic of the cowboy. "Who's this?"

Lora's dilated eyes got wider. "I don't know."

"Give me a name. I know he works for Max Devine because I've seen him at his ranch."

Lora chewed the end of her thumb before making a decision. "I think it's Zamora or something. Everybody calls him Z."

"What was he doin' here?"

"He owed me money."

"For what?"

"Dancing, what do you think?"

"Come on, Lora."

"Don't make me say anything. Please, Nick. Z's a killer. That's what he does. I hear things. Everybody stays away from him. He came from Mexico. When he shows up, people die."

CHAPTER THIRTY-SIX

I pulled into the parking lot of Lucky's Gym at four a.m. The dark building stared back at me like a man in a deep sleep. Lucky's Dodge Ram occupied the owner's parking place near the front door. I cut my engine and opened my window.

"Howdy. Thanks for coming."

Lucky smiled, exposing his missing front teeth. Usually, when he left the gym, he filled the blank space with two gold replacements, unless he expected trouble.

Sarge held up his camo travel mug in a morning salute.

"Wouldn't happen to have any more of that, would you?" I asked, pointing to the mug.

Lucky handed me a sixteen-ounce to-go cup from the minimart. The sides were hot, and it smelled fresh.

"That's what I call service," I said.

They piled into my pickup, and I filled them in on the situation while I drove. Since John Macrae added them to my payroll, they were eager to earn their money. They would have helped me without pay, but the money put everybody on a professional level. The plan was simple. Go to the poker house and see for ourselves if Lora had told the truth. I didn't need to tell them of the danger. I'd used them as backup before. They knew the drill.

Sarge loaded a Mossberg pistol-grip shotgun. He usually carried an

AR-15, but I told him the address was on a residential street. If we had to use weapons, I didn't want to risk a stray bullet through a wall causing collateral damage. A shotgun was deadly in close quarters but wouldn't penetrate drywall or siding.

Lucky always carried a 9mm, but he seldom had to use it at close range. His fists were faster and more deadly in a fight. "Where's Skeeter?" he asked.

"He's watching Diana at the house. I didn't want her involved with this."

"She was okay with that?" Lucky asked.

"She wasn't happy about it."

Lucky nodded like he understood her position. I didn't have time to explain mine.

"What about the back of the house?" Sarge asked.

"There's a six-foot board fence with a dog in the back. It borders a golf course."

Lora told me that Devine's bodyguard Z paid her in advance for entertainment. He kept her on a retainer. She was a particular favorite of the Bexar County judge. But she said next week's game would be canceled. They were using the house for a young guest.

I didn't believe her when she said Beau wasn't involved. I assumed she was covering for him, still trying to hang on to her pill connection. I did believe I'd made enough noise for the bad guys to come out of the brush. They were angry, they were dangerous, and they had no fear of the law. I was glad Lucky and Sarge came with me.

I waited at the neighborhood security gate for another resident to open the gate, then followed them in. Most of the houses were dark with only a few porch lights to light the houses. When I turned the corner to the party house, I saw Diana's town car. She saw me and waved through the back window.

"Looks like she changed her mind," Lucky said.

"Apparently," I said. Before I had a chance to get angry, she leaned out the back window and waved for me to park behind her.

I stopped and sent a text message to Skeeter. "*Where the hell are you?*" Instead of an answering text, a pair of headlights flashed from across the street.

"I guess the gang's all here," Sarge said.

"Maybe that's a good thing," Lucky said.

"Maybe," I said. I turned the inside lights off and stepped out. Diana met me at the back of her car.

"Nothing moving," she said in a whisper and popped the trunk.

Sarge and Lucky joined us.

"Thanks for coming, guys," she said to Lucky and Sarge, handing each of us an SAPD ballistic vest. She already had hers on.

"Do we know your son's in the house?" Sarge asked.

Diana shook her head. "I saw two men through the front window forty-five minutes ago. No sign of Aaron."

Skeeter joined us. "I found one surveillance camera over the front door and one on the back deck that overlooks the pool area."

"What's the plan?" Lucky asked.

They all looked at me. I focused on Diana. The fear and anger I'd seen earlier was gone. In its place were resolve and determination. She expected an argument. I didn't give her one. I glanced at Skeeter. He started to speak, but I raised my hand. Diana wasn't the kind of woman to sit on the sidelines when someone had her son. I was naive to think otherwise, and I knew nothing I said would change her mind.

"Sarge will come with me. We'll take out the back camera and break in through the kitchen. If Aaron's in there, we'll find him. I'll signal you when we're in position. Skeeter, can you provide a diversion so we can take out the guys inside."

Skeeter chuckled. "I got just the thing."

We waited while he dug in the back seat of his pickup and came up with a blue cable company shirt and khaki pants. He held them up. "Cable company," he said.

I checked my watch. Six a.m. "We wait till seven thirty. The cable company doesn't make house calls before then. In the meantime, Sarge and I will neutralize the dog and watch the back of the house."

Diana raised her eyebrow. "Neutralize?"

I showed her the plastic storage bag full of bacon-flavored doggy treats I'd borrowed from Sam's stash.

"Oh," she said. "I thought you meant—"

"You know me better than that." I took her hand. "If Aaron's in there, we'll get him out safely."

She pursed her lips in an effort to hold back her emotion. All the worst-case scenarios had been playing in her head since we read the warning note. She was a by-the-book detective, but if we found Aaron inside with these men, she would be torn between reading them their rights and shooting them in the head.

The watch dog in the backyard turned into a pushover. I had him literally eating out of my hand the moment he smelled the bacon bits. The next part was the difficult part. Waiting. Sarge settled in behind the utility shed with his back against the wooden fence and quickly became a lawn gnome. Waiting was second nature to him. A habit formed during his long Army career. For me it was much more difficult. I had plenty of hunting experience and understood the necessity for stillness, but it didn't make the exercise any easier. To make matters worse, my new doggy friend wanted to play. He was a hundred-pound pit bull and shepherd mix with short black-and-brown hair. He looked intimidating until he smelled bacon. He licked my face and hands, climbed on my back, and finally lay down beside me on the grass and went to sleep.

By seven o'clock, the eastern horizon flushed orange. I signaled Sarge. He approached the side of the house away from the angle of the surveillance camera. For a man pushing seventy, he moved like a big cat out for the hunt in the early dawn light. He reached under the camera and cut the powerline with a Leatherman tool.

I jogged to the house and tried the handle on the back door. The knob was locked but not the deadbolt. They must have figured they didn't need it with the dog. I slipped my folding knife into the jamb and popped the door open.

I paused to listen. The TV played a national morning news program. I checked my watch. Seven twenty-nine. A message appeared on my cell phone. Skeeter was right on time.

"*I'm going in*," he texted.

A second later, the doorbell rang.

A man's voice said, "What the fuck?" He sounded groggy from sleep. Furniture creaked and bare feet slapped on a tile floor.

I moved at a crouch toward a hallway that I hoped led to the spare bedrooms.

I heard a door open and another man's gruff voice said, "Who the hell is it?"

"Looks like the cable guy," the first voice said.

"See what he wants. Jesus, what time is it?" Gruff Voice asked.

I heard the distinct sound of an automatic pistol being armed. I knew Skeeter would have only a clipboard in his hands. He wasn't wearing a ballistic vest because he said it looked too obvious. He was right. The thugs we were after would instantly spot it and bolt or simply shoot him in the head.

Once before, I'd sent him as a decoy while I did recon. That time, he took a bullet in the chest. I was counting on Sarge to take out the man and his weapon; otherwise, Skeeter would be once again a sitting duck.

I moved to the first bedroom door and eased it open. The room was empty except for a stack of cardboard boxes in the center of the room. No furniture and no Aaron.

The front door opened. Skeeter's said, "Cable company. You set up an appointment yesterday for seven forty-five. I'm a little early. I hope you don't mind."

I smiled to myself. Skeeter could have been an actor. He was very convincing.

"Nobody called the fucking cable company, dude," the man said.

I moved down the hall to the next room. Empty. No Aaron. That left the upstairs area.

"I have the order right here," Skeeter said.

When I peered around the doorframe into the living room, Skeeter held a clipboard at arm's length with his metal prosthesis. A heavyset man with a scraggly blond beard and dirty gray T-shirt stood just inside the door. His right hand held a pistol concealed behind his back.

A skinny younger man in jean shorts and no shirt stood in an inner doorway. He had a sunken chest and three days' growth of beard. He rubbed his arms and chest, fidgeting like he needed a morning drug fix.

Both men focused on the oversized black man with the hook hand standing at the door.

"My boss will kill me if I don't check it out," Skeeter pleaded.

Sarge inched out of the kitchen, holding a black tactical knife. His focus was on the man at the door holding the weapon. I ducked behind the couch and slid across the tile floor toward Skinny.

The doorman moved his right hand up. "You can't come in here, fucker," he said.

"Come on, man. I'll just be a second. You don't want me to lose my job. Look at the order."

Skeeter held the clipboard up to the man's face. It was a good strategic move because it blocked his vision. Skeeter didn't know for sure what the man held behind his back, but I could bet he was thinking the guy had a weapon.

I waited for Sarge to make the first move. When he did, I would spring for Skinny. So far, the upstairs remained silent. With any luck, these two were the only two adults in the house.

"Get the fuck outta here!" Doorman said and moved his right hand up.

That was all Sarge needed. He dove forward and latched onto the man's wrist.

I waited a half second later for Skinny to make his move. When he did, I pounced on his back and pinned him to the floor with my knees. I brought out a zip tie and secured his hands behind his back before he could squirm.

"Don't move," I said, pressing the barrel of my Springfield .45 to the base of his skull. He lay still. "Cross your ankles," I ordered.

He crossed his ankles in the air, and I secured them with a second zip tie.

When I looked up, Sarge had his man on the ground, out cold. He didn't take any chances.

Skeeter walked through the front door and surveyed our work. "Did that guy have a pistol?" he asked, pointing to the weapon on the floor.

"I believe he did," Sarge said, picking up the pistol and emptying the bullets.

Skeeter let out an audible breath. His good hand shook.

"You weren't ever in any danger," I told him.

"You're full of shit," he said.

There was no sign of Aaron or any indication that he had ever been there.

"Did you find him?" Diana burst into the room out of breath.

"He's not on the ground floor. Check upstairs."

Skinny tried to twist his head to get a look at Diana as she came into the room. I jammed my pistol into the back of his neck.

"Face down," I reminded him.

Lucky and Diana jogged up the steps. I followed.

A large round table took up most of the space. Diana cleared the bathroom, and Lucky and I took the back room where I'd watched the ladies lead the poker players. The room had a bed and a dresser. All neat and tidy. Aaron wasn't there.

We met downstairs and went through the spacious kitchen. Except for two empty burger boxes that looked left over from last night, the space sparkled.

"What's that?" Sarge asked, staring at something near the back door.

Diana saw the object at the same time and rushed to pick it up. "It's his. It's Aaron's," she said, her voice quivering.

She held up a four-inch round piece of cardboard with the silhouette of a coyote stamped on one side and the outline of a coyote footprint on the other, one of the pieces from the tracking game. If there was one left on the kitchen floor, maybe Aaron dropped it on purpose.

"He's alive, and he's thinking," I said. "He knows we're coming after him."

"You think he left it there on purpose?" Sarge asked.

"No doubt about it. Aaron wouldn't part with those pieces," Diana said. "He wanted to be like Davy Crockett."

The doorman made a groaning sound. We all turned to him and his skinny sidekick.

"Maybe they know where he went," Sarge said.

Sarge was an expert. Interrogation was his specialty. He never talked much about it, but I'd gathered bits and pieces of what he'd done during his special ops career and how he managed to get information. We'd swapped notes when I asked him about his success rate. I had no doubt his methods would produce quick results.

"Let's go," I said to Diana.

"What? No. We need to find out what they know."

"I'll get whatever they know. Trust me. You shouldn't be here," Sarge said.

"He's right." I took Diana's elbow. She reluctantly let me lead her out the front door.

CHAPTER THIRTY-SEVEN

Maya agreed to help Nick before he finished explaining the plan. She owed him her life. Nick saved her from the filthy brute who was going to take her out of the country. She'd been a fool for trusting the man, but she realized how vulnerable she was and how easily that scumbag manipulated her feelings. She knew she'd been fortunate that Nick hadn't given up on her even after she ran away twice. A year after her ordeal, she was still feeling the effects of the kidnapping and abuse. She'd been living with her grandparents since Nick found her and brought her home, and next fall she would be ready to go back to school and finish her high school diploma.

Her grandfather stopped his pickup at the Devine ranch gate and turned to study his granddaughter in the passenger seat.

Maya felt her cheeks flush. She wore more makeup than she normally did for a day in the saddle. Her lipstick matched her dark red western shirt, and instead of her normal braids, she wore her shoulder-length raven hair loose and curled at the ends under her black cowboy hat.

"You're sure about this?" he asked. When Nick came to him for help, he couldn't turn him down. He didn't want to involve Maya, but it was her decision. He had made peace with the reality that his granddaughter was very headstrong and opinionated. She was very much her own woman who would make her own decisions whether he agreed with them or not. Helmut also realized that after what she'd been through, she could handle going undercover to gather information from Devine's mix of cowboys and private guards better than he could.

"Remember what Nick said—" Helmut started to say, but Maya cut him off with a wave of her hand.

"We've covered it, Grandpa." She regained her composure and touched his weather-beaten hand. "Nick needs this information. Diana needs this information. If they're hiding Aaron anywhere on the property, I'll find out."

The tall, clean-cut gate guard tapped on the driver's side window. He wore a wide-brimmed silver cowboy hat pulled low over his freckled face.

Helmut ignored him. "But if you can't get the information..."

"I'm not gonna do anything stupid." Maya smiled, leaned over, and kissed the old man on the cheek.

"What was that for?" A show of affection always flustered Helmut.

"For caring," she said with a twinkle in her eye. She loved seeing his reaction.

Helmut turned to the young cowboy and rolled the window down.

"Hey, Mr. Geisler. Maya." The young man's eyes went to Maya's red lips, then down to her tight-fitting western shirt and quickly back up.

"Hey, Glen. Haven't seen you in town lately," Maya said, rewarding him with a coy smile.

"I've, huh, we've been working overtime."

"Too busy for us regular folks," Maya teased.

His freckled face flushed red.

Helmut suppressed a grin, knowing exactly what she was doing.

"Heck, Maya. You—you know that ain't true," Glen stammered.

Helmut cleared his throat. "You gonna let us in or you gonna stand there gawking at my granddaughter all day?"

Glen suddenly stood rail straight. "Sorry, Mr. Geisler. Of course."

Maya giggled.

Glen hustled back to the gatehouse. The twin panels of the enormous gate began to swing open.

Helmut rolled up the window of his F-150 ranch pickup and shook his head. "You're playin' with fire, young lady."

"I can handle myself."

"I'm not worried about Glen. He's a good kid. Devine has some real thugs workin' for him out here. We've seen 'em before."

"Grandpa, I'll be fine."

Helmut drove through the gate, pulling the two-horse stock trailer that carried Maya's prize-winning barrel-racing horse. Max Devine made his arena available to the public on Wednesday of every week unless he had a special event. His only requirement was that you called in advance to reserve a spot. Devine provided steers and calves for roping in the morning. Early afternoon was reserved for barrel racing. Bronc and bull riders came to practice in the late afternoon. Most of the riders who came early stayed to watch them practice. Devine paid an EMT crew to stand by and catered barbecue for anyone who wanted lunch and dinner.

Maya started barrel racing last summer as a way to take her mind off the horrific ordeal she'd been through. She'd been riding horses since she was a little girl and was glad to get back in the saddle.

Helmut parked beside a dozen other pickups and trailers in the mowed pasture behind the arena, and they unloaded Maya's six-year-old sorrel quarter horse gelding. She named him Star because of the splash of white hair on his forehead.

"Start him out easy. Take a lope around the pasture to warm him up. I'll go see when your time slot to ride will be," Helmut said. "That will give you a chance to take a look around."

"Go, Grandpa, you're making Star nervous," she said.

When Helmut walked away, Maya tied Star to the side of the trailer by his halter rope and hoisted the blanket on his back. She'd been up early giving him grain and rubbing him down for the day's activity. She opened the saddle compartment in the front of the trailer and slowly pulled out her saddle.

She heard the small ATV engine noise rumbling toward the trailer and checked to be sure Glen was the driver. She'd met him at the Christmas party at church a couple of months ago, and every Wednesday when Helmut brought her to Devine's ranch to practice, Glen made a point of stopping by their horse trailer. They hadn't officially gone on a date but did meet for ice cream at the Dairy Queen last week.

When the ATV got closer, she accidently dropped her saddle in the dirt, then slowly bent to pick it up. The move had the desired effect.

"Need some help?" Glen said, cutting the engine and coasting to a stop.

"I thought you were on gate duty," Maya said, rewarding him with a smile.

Glen hustled over, picked up Maya's saddle, and wiped the dirt off with his hand. Star sidestepped away from him and gave a snort when he hoisted the saddle over the horse's back.

"Easy now," she cooed to the horse.

The horse relaxed at the sound of her voice.

"He only likes me to saddle him," Maya said.

"He's a fine animal," Glen said, stepping aside and letting Maya pull the cinch under the horse's belly.

Maya brushed against Glen as she reached for Star's padded breast collar. "I wanna warm him up before we go through the barrels." She slipped Star's silver-studded bridle over the horse's ears. "Where's your mount? I don't wanna get lost." She took the latigo and let her hand rest for a moment on his before she tightened the cinch.

"Uh—you can't—you shouldn't be—you have to stay..." The end of his sentence trailed off when Maya launched herself into the saddle in one fluid gymnastic movement.

"I know all that," she said. "I've been here before, you know," she teased.

Glen put his right hand on her thigh and the other on the left rein. He looked up at Maya with a sheepish grin. "Then you know the rules," he said, making an effort to sound gruff and authoritative. "Stay near the arena and the parking area."

Maya laughed and grabbed his cowboy hat.

Startled, Glen let go of the rein and reached for his hat.

Maya spurred Star in the flank, and the horse spun around the young cowboy like he was a barrel in the arena and took off across the field.

"Maya!" Glen shouted to the cloud of dust Star kicked up as he sprinted away.

Maya knew she wouldn't have to go far before Glen mounted a horse and came after her. The cowboys kept saddled horses ready to ride in the stock pens behind the arena chutes in case they were needed to wrangle rodeo stock or, as in her case, visitors who wandered too far from the designated grounds.

After her ordeal with Russell Stevens, or the "Dragon" as he liked to be called, Maya understood the limits of her charm and allure. Boys like Glen were easy enough to manipulate. Some men, like the Dragon, weren't so innocent. Maya didn't recognize the difference until it was almost too late. The Dragon sold her and three other girls and was in the process of flying them all out of the country when Nick Fischer found her. The thought of what might have happened still gave her nightmares.

The gate at the end of the pasture was open, but she pulled Star's reins and forced him into a fast walk. She didn't want to reach the gate before Glen found her. The gravel road through the open gate led into thick oak and mesquite brush between two limestone cliffs.

"Maya!" Glen yelled from a hundred yards away. He was riding a red roan horse that was near to Star's big seventeen hands.

Maya didn't wait. She placed Glen's hat on the gate post and spurred Star through the gate and into the brush-lined gravel road. This was the section of the property Nick Fischer told her he was interested in knowing more about.

Maya rounded the first bend in the road and reined Star to a stop. She wasn't under any illusion that what she was doing wasn't dangerous. The other guards on Devine's payroll always traveled heavily armed. She suspected none of them were real cowboys like Glen.

In a few moments Glen appeared, riding at a gallop. He jerked his reins to avoid crashing into Maya and Star.

Maya laughed at Glen's surprised and exasperated expression. "Where're you goin'?" he shouted when he finally got his mount under control.

"I told you I wanted to warm Star up before I took him in the arena."

"You know this pasture's off limits."

"The gate was open."

"That's because—that's when—it ain't supposed to be open," he stammered.

Maya jumped off her horse and led him to the small creek that flowed over the road. The water was clear and bubbled over flat limestone slabs of rock that were covered with bright green moss.

"Be careful," Glen said. "The bottom's real slippery."

Maya recognized the slippery moss but ignored Glen's warning. "Star needs a drink," she said over her shoulder. "This is a pretty spot. Why's it off limits?"

Glen swung his right leg over the saddle horn and slid to the ground. "It's an exotic animal pasture. Mr. Devine only lets hunters in here. They pay big bucks. He don't want the animals disturbed."

Maya dropped Star's reins and let him stand in the creek bed. The horse ducked his muscled neck and sucked in the cool water.

"He's bringing in another load of animals today," Glen said.

"What kind of animals? Can I see them?"

"Huh—well—I don't know—"

"Oh, come on. Where do they unload them?"

Glen took off his cowboy hat and ran his fingers through his short blond hair. "About a quarter mile up this road, there's a high-fenced pen and a couple of bunkhouses for the hired hands. But I don't know what time they're comin'." He reached for Star's reins. "We should be getting back."

Maya took a calculated step into the creek. The water was ankle deep on her boots. Both her feet slipped on the slick moss, and she landed on her butt in the water.

Glen immediately roared with laughter, startling his roan horse. The animal reared and pulled away from his grip, then turned and galloped back toward the arena.

Maya grabbed Glen's heel and pulled. He fell back into the water beside her. Now, it was Maya's turn to laugh. Star raised his head and snorted. He was bombproof. Helmut trained him well. He'd seen too many accidents caused by spooky horses, and he wasn't about to risk his granddaughter's safety.

"You're gonna get me fired!" Glen's voice sounded angry.

"Oh, come on. For slipping in the water?" Maya playfully splashed him in the face. She'd managed to pull the two top snaps on her western shirt open, revealing the top of her red lace pushup bra.

Glen noticed. His gaze was immediately fixed to her exposed cleavage.

"We can't go back right away. We're all wet," she said, giving him her best coy smile.

Glen's face was flushed red despite the cool water. He opened his mouth to speak but nothing came out.

"Let's go up to the bunkhouse and dry off," she whispered. She stood and took his hand. Glen followed her out of the creek to the road. Star walked behind them like a maiden aunt chaperone.

The two walked through another open gate and approached a high-fenced pen surrounded by four limestone bunkhouses. Devine didn't build anything cheap, and the buildings, although small, were nicer than most of the houses on the west side of San Antonio.

Glen opened the pen, and Maya led Star inside. The fence was eight feet high and solid wood, built to hold wild game. The solid panels allowed the wranglers to move outside the pen without spooking the animals while they prepared them for release into the pasture.

The door to the nearest bunkhouse was unlocked. Glen and Maya went inside. There were four bunk beds against the front wall, a table in the corner, and a kitchen area in the back next to a toilet and shower room.

"This is cozy," Maya said. "Is this where you sleep?"

"Not me. Only the permanent employees bunk here."

"You mean the thugs with guns?"

"Yeah, pretty much."

The room was tidy and clean enough for a bed-and-breakfast.

"There's probably towels in here." Glen went into the shower room. When he returned with a white bath towel, Maya had her wet shirt off.

She faced him with only her red lace pushup bra and a smile. She let him take a good look before holding out her hand for the towel. "Well, hand me the towel before I catch cold," she admonished him.

Glen's face turned beet red. He handed her the towel and turned to look out the window.

"What time did you say they were bringing the animals here?"

"Oh, shit," Glen said, remembering why they weren't supposed to be there. He checked his wristwatch.

Pickup engine noise filtered through the limestone walls.

"They're comin'," Glen said, panicked. He went to the window and peeked through the curtain.

Maya stood behind him watching a dark green dually pickup pull into the yard.

"Where're the animals?" Maya asked, noticing the pickup wasn't pulling a trailer.

The dually slowed enough for Maya to see a stern-faced driver wearing a beard and a brown cowboy hat. A bald man sat in the passenger seat, holding a rifle. In the back seat she saw a little boy. Aaron Ochoa.

CHAPTER THIRTY-EIGHT

Diana and I waited for Maya and Helmut at the German Bakery in Fredericksburg. I ate a plate of sauerkraut and local sausage and skipped the beer in favor of unsweetened tea. I had a feeling the night would challenge my senses, and I wanted to be sharp. Diana was too nervous to eat. She ordered a blueberry kolache but cut it into six pieces and only nibbled at one.

"The whole thing doesn't make sense," she said. "Kidnapping is a game they play in Mexico, not San Antonio."

"Maybe they have Mexican ties."

"Cartel?"

"Makes sense. Frank and Fahl are dealing pills on a large scale." I finished my tea.

Diana pushed her kolache plate in front of me.

I couldn't resist taking a taste. "Hanging Danny Sanz off a bridge sounds like something I read about happening in Nuevo Laredo last year. Part of a cartel turf war."

"We definitely have cartel influence in San Antonio, but Devine doesn't fit the mold."

"He's got big money, and nobody knows where it came from."

"You think he's using the Willow City ranch to launder money?" she asked.

"Could be. He's buying exotic animals and selling hunts. He can set his own price."

The waitress refilled my empty tea glass. Diana waited until she left. Her eyes settled on me. "I don't like it. What if those guys just made up a story to keep Sarge from torturing them?"

I reached under the table and took her hand. "I know you don't like my hunches, but I have a gut feeling Aaron's on Devine's ranch. Whoever took him is smart, but not that smart. They wouldn't question dropping the animal track game pieces. Aaron did that."

"There's no cell phone service in most of that area north of Willow City. It's thirty miles from town. They need us to disappear without a trace. The ranch is the perfect trap."

My phone rang. The caller ID said Maya. I accepted the call and pushed the speaker icon.

"I saw him," she said, out of breath. "I saw Aaron."

"We'll meet you at your Grandpa's," I said.

Diana was already out the door.

I paid the check and hurried after her.

She was too full of anticipation to talk on the fifteen-minute drive out to Helmut's ranch. Her eyes were closed, and I knew she was saying a prayer for Aaron's safety.

"Put in a good word for us," I said. She nodded.

• • •

Helmut and Maya were waiting for us on the porch of his single-story, limestone-block ranch house. I parked beside his horse trailer, and both met us in the yard. The design was the same as my own family homestead and one of only a handful of original German immigrant houses built in the nineteenth century still occupied.

"How did he look? Was he okay? Was he tied up?" Diana fired questions.

"I only saw him for a second. He was in the back seat of a pickup truck."

Diana digested that information. I put my hand on her shoulder to calm her down.

"Sorry. I'm all worked up."

We went inside, and Maya told us her story about how the young cowboy, Glen, had taken her to the bunkhouse where they'd seen the green dually with Aaron in the back. Glen had told her about another older bunkhouse that used to be the original ranch house. It was farther up the gravel road and was probably where they were taking Aaron.

She was very sure that Glen wouldn't tell anyone what he'd seen or that he had been in the bunkhouse with Maya.

"Are you sure we can trust him? He does work for Devine," I said.

Maya hesitated. She was wondering the same thing herself. "I trust him. He wasn't supposed to be there, with me. If he told, he'd be fired."

CHAPTER THIRTY-NINE

Glen Zech sat in a corner booth at the Fredericksburg Dairy Queen next to Maya. He fiddled with the straw in his milkshake and looked uncomfortable. I studied him from the other side of the booth. Diana sat beside me. Glen felt three pairs of eyes trained on him in an intense effort to read his character.

"I know a Kris Zech from Mason County. Any relation?" I said, starting the conversation with family. I didn't have a lot of time, but I needed to know if we could trust him.

"Yes, sir. He's my cousin," Glen said.

"Yeah? We hunted together a few times."

"He told me. Everybody knows about you, Mr. Fischer."

"Where is he now? Still workin' at the feed store?"

"No, sir. He finished up his degree in wildlife management. He's workin' for a rancher down in the valley."

"Y'all do any good in football last year?"

"Not much. Johnson City beat us again." He shook his head in shame when he said it, reliving the disgrace of getting beat by an archrival.

"That's too bad. I watched a few games in the Puncherdome." The Mason High School football stadium was a converted horse racing venue that fans of Puncher football had affectionately named after the home team. "What about you? You gonna work for Devine all your life?"

Glen stole a glance at Maya. She rewarded him with a smile.

"He wants to join the Marines, like you did," she answered for him.

"How old are you, Glen?"

"Twenty-one. I know I'm gettin' a late start, but when this job for Devine came up, I couldn't pass it up. I get to ride almost every day."

"You can do that on your family ranch."

"Not and get paid for it."

"Joining the Marines is a big step. You won't be ridin' horses."

"I know that. I wanna do my part."

"Why not go to college?" I asked.

"I want to, eventually. I figured the GI bill would help with that. My family's not rich."

Maya smiled. She liked what she heard from Glen. I gauged her reaction, knowing her instinct about his character would be a good indication of whether we could trust him. Diana took my hand under the table and squeezed. She shared a reassuring nod with me. For once I agreed with both women. The kid from Mason, Texas, had his heart in the right place. He didn't seem to know about the kidnapping or that his boss might be involved in something illegal.

"I asked Maya to introduce us because there's something going on out at the Devine ranch you need to know about. Once I tell you, you can walk away, or you can help us. But you won't be able to go back to work for Devine. If you wanna join the Marines, now would be as good a time as any."

The kid's face flushed. He felt the heat from Maya's and my steady gazes. I was forcing him to make a big decision. I didn't feel guilty about it. When I was his age, I was on my second deployment to Afghanistan. My childhood hadn't been as sheltered as Glen's. My dad was a law man who died in the line of duty when I was in high school. The worst that had happened to Glen was probably getting beat in football by Johnson City. That was a tragedy, but one on a different level.

Maya reached for his hand above the table. It was all the persuasion he needed.

He took her hand and a deep breath to calm his nerves. Bootcamp was going to open his eyes. I wished I could see his reaction when he first stepped off the recruit training command bus and came face-to-face with that first Marine Corps drill instructor with an attitude who would make his life uncomfortable for the next thirteen weeks.

"I'm ready," he said with more confidence than I expected.

I ordered a refill of coffee and looked around the small fast food restaurant. There was a young family with four kids all under nine years old at a corner booth. Four high school girls sat next to them, all glued to their cell phones. An older couple sat on either side of a pretty young girl no more than six, all eating vanilla ice cream cones with contented smiles. It reminded me of my own high school days when the Dairy Queen was the place to hang out after football games or on the weekends when we weren't at the river.

Glen ordered a double cheeseburger and another milkshake. Maya ordered the chicken BLT salad and a Diet Coke. After the food came, I told Glen the story of Aaron's kidnapping. He didn't interrupt. I let Maya describe her own part in what had happened at the ranch that afternoon. As I suspected, in light of her newfound affection for Glen, she didn't let on that the whole encounter had been a setup. What mattered was that Glen was willing to help us get back on the Devine ranch and lead us to the old house where we suspected Aaron was being held.

"I still can't believe Mr. Devine has anything to do with it," Glen said when I was finished.

"We don't know that he does know anything about it," I said. "Whoever is behind it will get what's comin' to them. The main thing now is for us to get Aaron back safely."

"I understand. I'll do whatever I can to help."

"Thank you, Glen," Maya said, and rewarded him with an impromptu kiss on the cheek.

CHAPTER FORTY

Skeeter picked up Lucky and Sarge and arrived near the Devine ranch gate an hour after my meeting with Glen. They were waiting for my signal on the county road just outside the perimeter fence. The idea that this was a setup kept creeping into my mind like the lingering image from a bad dream. Sarge was an experienced interrogator, but he did say they gave up the information quickly. This isolated ranch was the perfect place to get rid of the evidence.

One thing I was sure of, whoever had Aaron would kill him if we contacted the police or the FBI. Neither service would have been useful in mounting a rescue mission on a remote ranch. Both had units that could, if given time, respond to a hostage situation in an isolated area, but we didn't have time. The same gut feeling that spoke to me about the trap urged immediate action or risk never seeing Aaron alive again. Like the early settlers to the Texas Hill Country, we were on our own.

Glen told me that Devine kept ten full-time hands. At least those are the ones he counted, not including the one called Z. Three were local boys like himself. Seven were older and operated mainly as security guards. Glen, being the good-natured country boy that he was, tried on several occasions to engage the guards in conversation, but they never gave out any details about their specific job function. The only thing clear to Glen was that they weren't cowboys. They mostly rode ATVs and pickups and were always heavily armed with Glock 9mm pistols and Colt AR-15s in .222 and .308 caliber.

My plan involved using Glen and Maya as decoys to get Diana and me onto the ranch. Given another day to plan, I would have preferred to draw out our route on a topo map and program it into the GPS. Then I would have set up a mock staging ground and executed several practice runs. Sarge and I'd both trained for and experienced night ops, but we didn't have time.

Those nighttime raids ran through my head as I lay flat beside Diana in the bed of Glen's pickup. I tried to recreate the thought process I used then to clear my head and focus on the mission. On deployment, we used to say, "Don't think about the ones back home or you'll never see them again." The idea was simple—anything that interfered with reaction time could mean the difference between life and death for yourself or those around you. On tonight's mission, I had a personal attachment to the target and the woman lying beside me. Both drove the process and interfered with it at the same time.

The night was dark and still and hovered near forty-five degrees in Fredericksburg, which meant at least five degrees colder in the dry hills north of town. The short drive from the Willow City barbecue where I'd left my pickup had caked both of us in dust.

"Hey, Marty," Glen said to the night gate guard. "You remember Maya?"

Devine always hosted a dance and barbecue after the Wednesday rodeo practice that sometimes went late into the evening. He wanted a properly dressed, Hollywood cowboy on the gate to keep up appearances.

"I danced with you at Hondo's," we overheard Maya remark.

Diana and I listened and hoped the night man wouldn't get the urge to peek in the back of Glen's pickup. The lights from the flashing Yosemite Sam sign reflected off the pickup windows and made our skin glow neon red and blue.

"Yeah, sure. What're y'all doin' out here so late?"

"Maya wanted to hear the band if they were still playing," Glen said.

"They're still there, but they moved inside the barn. It got too cold for everyone."

"Seen Z around?" Glen asked.

"Haven't seen him since this afternoon."

I heard a motor hum. Marty was opening the gate.

"Hey, Marty," Glen said. "I ever tell you, you look like Woody from *Toy Story*?" Glen's and Maya's muffled laughter came from inside the pickup cab as we drove through the gate.

"Hey, fuck you," Marty called after the pickup.

When the lights from the front gate faded, Glen slowed and unrolled the back window separating the cab from the pickup bed.

"Y'all all right?" he asked.

"I forgot how uncomfortable the bed of a pickup was."

"Why do they even call it a *bed*? I'll never walk again," Diana said.

"Drive slow and head toward the arena like you're going to the dance. How many vehicles do you see?"

"About a dozen pickups," Glen said.

I heard him clear his throat. "We got trouble," he said, his voice tense. "Two ATVs just took off from the main house. They're headin' our way."

"Okay, don't panic. Keep going unless they stop you."

"They're comin' from the passenger side and comin' fast."

"We need to get out," I said.

"They're coming down the road. There's a curve around an oak mott about a hundred yards ahead."

"Let me know when they're behind the trees. We'll slip out the other side of the pickup. How far's the bunkhouse?"

"From here it's about a mile and a half."

"Okay, we'll meet you there."

"Now," Glen said in a whisper. "They're behind the trees. Go, now."

Diana and I slipped over the side of the pickup and dropped to the white caliche road. Glen had slowed to a crawl but was still moving. We both recovered and ran into the waist-high grass. The pasture near the house was carefully landscaped and irrigated. In a few weeks, it would be a solid blanket of bluebonnets, primrose, and Indian paintbrush flowers.

I heard the ATVs before I saw the headlights. The balloon tires on the vehicles kicked up rocks on the loose caliche fifty yards from our position.

I motioned Diana to follow me behind a large live oak tree. I didn't want to risk running through the knee-high grass. There was no moon, but the movement alone would give us away. If the men coming on ATVs were part of Devine's guards and they had any training, movement in the dark would quickly give us away.

A cloud of white caliche dust engulfed Glen's pickup as the ATVs stopped beside it. Glen left his headlights on. The two men on the ATVs shielded their eyes from the bright light.

"What do we have here?" a short stubby man called out when he stepped off his ATV.

We were close enough to see his pockmarked face in the headlights. He wore a Carhartt jacket and a green John Deere cap. The other man held an AR-15. Both had pistols on their belts.

"I don't like this," Diana whispered in my ear.

I used the tree to rest the barrel of my own AR-15 chambered for .308. The pickup headlights created a perfect silhouette target of both men.

"I've got 'em covered," I whispered back.

"I worked this afternoon. Just coming back out to the dance."

John Deere stopped beside Glen's open window. "It's little Glen from Mason," he called to the taller man.

"Fresh meat," the other man said. He pushed his AR-15 through the passenger side window. I could see his leering expression in the dome light. A gold cap sparkled from his left front tooth.

"My, my, my," John Deere said.

Both Maya and Glen stared straight ahead.

"You're out late, cowboy."

"Marty said the dance was still going on," Glen said. His voice was clear and confident.

"Who's the chica?"

"My girlfriend."

"Do you like to ride?" the man with the gold tooth sneered.

"Yeah," Glen said. "She's a barrel racer."

"The girl knows what I'm talkin' about," Gold Tooth said.

The two men laughed.

I took steady aim on the man's gold tooth. The suppressor would muffle the shot. John Deere stood by the passenger door. He would need to reach for his pistol and turn. My second round would put him down before he could get off a shot.

"Watch your mouth!" Maya shouted and slapped Gold Tooth hard across the mouth.

I hesitated, waiting for the man's response. Although we needed Glen and Maya to access the property, this situation was the one I wanted to avoid.

Diana put a hand on my shoulder. "Wait," she whispered.

If either one of the men laid a hand on Maya, they would go down.

Suddenly, they both burst out laughing.

"You got yourself a live wire, son," John Deere said, slapping Glen on the shoulder. "I hope you can handle her."

"You need any help, just give us a call," Gold Tooth added.

We watched the two guards shine their flashlights into the bed of the pickup, then return to their ATVs. Diana squeezed my shoulder. I smiled and shook my head. She knew how close I'd come to pulling the trigger.

"Maya's all grown up," she whispered.

I still thought of Maya as the naïve young girl who briefly let herself be taken in by a ruthless trafficker who nearly sold her out of the country. The truth was, she was a woman of the world who had learned the hard way how to deal with thugs and degenerates.

CHAPTER FORTY-ONE

Diana and I jogged through waist-high grass to the cross fence separating the front pasture from the section of land containing the bunkhouse. Ambient light from the ample stars made travel in the carefully maintained pasture relatively easy. The dense brush on the other side of the fence would slow our progress.

I searched the edge of the brush across the fence, then heard a low whistle.

Skeeter, Sarge, and Lucky were waiting just over the fence in the shadow of a mesquite tree. I pulled the tightly strung wire up from the ground so Diana could crawl under. The space wasn't big enough for me, so I climbed the wire. Luckily the ten-foot game fence was strung tight enough to hold my weight.

When I hit the ground on the other side, I saw headlights pass through the gate five hundred yards from our position. I hoped it was Glen's pickup heading to the bunkhouse. If it wasn't, our cover was blown, and we'd need a new plan.

"Everyone all right?" I asked in a low voice.

All three nodded.

Sarge gripped a small five-inch tactical flashlight in his palm, adding a reddish tint to his black face paint. Skeeter and Lucky wore the same makeup. Both had dark complexions and laughed at Sarge's insistence that they wear makeup, until he told them it was the oil and sweat on the skin reflecting light that attracted the enemy at night and made them an easy target, not necessarily skin tone.

Skeeter and Lucky wore short black jackets and dark jeans. Sarge was dressed head to toe in black tactical gear he'd acquired from his long military career. He was slight built and agile. In the dark, nothing he did or said gave away his age.

"Glen said there's a creek between here and the bunkhouse. We'll stop there, and Sarge will go ahead to scout the bunkhouse."

Diana cleared her throat, but Sarge took off at a fast pace into the underbrush, and I followed, not giving her a chance to protest. She wanted to be the first on the scene because we were after her son. Sarge suggested that a silent insertion would be more likely to produce the desired effect. When I explained what his military jargon meant, she deferred to his judgment. The alternative was calling in the local sheriff and charging through the front gate with a dozen deputies, a move guaranteed to get Aaron killed. Sarge was the most experienced at this kind of operation. Even pushing seventy, he hadn't lost a step.

Skeeter followed last. The big guy was able to keep up even though he hadn't been on the gridiron since college and hadn't lifted a finger to exercise since the car wreck that left him without a forearm. Like Colton Macrae, he was a natural athlete.

Sarge slowed briefly to ford the creek, more for us to see the natural rock bridge he used to cross the water than because he needed to break stride. Deep shadows from live oak and mesquite trees covered the small rocky stream. When we were all safely across, Sarge disappeared into the brush without a word.

I took Diana's hand in mine while we waited. Her cold, clammy fingers trembled. I rubbed her palm and heard her let out a breath of air. We were going after her son, but she was a veteran police officer, and I trusted her to hold it together.

Skeeter checked the loads in his Mossberg pistol-grip shotgun. Lucky watched him in the dim light. Both seemed absorbed in their own thoughts. Skeeter had been around me enough to know what was coming. For Lucky, fighting was in his DNA. He'd grown up on the mean streets south of the border and understood better than any of us what kind of trouble the cartel could bring, if that was who we were up against.

Before I had asked them to join, I'd made clear my suspicions. Frank and Beau were dealing opioid pills in large quantities, and Devine would be the most likely businessman to launder the kind of money they were making. I knew I was wasting my breath, but my point was to warn them and let them know the danger. Of course, they both agreed to come with us. Cartel or not, we all feared for Aaron's life and were anxious to get started.

A coyote yipped somewhere between us and the main gate. Another responded. They were teaming up for a night hunt. A hoot owl called from the oak tree across the creek. I thought of a thousand other winter nights like this that I'd built a fire and stared at the flames. I'd camped, hunted, and partied in these Texas hills my entire life.

Diana pushed closer into my shoulder when the owl hooted again. She was raised in a small town but couldn't wait to move to the big city of San Antonio when she graduated high school. She hadn't spent much time in the brush. Her father hadn't taught her to hunt, and she hadn't pursued it like her brothers had. She liked going with me to the ranch and even riding horses, but I didn't know whether it was genuine affection or if she was mainly attracted because Aaron went wild every time he came with her to the ranch. She trusted me now, but I wondered if it was because she had no other choice. Another case and another circumstance that didn't involve her son might bring different results. If her son was removed from the equation, would she have agreed to my plan and my tactics? I didn't know the answer to that.

When the owl hooted a third time, Sarge reappeared, like a shadow in the moonlight. He moved with the quiet practice of a whitetail deer in the underbrush, rarely making a sound. He touched my elbow before I knew he was there. I realized I'd been distracted by my thoughts of Diana. It was a big reminder of why I didn't want Diana along, but there was nothing I could do now except clear my head and focus on the mission.

"Glen and Maya are at the bunkhouse," he whispered. He turned immediately and went back the way he'd come.

I pushed Diana ahead of me and followed. Skeeter and Lucky brought up the rear.

In less than ten minutes, we came to the cleared area around the corral and bunkhouse. A nightlight illuminated the empty corral and showed Glen and Maya waiting for us on the porch.

We all went into the front room of the bunkhouse and stood around the wooden table while Glen sketched the layout of the old house. The structure resembled my family ranch house except it was one story. Like most of the old and new ranch houses in the area, it was built with large slabs of limestone rock. The wooden front porch was covered but still part of the original structure, which meant any approach up the steps would make the old timbers creak and groan. A big picture window overlooked the porch. Two kitchen windows faced the corral off the back of the house. There were three bedrooms that each had a single window. Two on the left side and one on the right.

The corral and two-story barn sat twenty-five yards from the kitchen door. Glen said it was rarely used except for horses and was mainly empty during the spring. It was one of the few structures that hadn't been rebuilt. Glen had stumbled upon it while chasing a stray yearling buffalo. None of the cowboy hands were allowed around the house. It was reserved for Devine's collection of bodyguards.

I left Glen and Maya at the bunkhouse with instructions to park his pickup across the gravel road to block the exit. Both seemed nervous, especially Glen. He was the only one who had seen and worked with the men we were up against, and he seemed to think they were a rough bunch. I assured him we could handle them.

We took off on foot up the road. The light color gravel reflected enough light to make travel easy. Sarge led the way, followed by Skeeter, Lucky, and Diana. I brought up the rear. There was a locked gate two hundred yards from the house that sat in the middle of a meadow at the base of a steep limestone cliff. The creek that we'd crossed earlier ran through the old corral and meandered down the meadow.

The house and grounds were completely dark. No lights on inside the house. The dark green dually pickup Maya described wasn't there. In its place was a red Ford. I checked my watch. Three a.m.

Something on the porch moved.

Sarge scanned the area with his night vision binoculars.

I motioned everyone to the side of the gate under the shadow of a maple tree.

When Sarge joined us, he said, "There's a man sitting on the porch with a rifle across his lap."

An idea popped into my head. It would work, if the porch guard was operating on only a few hours of sleep. "I'll work my way over to the creek and follow it up to the corral. That will put me behind the house. I'll make enough noise to get the guard's attention. Make it count. I don't wanna get shot out there."

"I'll take care of him," Sarge said. His flat direct voice showed no emotion. He was a dangerous man, and I was glad he was on our side.

"When you do, I'll check the windows and see if I can locate where they're holding Aaron," I said. "If we're lucky, he's sleeping in one of the rooms alone. Once he takes care of the guard, you two go to the front door and wait for my signal." I pointed to Diana and Skeeter. "Lucky, follow the fence line and come out on the east side of the house. You'll have my back while I'm checking the windows in case there's another guard stationed outside the house. These guys are supposed to be professionals. Be on the alert."

"Be careful," Diana said before I could turn away.

"If he's there, will get him," I said. We all hoped he was there and didn't want to think of the alternative.

Diana hesitated. She chewed her bottom lip. She was an SAPD detective, but this kind of operation wasn't in her wheelhouse. She was outside her comfort zone, but she knew her son was out there somewhere. Finally, she nodded, and I took off at a fast jog through the underbrush.

CHAPTER FORTY-TWO

Running through a remote pasture in Central Texas challenges the reflexes and the senses. Every wrong move draws blood from the needle-sharp thorns that arm every tree and shrub. Add night, unstable footing, and the adrenaline rush from anticipating armed confrontation, and I felt lucky to make it to the creek with only a cut cheek and bruised left knuckle.

I was no match for Sarge's silent nighttime movement, but there were plenty of animals in this pasture that would make noise. The buffalo, the longhorn cattle, the elk herd, and wild hogs always raised a ruckus going to water at night. I counted on being heard and not seen. I wanted the guard to get suspicious and move off the porch so Sarge could take him out.

I paused at the edge of the creek to give Sarge time to get in position. After five minutes, I began moving up the stream bed toward the house. The thick brush I'd run through quickly dissipated. The field had been cleared with a bulldozer in a one-hundred-yard circle around the house. I crawled on my belly to a suitcase-sized boulder an ancient flood had washed off the hillside.

The guard stood in the yard seventy-five yards away, aiming a rifle with a prominent scope directly at me. The scope would no doubt have night vision capabilities. I froze. Movement would give me away before anything else. The guard wouldn't hesitate to pull the trigger. He wouldn't give a damn what animal he killed. He probably had instructions to shoot first and ask questions later.

I studied the man's silhouette. He wore a bulky jacket and blue jeans. His face was behind the scope, but he wore a black baseball cap.

I was aware that the watch cap on my head made a fine target. The rest of my body was behind the rock. There's nothing like the feeling of being caught in the crosshairs of a high-powered rifle. I'd been on the other end many times, looking for a clear shot. The guard would be slowly scanning the creek bank for a solid shadow with a smooth silhouette that distinguished itself from the surrounding brush and grass. Once he found it, he would wait for movement to confirm an enemy position. If he was zeroed in on my watch cap, I would never hear the shot. The bullet would reach me before the sound.

My scalp itched. A fire ant crawled up the exposed wrist on my left hand. When it hit the hairs on my arm, it would realize where it was and plunge its fangs in deep. Fire ants were fearless and ambitious. Their job was to return food to the nest no matter what size. Two more followed their fellow worker. The nest was a foot from my elbow. I had to move soon or be in a world of hurt.

The guard took a step forward, his eye glued to the scope that didn't waver from my position. He'd seen my silhouette. All he needed was movement to confirm I wasn't part of the rock, then he would pull the trigger.

Another ant sank his teeth into my wrist. Despite the cool night, sweat dripped from my eyebrows and into my eyes. I gritted my teeth as the searing pain from the ant bites radiated up my arm. Where the hell was Sarge?

A silent shadow moved behind the guard. Like the sudden swoop of a nighthawk, the shadow landed on the guard and took him to the ground. The movement stopped in less than five seconds. I waited to see which man would get back up.

When a slight-built figure stood, I breathed a sigh of relief and quickly jumped to my feet and brushed off the fire ants.

Sarge pulled the guard out of the yard and into the deeper shadows beside the house. I studied the compound. No other movement caught my attention. The creek offered no more cover from this point to the corral. With the guard gone, there was no point in continuing in the same direction. So, I jogged directly toward the house.

Sarge met me at the kitchen window. I motioned for him to circle the house to the east where Glen had indicated there were two more bedroom windows. I took the west side. If the old house had a similar layout to my family ranch house, that room would be the master bedroom.

I edged close to the windowsill. The frame showed a two-inch gap. Someone had left it open to let in fresh air. It was an old-style sash weight window that would probably wake the dead if I pried it open any farther. I let my eyes adjust to the darkness of the room. The outline of a four-poster bed stood next to the window. A large wooden armoire rested against the wall. The place hadn't been touched since the original inhabitants moved out a hundred years ago. The door was closed, a single, empty, highbacked wooden chair stood beside the bed.

I pressed my ear close. The sound of a soft whistling snore escaped the two-inch opening. Someone was sleeping in the bed.

I search the yard and found a discarded wooden pallet. Leaning it against the wall, I climbed up beside the window for a better angle to see into the room and determine who slept in the ancient bed.

The frayed remnant of a white lace curtain partially blocked my view of the outline of a man lying on a bare mattress. He was barefoot, with boney legs and clad only in jean shorts.

I put my hand under the window and pushed. The old wooden frame rose with surprising ease. I waited and watched the figure turn slightly. The snoring continued. I put my boot through the opening and found the floor. The old wooden planks squeaked under my weight.

The man snorted in his sleep and said something unintelligible.

I searched the dark room for a weapon. A pistol rested on the nightstand between the window and the bed, and a pump shotgun leaned against the wall near the door, exactly where he would need them if he was under attack.

I took another step closer to the bed. The skinny man moved now. He was awake and reaching for the pistol. I brought the butt of my AR-15 down on his forehead.

Skinny abruptly went back to sleep.

I zip tied his hands behind his back and walked to the door. The rest of the house was quiet. I pulled the door open and moved into the hallway. I stood still for a full minute, listening for any sign of other guards. Nothing.

I crept to the kitchen. Empty. The next hallway led to the other bedrooms. I opened the doors one by one. Empty. The front room was the same. The house was as Glen described it, but there was no sign of Aaron.

I flipped on the light and slowly walked out on the porch with my hands visible.

"All clear," I yelled.

Diana jogged out of the shadows. "Is he here? Did you find Aaron?"

"One other guy sleeping inside. I tied him up on the bed." When I spoke, I heard a shout from the bedroom. The man must have regained consciousness. "Turn the lights on. Let's search the place."

"I'll check it out," Diana said and jogged into the house.

Skeeter and Lucky appeared out of the shadows.

"Check the corral and the barn," I told them. They hustled out of sight.

Sarge entered the pool of light, dragging the unconscious guard who had held me in check with his night vision scope. He was clean-shaven with a bald head. Blood oozed from a mark above his left temple.

Sarge propped the man up against the bottom porch step and handed me the rifle he was using.

"Nice weapon." I ran my palm over the Remington Model 700 black composite stock and read the .338 Lapua Magnum stamp on the barrel. It was the same model weapon Danny Sanz had used. If the guard had fired and hit his target, there wouldn't have been anything left of my ugly mug.

I peeked through the scope. Instead of light, it showed shades of gray. I moved it through the pasture and picked up the red heat signature outline of a longhorn cow near the corral. The thermal image of my head, even covered with a watch cap, would have been a solid red oval. I wondered why he hesitated to pull the trigger.

"He was here," Diana said. She stepped back out on the porch holding a four-inch round piece of cardboard with the silhouette of a turkey stamped on one side and the outline of a distinct three-pronged footprint on the other.

I stormed past Diana and into the bedroom.

Skinny had the zip tie around his wrists hooked on the end of the bedpost, trying to free himself. "You can't be here," he whined. "This is private property, fucker."

I grabbed him by his scruffy dark hair and yanked him off the bedpost. "Where's the boy?"

"Let go of my hair, man."

I pulled him through the front room and out onto the porch. Diana stood aside while I shoved Skinny down on the bottom porch step beside the bald guard.

"Talk," I insisted. "I know Aaron was here. Where is he now?"

"Fuck you!" he hissed.

I hit him on the left ear with the back of my hand. "Wrong answer." I was tired of playing hide-and-seek with Aaron's kidnapper.

Skeeter and Lucky returned from searching the barn and corral.

"All clear," Skeeter said. "What's up?"

Diana held up the turkey track. "Aaron's been here."

The unconscious guard groaned and opened his eyes.

"Maybe his buddy will talk," Sarge said and grabbed the man by his shirt collar. "Rise and shine, tough guy."

The man slowly regained his senses. "Who're you?"

Sarge pressed the razor-sharp edge of a seven-inch commando knife to the man's neck. "I'm the evil spirit here to drink your blood." Sarge's voice was cold and ruthless. "Give me an answer or I'll slit your scrawny throat."

The man's face turned a shade of gray. There was an edge in Sarge's voice that no one could ignore or mistake for anything other than real and authentic.

I noticed a slight smile creep over Lucky's face before he turned away. He was the only one of us who had ever heard Sarge unleashed.

"I don't know nothin'," the man said, his voice trembling.

"Take that to your grave," Sarge whispered and pressed the knife harder into his neck.

A trickle of blood drained down the man's skin and soaked into his dark green shirt collar. He flinched.

"Wait! The boy's gone," he blurted out.

"We already know that," Sarge said and sliced deeper.

"Jesus, don't kill me. I don't know where he took him."

"Who took him?" I asked.

The man sucked in quick breaths through clenched teeth. He felt the knife on his neck. "It was Z. He brought the kid out here. He didn't tell us why. I didn't know who he was."

"Why did he leave?" Diana asked.

"He didn't tell us. I swear. He took off about two hours ago."

Sarge eased the pressure on the knife.

"Why were you still out here?"

"Z said someone was coming. Said we were to take out whoever came."

"You mean kill us?" I asked.

The man nodded.

"What about Beau Fahl?" I asked. "Where's he?"

"I don't know."

Sarge held the knife edge up to his mouth and smiled. "If you're lying, I'll drink the rest from your jugular." He licked the blood off the blade.

"It's the truth. I swear to god, man."

No one had any doubt that Sarge would follow through on his threat.

Sarge turned to the other man on the porch step. Skinny shivered, and his skin turned white as much from the cold as from Sarge's menacing grin.

"That's gospel, dude. He—he's telling you everything. We were supposed to take out anybody who came through the gate."

"What's Z's phone number?" I asked.

Skinny hesitated.

Sarge lifted the knife.

"It's in my phone," he shouted.

Skeeter plucked a cell phone from the man's back pocket. "Let's take a look."

The screen wasn't locked, and Skeeter thumbed through the recent calls and messages. "Here we go. Z. At least it's easy to spell," Skeeter said with a deep baritone chuckle.

"Can you trace the number?" I asked him.

Skeeter looked at Diana, then back at me. He cocked his left eyebrow. "That requires a warrant. You know that."

"Don't give me that shit, Skeeter. This is my son we're talking about."

"Can you get a warrant?" I asked her.

"You know that by the time I get back to San Antonio and get the warrant, Aaron could be gone for good."

"You want me to bend the rules?" Skeeter asked.

Diana's eyes narrowed. "You're goddamn right!"

CHAPTER FORTY-THREE

I left Sarge at Devine's along with the skinny guard in case by some chance Z returned. Skinny begged me not to leave him alone with the "commando" as he called him. Sarge's tactical gear and his demeanor brought the specter of death. I told him that if we found the boy alive and well, I would put in a good word for him. Sarge just smiled. Skinny wet his jean shorts.

We needed cell phone service in a hurry. Helmut's ranch was the closest place that had reliable bars and a much-needed cup of coffee while we put my plan in motion. Z and Aaron were two hours ahead of us, and we couldn't risk the hour's drive to San Antonio before we made contact.

Lucky got out and opened Helmut's ranch gate. The welcome blast of fresh air eased some of the tension in the cab of my pickup. Diana sat in the front passenger seat laser-focused on our next moves that could result in either the rescue or the death of her son. The guard, Vic, who had held me in his thermal scope sights only thirty minutes ago, sat in the middle of the back seat, probably wondering how or if he would make it through the night alive. Skeeter sat beside him, impassive as always and hard to read. He tapped his metal hook on the armrest, keeping a steady beat to a song only he could hear.

When Lucky climbed back in the pickup, I drove to the house. I thought over the series of events leading from the time of Colton's murder to now. I'd spent most of the time after the wrong man. Beau Fahl was a part of the operation, but the man they called Z gave the orders, and he seemed to be directly under Max Devine's control. If it was true that Devine was connected to a Mexican cartel, the unlimited access to money at his ranch made perfect sense. It would also explain why no one seemed to know exactly where he came from or how he earned a living.

I smelled the camp coffee before Helmut opened the door and ushered us all into his kitchen. While we sat around the table, Helmut lifted the old blue enamelware coffeepot off the burner with a dishtowel, then dribbled cold water over the steaming brew and filled a porcelain cup for each of us. Like my grandpa, he'd never owned a coffeemaker. The water at the end was the key to taking the bitter edge off camp coffee and caused the larger loose grounds to settle to the bottom. The smaller chunks filtered through your teeth.

At this point, a few stray coffee grounds were just what I needed after spending most of the last twenty-four hours on the go and in harm's way. The others around the table felt the same and gratefully sipped from the steaming cups. Even Diana, who never took a sip of coffee that wasn't three quarters cream and sugar, wasn't bothered by the extra jolt of caffeine. We were all bone-tired and running on adrenaline and the hope of finding Aaron alive and well.

Skeeter logged into his laptop and set up the program that would give us Z's location once the guard, Vic, dialed his number and hit connect. The backup plan was to get a warrant and use the SAPD system. Diana had already placed the call and put that into motion. Skeeter's method could save us six hours or more, time we couldn't afford to lose. Diana understood this and felt it more than any of us.

Maya and Glen sat together at the table. He seemed surprisingly calm. I couldn't help wondering if he was putting on a show of courage for her benefit. The more I thought about Devine's operation, the less I was willing to trust anyone associated with it. That included the young cowboy.

"I'm ready," Skeeter said, looking up from his laptop.

All our eyes turned to Vic.

He studied us in return, still not sure what his fate would be. I had no pity for him. He'd come within a nanosecond of killing me in Devine's pasture and would have willingly done so if Sarge hadn't taken him down.

He cooperated for the most part in fear of being left with Sarge. I hoped it was enough to force him to continue.

"Cut him loose," I said to Lucky.

Lucky produced a switchblade knife and quickly separated Vic's hands from the zip tie.

Vic had been silent and sullen. I'd bandaged the knife cut Sarge left on his neck, but he had refused my offer of water.

"This is your chance," I told him. "If you blow it, I'll turn Sarge loose on you again, and you'll be on your own."

"You'll let me go if this works?" he asked.

"No. You'll still have to answer for kidnapping a little boy," Diana said. Her voice had regained the edge that served her so well as a detective.

"I told you, I didn't kidnap nobody—"

"Save it," I jumped in, cutting him off. "If that part's true, you won't have anything to worry about. Just remember what to say when Z answers."

Vic nodded. "Z will speak Spanish. Do you understand?"

"Some," I said.

"If I don't reply in Spanish, he'll be suspicious."

"I speak Spanish," Diana said.

"All right," I said. "Write down what he says if I don't understand."

Maya went to the kitchen drawer and pulled out a pen and notebook and handed it to Diana.

Skeeter didn't need much time. Once Z answered his cell phone, he would have the information he needed, and we would know where he was within a few blocks.

Skeeter dialed Z's number, put the phone on speaker, and placed the phone on the table.

"*Sí?*" It was Z, or we hoped it was. The voice was gruff.

We all held our breath.

Helmut set the coffeepot down on the gas stove with a clang.

I held up my hand for silence.

He gestured an apology.

"*Vinieron por nosotros,*" Vic replied.

"*Cuando?*"

"*Hace una hora.*"

"*Que pasó?*"

Vic focused on my face.

Diana scribbled the English translation as fast as she could, but I held up my hand. So far, I understood that Vic told Z we came to the ranch an hour ago.

"They came on foot through the pasture. One looked military. Forehead full of scars. The other was a big black guy with a metal hook."

"*Y la mujer policía?*" Z's voice rose in excitement.

"*Muerta. Todos muertos.* I got all three comin' across the field. They showed up nice in my thermal scope. I told you we wouldn't have a problem."

"*Bien por ti, hombre!*" Z exclaimed.

Diana's lips pursed, holding back the wrath of a mother bear missing her cub.

I pointed to the map on the laptop screen to remind Vic to get to the point. We needed to know where Z was going.

"*Vas a volver?*" Vic asked.

All eyes were on the blue dot blinking on the map near the San Antonio zoo, north of downtown.

"*Dos días.*"

"*Cuando nos pagan?*" Vic asked.

I glanced down at Diana's translation. He'd asked about getting paid. I raised my eyebrow at Vic. Money was something he'd failed to mention, and I wondered if he was trying to tip Z off. I moved my finger across my neck and mouthed, *Hang up.*

Vic held up his hand, signaling for me to wait.

Before I could reach for the phone, Z responded.

"*Tranquilo, hombre. Deshazte de la evidencia. No vuelvas a hablar de esto. Entendes?*"

"Sí."

The line went dead.

"How'd I do?" Vic asked.

"That depends. What was the last line?"

"He said get rid of the evidence and don't say anything."

"He meant bury the bodies?"

"Yeah, man."

I looked at Diana for confirmation.

"That was it. We were supposed to end up in the pasture, never to be heard from again." She leaned over the table into Vic's face. "How many bodies are buried out there?"

Vic studied his hands.

"One thing at a time," I said. "How much money were we worth?"

"He gave us each a grand up front. Five more if we—if we stopped the threat."

"Killed us?"

"We're guards. That's what we do. Protect whatever the boss says. You were trespassing on private property."

"Always figured I was worth at least ten grand," I said.

Skeeter chuckled, then cut it short when he realized he was the only one laughing.

Lucky zip-tied Vic's wrists behind his back.

"Come on. Is this necessary? I did what you asked."

"We haven't got the boy back yet," I said.

Skeeter looked up from the map on his laptop. "Guess where Mr. Z just parked his pickup?"

We turned our attention to him.

He pointed his metal hook at the screen.

CHAPTER FORTY-FOUR

Lucky tied Vic's hands and feet, and Helmut locked him in the tack room of his barn. Maya and Glen wanted to go with us to San Antonio, but this time I made them stay home. Both were young and needed sleep. Neither would be of any help for what I had to do.

The whole kidnapping seemed to be a setup from the beginning to lure Diana and me off the grid. I thought back to the house in San Antonio and the tracking game clues Diana found there and in Devine's old ranch house. Finding them urged us on. The game pieces put a face on the trail we followed. We all felt we were getting close. But the Willow City ranch seemed to be as close as we were supposed to get. Z had created a trail he knew I would follow.

Speeding toward San Antonio, I thought about Glen. Was he part of the plan? He gave all the right answers when I questioned him. On the outside, he played the part of a Central Texas cowboy, but it could have all been an act. Devine's entire ranch setup with the rodeo arena and the imitation pioneer fence had the artificial feel of a California theme park. I knew Glen's family. The Zech clan were early settlers of Mason County and had been in Central Texas as long as the Fischer family. Z could have persuaded him to participate or paid him enough money to be an unwilling partner, but I didn't want to believe that.

I reached for my cell phone.

"What's up?" Diana said.

"I wanna check on Sarge," I said.

Dawn added a soft orange light to the surrounding hills. Traffic was beginning to pick up as we neared Boerne on the outer limits of Bexar County. I was hoping to beat the eight o'clock peak travel time marred by the perpetual I-10 construction, but that didn't seem likely. Skeeter and Lucky followed close behind in Skeeter's pickup.

I hit Sarge's speed dial number. He was still at Devine's ranch babysitting the skinny guard. That put him roughly thirty miles from Helmut's front door, most of it on dirt and gravel backroads.

He picked up on the first ring. "Yep."

"Everything all right?" I asked.

"Peachy. What's up?"

I filled him in on my theory of Glen's possible involvement. When I was done, he already had Skinny's pickup started and Skinny in the back seat.

"I'm on my way," he said.

"You think Glen's in on it?" Diana said when I disconnected.

"I don't know. If he is, Z already knows we're on our way."

"That would explain why Vic cooperated," she said.

"I thought he was scared of Sarge, but you're right."

"I can't believe such a nice kid would be involved."

"I trusted him too, but he did seem a little too eager to please."

I rang Maya's number. I didn't know how much of my theory to tell her for fear of putting her in danger. I let the phone ring until it went to voice mail, then left her a message to call right away.

The ring must have woken her, because she called back immediately.

"Hey, Maya, is Glen with you?" I asked.

She hesitated. I heard her breathing on the line, no doubt trying to wake up and clear her head.

"Give me a minute," she said. "He was sleeping on the couch."

I shared a look with Diana. She bit her bottom lip.

"He's here," she said. "He's still on the couch. Do you wanna talk to him?"

"No," I whispered. "This is very important. He may be involved."

"What?" she said, too loud.

"Keep your voice down. I don't have time to explain. Find his cell phone and take it to your bedroom."

"Okay," she whispered.

We waited several tense minutes. Brake lights stretched out ahead of my pickup as the three interstate lanes abruptly narrowed to two. I hugged the concrete barrier in the left lane.

"Got it," she said.

"Are you in your room?"

"Yep," she said. "I've got the phone, and it's unlocked."

"Check recent calls or messages."

"No calls since yesterday."

"Messages?"

"Nothing."

I told Maya my suspicions about Glen's involvement and that I was sending Sarge to her house. She didn't believe that Glen could be involved but had been through enough problems of her own not to question my judgment. She only said that she hoped I was wrong.

"If I'm wrong, you never have to mention what I said. Toss the phone under the couch and pretend he lost it there. I'll call Sarge and tell him what you found. He'll know what to do."

CHAPTER FORTY-FIVE

I parked on the street in front of Lora's condo at six thirty a.m. Diana and I split up and covered the visitor parking lots on both sides of the building. We were looking for the game-warden-green pickup with dual back tires.

When I didn't see it on the west side lot, I jumped the barricade and entered the residents' covered parking garage. Lora's white BMW occupied her numbered space. I wondered how deeply she was involved. Z and Beau Fahl were not the kind of naïve young veterans she normally preyed on. Both were evil. I knew she was coldblooded, but I didn't think she would go as far as murder and kidnapping. Something else was driving her. Maybe it was fear or maybe the pills were her undoing. Opioids ruined every life they came in contact with.

Skeeter stopped beside me on the street.

"Anything on the surveillance camera?" I asked.

"Nothing. He must have cut the power. The camera's dead."

Diana jogged around the side of the building. "I found Beau's pickup," she said. The deep creases in her forehead gave away the pressure she felt. Was her son there, and would we be able to rescue him alive?

"If Z's not here, he hasn't been gone long," I said. "We'll find out where he went. As far as we know, he thinks we're dead. We have the element of surprise."

"Unless Glen tipped him off," Diana said.

I shook my head. She was right. If the country boy from Mason County was involved, our chances of seeing Aaron again were less than zero. Diana and I both knew it. I opened my truck toolbox and took out the ballistic vests. Diana and Lucky slipped the protection on over their shirts. If they were waiting for us, we would be ready.

Skeeter already wore his size triple X vest. After taking a bullet on the Marcus Lopez case, he special-ordered one in his size and always kept it behind the seat of his pickup just in case. The extra bulk of the vest on him looked like a football uniform.

Cars trickled out of the parking garage. Residents with day jobs going to work. They all slowed for a good look at the small assault team forming in front of their condo.

I knew the layout like the back of my hand and sketched the floorplan of Lora's condo on a piece of notebook paper. The kitchen was inside the door and to the right. The two bedrooms were down the hall to the left. Lora's room was at the end. The spare bedroom had a bed but was full of boxes and Lora's extensive shoe and clothing collection. The living room was straight ahead.

If they weren't in the kitchen or the living room, I would clear Lora's bedroom.

Diana would follow me and take the spare bedroom. If Aaron was there, he would likely be locked or tied up in that room. Lucky would clear the small pantry and take up a position in the kitchen. Skeeter would cover the front door in case Z or Beau called in backup or nosy neighbors congregated in the hall.

I took the east side stairs, and Lucky and Skeeter took the west side. Diana rode up in the elevator. Skeeter carried a heavy three-inch metal pipe that was three feet long with rebar handles that I used for tamping metal fence posts. Every time I drove out to my ranch, I found a loose or broken post that needed repair, so I kept it under the toolbox that stretched across the pickup bed. The whole thing weighed thirty-five pounds with an extra hunk of steel welded on the end that made it look like a battering ram. It had come in handy before. One good swing usually did the trick on a deadbolt lock.

When we met at the door to Lora's condo, Diana and I drew our pistols and moved to either side of the door. Lucky would enter behind us.

Skeeter faced the door, holding the post driver by the handle, his pistol-grip shotgun slung over his left shoulder. It would have been better had he practiced the move a few times. In the Marines, we drilled locked door entries until we were blue in the face, because any number of things could go wrong. A booby trap could blow up in your face. The inhabitants could shoot through the door. The door could be solid reinforced steel and fail to open on the first swing, alerting the targets.

I hoped for the best and nodded for Skeeter to go ahead.

Skeeter swung the metal pipe, throwing all his three-hundred pounds behind it.

The metal door caved in, and the wooden jamb split almost in two, opening a one-inch gap in the doorframe.

"Back!" I yelled at Skeeter.

He moved sideways, and I kicked the handle.

The door slammed against the interior wall, spraying splinters on the white carpet.

A woman screamed, "No!"

Blood covered her face and naked chest. She stood in the kitchen pointing a pistol at my head. Her tangled blond hair covered her face like some wild animal caught in a trap.

I didn't recognize who it was.

She fired over my head.

I dove at her legs and took her to the floor. Her pistol clattered on the fake marble countertop.

The woman rained blows down on the back of my head until Lucky grabbed her from behind and zip-tied her wrists.

"Don't touch me!" she screamed.

"Calm down," I said, examining her wounds. "We're not gonna hurt you."

Diana handed me a kitchen towel. I wiped the woman's face and neck.

"Lora?"

A four-inch gash from her ear to her chin marred her once pretty face, and a bloody Z was carved into her enhanced breasts.

She gulped a huge breath of air. "I thought you were him. He—he said he'd come back."

"Who?"

"Z."

Lucky handed Diana a bathrobe he'd found in the hall closet, and she wrapped it around Lora. "Is my son here?" she asked.

Lora nodded, hyperventilating too heavily to speak.

"He's here?" Diana asked. I heard the excitement in her voice.

We didn't wait for Lora to answer. Diana followed me into the living room. Skeeter was on his phone talking to the 911 operator. Beau Fahl lay spread eagle on the glass coffee table, beaten to a pulp. Red blood splattered the white furniture and walls like a 3-D Jackson Pollock painting and dripped from his face and chest into the white carpet. He hadn't been dead long.

I sprinted down the hallway toward Lora's bedroom door. Diana followed. "Take the spare bedroom," I yelled, then hit the door with my shoulder. The door burst open, and I tumbled headfirst into an empty room.

"Nick!" Diana yelled from the spare bedroom.

I scrambled to my feet and ran down the hall just as she emerged. She held up a round cardboard disk with the silhouette of a gray fox.

"He was here," she said. "My baby was here."

I followed her back into the kitchen, where Lora had collapsed on the floor. Lucky stood beside her. Diana holstered her pistol.

"Where is he?" she asked in her cold, hard detective voice.

"I don't know," Lora said.

Diana slapped her hard across the unmarked cheek. The blow rocked Lora's head back and came so fast Lora's mouth was still open.

"Try again," Diana said in the same cold voice.

"I don't know. I swear to god, I don't. Z took him and left." She opened the robe for us to see the scars on her breasts. "Look what he did to me!" she screamed. "Look what he did to Beau! He's an animal. I can't ever work again."

"Why kill Beau?" I asked.

She took several big gulps of air.

I poured her a glass of Jack Daniels.

She sucked it down and got her breathing under control. "Beau wanted more. A bigger cut of the business. He had plans." She sobbed as if she had been part of his plans from the beginning. "He said he—he earned it. Z just laughed at him." She paused to wipe the blood and tears from her face with the edge of the bath towel. "Beau said Frank already agreed. Beau had people lined up. Some bikers he recruited for distribution."

"What happened?" Diana asked.

"Z said Frank was done. That his part in the business was finished. Beau refused to believe him, so Z killed him. Killed him like he was nothing. I screamed at him to stop, and he started on me."

I glanced at Beau's bloody body. Z beat the life out of the brute who kicked my butt in the MMA cage. I searched for gunshot wounds but found none. He'd killed him with his bare hands.

"Where did he go? Do you have any idea where he would take the boy?" Diana asked.

"I—I don't know. I really don't know." Tears flooded her cheeks, mixing with the blood from her cut face.

"The ambulance is on its way," Skeeter said.

I poured Lora another glass of Jack.

She swallowed it like water.

I leaned down next to her. "You need to tell me everything you know. A little boy's life depends on your answers. Do you understand?"

Lora slowly nodded.

"When you told me about the poker house, was that a setup?"

She nodded again. "Yeah."

"So we were supposed to go to Devine's ranch?"

"That's right."

I heard the ambulance outside the building.

"Z thinks we're dead. He killed Beau," I said, thinking out loud.

"He told her the business was finished," Diana said, continuing my thought.

"It means he's got one more stop," I said. "Pray to God Glen's not involved."

We ran toward the door with Skeeter and Lucky behind us. The EMT passed us in the hallway.

CHAPTER FORTY-SIX

I sped past the Dominion golf course and pulled up to the security gate of San Antonio's most exclusive neighborhood. Diana had her badge out ready for the guard, but no one appeared. Lights illuminated the closed entrance, but the guardhouse was dark and empty.

"I thought they manned this gate twenty-four seven," Skeeter said.

"They do," Diana confirmed.

I bailed out and jogged to the guardhouse. The door wouldn't budge. I knocked. "Anybody home?" I pressed my cheek against the door glass and saw the tip of a boot on the floor. The guard was sleeping or hiding or something worse. "Can you hear me?"

Nothing.

Lucky looked in the back window. "He's dead."

I smashed the butt of my Springfield .45 through the door glass and opened the lock from the inside. The night shift guard on the floor had gray hair streaked with bright red blood. I checked his pulse. His lifeless skin was still warm to the touch.

"We're on the right trail," I said. "This looks like Z's work."

"The dude don't mess around," Skeeter said. He stepped over the lifeless guard and studied the electronic board on the wall. He made some adjustments on the console, and the main gate swung open.

We piled back into my pickup, and I gunned the F-150 through the open gate. Skeeter found Frank's address on his phone GPS.

"Take a right up here," he said. "It's the house at the end."

I cut the headlights and coasted to a stop behind a game-warden-green dually. The thick oak trees around the cul-de-sac created dark shadows on the street. We jumped out and jogged toward a Spanish-style house decorated with strings of white lights, like the San Antonio missions during Christmas.

We gathered at a bronze Catarina fountain in front of the main entrance. The lights were on in the main building, but there was no sign of life. I hoped we weren't too late.

Skeeter held up a satellite image of the compound on his cell phone. I could see the pool in back and the lighted path through the landscaped brush leading to the back of the house.

"He's an easy man to track." Lucky pointed to the garage, where a man dressed in khaki pants and a black jacket lay sprawled on the ground in a pool of blood.

Skeeter picked up the man's two-way radio and listened. Nothing but static.

Skeeter and Lucky circled the side of the compound. Diana and I went to the main entrance. We planned to meet at the pool behind the house. The still night air chilled my hands, and I rubbed them together to generate some heat before I pulled my Springfield and checked the two extra magazines in my back pockets.

Diana had on black leather shooting gloves and held her Glock 9mm chest-high and pointed down. She wore her dark hair pulled into a tight ponytail, and her detective badge hung from a lanyard around her neck.

A sliver of light cut around the edge of the front door. I nudged it further open with the toe of my boot.

An impressive Lady of Guadalupe shrine greeted us in the entryway. Diana crossed herself. I saw her lips move in a silent prayer. We could use a Hail Mary against Z.

We continued down the hallway. My boot heels echoed off the stone walls and arched ceiling. The house was a palace bought and paid for with the countless lives destroyed by Frank's opioid distribution.

A metal clang like a baseball bat hitting a light pole shattered the silence. I sprinted to the end of the hall, Diana on my heels. We heard a muffled cry like a bull moose shot in the gut.

I waved my hand for her to slow down, not knowing who or what we would find. We crept through a large living room the size of a motel conference room with a massive river rock fireplace and trophy animal heads lining the walls. The stuffed mounts seemed to glare down at us when we paused to listen.

Another wounded animal sound. More like a groan. Came from the pool area. I motioned Diana toward the shattered door. Glass crunched under our boots as we crept our way onto the patio that surrounded an oval-shaped pool. A cloud of steam rose from the heated water, obscuring our view and mixing with the low-hanging morning clouds.

We inched our way forward in the fog. An overwhelming stench hit me in the face. A mixture of blood and excrement. The scent of death. I immediately thought of a gut-shot animal.

Then a slight breeze picked up, giving us a clearer view of the far side of the pool.

We both brought our pistols up and froze. Two naked bodies seemed to hover three feet above the deck like ghostly apparitions.

We skirted the edge of the pool.

Doc Frank's enormous bulk hung beside an older woman. Their naked bodies glowed with a bluish tint in the early morning light. A thick rope linked both bodies to the wrought iron railing.

At the same moment, Z stepped out of the shadows and stood on the raised deck above the bodies like some actor playing a western devil on an outdoor stage. His brown cowboy hat obscured his face in shadow, adding to his sinister aura. In his right hand he held a Colt 1911 pistol. In his left he held a rope attached to Aaron's neck. The boy was gagged and blindfolded with his hands tied behind his back.

"You move pretty good for a dead man," Z said, his voice dry and cold with a thick Mexican accent.

"The news was premature," I said. "Let the boy go."

"I cannot do that, my friend." He showed no indication that he thought of Diana and me as a threat of any kind.

"Aaron, honey. It's all right, now. Mommy's gonna take you home."

The boy made a sound through the gag.

"Turn him loose. It's over," Diana said. "I'm a police officer. Backup is on the way." She held her SAPD detective badge up for him to see.

"That means nothing," Z said. "It's over when I finish here. No one can stop me."

He spoke with supreme confidence in his ability. After seeing his handiwork with Beau Fahl and now Frank, it was easy to see where his cockiness came from.

"Let my son go and give up your boss. Maybe you can beat the death penalty," Diana said.

"Devine is your boss, right? He calls the shots?" I asked.

"You don't know nothing," he said and tugged the rope tied to Aaron's neck.

The boy didn't make a sound.

"Forward," Z ordered the boy. Aaron took a step closer to the iron rail. Z grabbed him by the arm, lifted him like a bag of potato chips, and set his feet down on the top of the rail. Aaron balanced precariously on the thin metal.

I'd faced bad men doing evil things, but Z was the closest thing to a devil incarnate I'd ever encountered.

Z looped the free end of the rope around the top of the rail. A false step would send Aaron over the edge and break his neck. "Tell your partner to step out of the trees and join you by the pool," Z said, still holding the 1911 pressed into Aaron's small head.

"Come on out, Skeeter," I yelled, hoping the emphasis I placed on his name was enough to keep Lucky in the shadows. Z had no reason to suspect there were four of us.

Skeeter walked out of the shadows and took the steps down to the pool. He held the shotgun with his good hand.

"Drop the gun," Z ordered.

Skeeter tossed the shotgun into the manicured rose bed.

"Let the boy go and you can walk out of here. I'll promise you a twenty-four-hour head start." I was spinning a tale hoping to buy some time. I needed a clear shot when Z's pistol barrel was pointed away from Aaron's head.

"I don't make deals with the pretty detective or with you."

"I get that," I said. "Deals are a big *distraction.*" I emphasized the last word, thinking Lucky might get the hint and remember what I'd done for Sarge on the Devine ranch.

Aaron teetered on the edge of the thin rail, his hands tied behind his back, struggling to keep his balance.

Diana made an audible gasp. "No, Aaron. Hold on, honey! Stand still." She stepped around a patio table. The move gave her a clear run to the base of the raised deck should Aaron fall.

I focused on Z. "Let him go!" I yelled. "The boy can't possibly hurt you."

Light glinted off Z's white teeth. "Nothing personal. Just business."

His business was death, and he enjoyed his work.

"Drop the pistol!" Lucky yelled from somewhere behind the deck.

It was the distraction I was waiting for.

Z turned instantly and fired at the voice.

I raised my pistol and pulled the trigger, counting on instinct, countless hours of practice, and Diana's Hail Mary to guide my aim.

The .45 slug hit Z's forehead and took off the top of his skull. The brown cowboy hat fluttered in the air, and his body collapsed like a sack of deer corn.

Aaron lost his balance and tipped forward.

Diana screamed, "No!" and sprinted forward, arms outstretched.

Lucky appeared at the railing and grabbed Aaron's feet as he tumbled forward and hauled him to safety.

I ran up the steps, keeping my pistol trained on the spot where Z collapsed. If the devil was still breathing, he could still kill.

I knelt beside the expanding pool of blood that encircled Z's body. The top of his face was missing. He wouldn't kill again.

Diana untied the rope from Aaron's neck and pulled the dirty rag from his mouth. "Are you hurt?" She searched his small body for any signs of abuse.

Aaron focused on Z's gruesome face. "Is he dead?" he asked in a timid whisper.

"Yes, honey. He can't hurt you anymore," Diana said, holding her son as if he might disappear again at any moment. He wouldn't forget his ordeal, and it would be a long time before he got over it. Like the many frontier children who had witnessed the brutal slaughter of their family at the hands of Kiowa or Comanche, Aaron came face-to-face with a part of humanity that most children thankfully never see.

"He was a bad man," I said. "Now he's dead. Even a devil can't dodge a .45."

Diana covered Aaron with her jacket and walked into the house.

Lucky collapsed on the deck. Blood covered the left side of his shirt. I took off my jacket and pressed it into the wound.

"You're hit," I said. Z's shot had found its mark.

His breathing was shallow. He wouldn't last without immediate attention.

Skeeter made the call to 911 and gave them Frank's address.

CHAPTER FORTY-SEVEN

I stopped at the ranch gate and unrolled my pickup window. The air no longer held its winter edge. The stiff south wind brought moist salty air that smelled like the Gulf of Mexico. In the early dawn light, patches of bluebonnets and red Indian paintbrush dotted both sides of the road like paint spilled from a giant's bucket. Spring returned to Central Texas with its annual hope of life and new growth.

The doctor said Lucky would make a full recovery. After five days in intensive care and a half dozen pints of blood, he had insisted on getting back to his gym so that the high school kids had someplace to go after school. SAPD and the DEA were still unraveling Frank's intricate pill operation. With the FBI's help, a few more arrests were made, but no one was able to lay a glove on Max Devine. He was at the Houston Stock Show during the bloody weekend activities, and no one could find anything that linked him to Frank's business. Z had no criminal history. He had no history of any kind. No one matching his description, fingerprints, or DNA could be found in any database. It was as if the gates of hell had opened and he emerged long enough to terrorize Central Texas. I was happy to send him back where he belonged.

Lora was able to talk her way out of serious charges in exchange for information about Frank's operation and Colton's murder. She provided the murder weapon that matched the casing I found at the cattle barn. She convinced the DA that she had been under constant threat of physical harm. Maybe she was. The scars ended her dancing career, but I didn't pity her. She had information on everybody she ever met. I had no doubt she would leverage her knowledge to land on her feet again.

John Macrae was satisfied with the results. He would forever wonder if he could have bridged the gap between him and Colton. I liked to think he would have eventually gained his son's trust, if Colton could have beaten his addiction. He gladly paid me a bonus and wrote a check to Sarge and Lucky. Both donated the money to Lucky's Gym so they could continue to offer free service to the local high school kids.

The DA still wanted my license but could find no legal reason to take it or to press charges against me. I accepted a warning and a lecture from her only because Diana was present, and I had promised her I would hold my tongue. It helped that the DEA agent in charge was also there and acknowledged my help was instrumental in taking Frank's operation down.

I got out and opened the gate and heard a dog yelp. Sam was barreling down the gravel road toward me. Helen walked out of the barn and waved a dirty work glove in my direction. At the end of the day, I had my estranged mother, a happy Lab, and a long list of spring chores to do. With fences to mend and a new history of the Alamo to read, I knew I would be ready to go back to work in a few weeks.

Diana had also taken time off to be with Aaron and spend time with her family in Castroville. She felt that seeing me would be a constant reminder to Aaron of his ordeal. I didn't try to talk her out of it. She left her stuff at my house and kept my beer in her fridge. Maybe someday soon we could pick up where we left off. I hoped Aaron's wounds would heal in time. I knew we would always share a love for Davy Crockett and a passion for animal tracking.

Another pickup stopped behind me. Glen had come and brought Maya. He had not been involved with Z's operation and had proved to be more loyal to Maya than to Devine's ranch. Both had volunteered to help me catch up on the ranch work. I expected to see a lot more of them and was glad to see Maya happy. Trusting another man besides me and her grandfather was a big step in her own recovery.

THE END

If you enjoyed this Nick Fischer adventure, please stop by Amazon and write a quick review. Your support will be much appreciated.

Sign up for G.D.'s newsletter for a FREE copy of his latest short story and updates on new releases at GDObermiller.com.

DON'T MISS THE OTHER BOOKS IN THE NICK FISCHER SERIES.

RIVER WALK MURDER (book one)

Stonewalled by a dirty cop working for a corrupt politician, the family of a dead woman found in the San Antonio River turns to Nick Fischer for justice.

THE GIRL FROM CALI (book two)

Nick Fischer fights for justice in his old hometown when a local rancher's estranged granddaughter falls prey to a charismatic and ruthless sex trafficker.

RUNNING TARGET (book four Available September 2026)

Nick's past comes back to haunt him when he finds himself the target of a cartel hitman seeking revenge for his brother's death.

ACKNOWLEDGMENTS

I would like to thank my daughter Ruby and sister MaryAlice, who chided and encouraged me throughout the writing process. Also, I would like to thank the outstanding officers of the SAPD Citizen Police Academy for patiently answering my questions and showcasing the fine work they do to protect and serve the community. Finally, thank you to my editor Lisa Gilliam, for her patience and guidance. Prost!

G.D. Obermiller is a fifth-generation Texan who has worked as a cowboy, served as a Navy Corpsman, and taught college English. He's the author of four previous novels, several screenplays, and a one-act play produced in Austin, Texas. He currently lives in North Texas with his daughter and faithful Labrador retriever.

Visit G.D. online and signup for his newsletter to receive special offers and more information about the series.

GDObermiller.com
Facebook.com/GDObermiller
x.com/GDObermiller
Instagram.com/GDObermiller

www.ingramcontent.com/pod-product-compliance
Lightning Source LLC
Chambersburg PA
CBHW030825310726
48980CB00006B/642/J

* 9 7 9 8 9 9 3 8 5 8 8 3 8 *